W9-BTP-888

CLUB PICK

Dear Bookmarked Reader,

As a Franco-English writer living in Paris, France, I cannot begin to tell you how thrilled and honored I am that *Sarah's Key* has been chosen to be a Target Book Club Pick. I discovered Target quite recently, during a holiday with my family in California. *Why can't shops like these exist in France?* I remember thinking. My husband and son spent hours in the CD/DVD section, my daughter went crazy in the women's fashion department, and guess where I was? In the book section, of course, where I splurged on paperbacks I could take home.

I'm very aware that thanks to Target, my novel will find itself in the hands of many new readers, especially my U.S. readers, as I live in Europe. This is a fantastic and enriching opportunity for me.

Sarah's Key is a story of loss. Of family secrets. Of a silence that spanned sixty years. It is the story of France's darkest days and of the scars still left today. The story of two families, linked by silence, linked by sorrow.

But it is also the story of a woman and a man who were never meant to meet.

One of most wonderful things I've learned through *Sarah's Key* and the feedback I've been getting from readers and book clubs is that as a writer, you can really reach out and touch people in every sense of the word and that they want to thank you for it. I love it when my readers tell me "they couldn't put my book down" and had to stay up all night to read it! I also love it when my readers recommend my books to their friends and family.

I hope you will enjoy following my heroine Julia Jarmond, an American journalist based in Paris, married to a Frenchman. Commissioned to research the great Vel' d'Hiv' round-up that took place in occupied Paris during the war, Julia stumbles upon a family secret. But in her ardent quest for truth, she opens Pandora's box. As a mother, as a wife, and as a woman, nothing will be the same for Julia again.

If you want to contact me about *Sarah's Key,* you can do so through my blog: www.sarahskey.com

I'd be very happy to hear from you!

All best from France,

Tatiana de Rosnay

More Praise for *Sarah's Key*

"Masterly and compelling, it is not something that readers will quickly forget. Highly recommended."

—*Library Journal* (starred review)

"Already translated into fifteen languages, the novel is de Rosnay's tenth (but her first written in English, her first language). It beautifully conveys Julia's conflicting loyalties, and makes Sarah's trials so riveting, her innocence so absorbing, that the book is hard to put down." —*Publishers Weekly* (starred review)

"A journey of exploration into two separate worlds . . . universal lessons about our shared humanity . . . Well-written, informative, and exciting, this book deserves wide readership."

—Nechama Tec, Holocaust scholar and author of *Defiance*, a major motion picture

"In the story of young Sarah, her cruel parting in Paris from her mother, and her imprisonment in the camps whose savagery she survives, the reader is brought close to those flames by this remarkable novel written with eloquence and empathy."

—Paula Fox, author of *Borrowed Finery*

"Just when you thought you might have read about every horror of the Holocaust, a book will come along and shine a fierce light upon yet another haunting wrong. *Sarah's Key* is such a novel. In remarkably unsparing, unsentimental prose, Tatiana de Rosnay exposes a little-known crime committed against thousands of French Jews and their children, yet focuses her story through a lens so personal and intimate, it will make you cry—and remember."

—Jenna Blum, author of *Those Who Save Us*

"*Sarah's Key* is an absolute page turner about France's darkest days. . . . Readers are swept away on an intriguing and disturbing journey into the past. *Sarah's Key* unlocks the door to a powerful, haunting secret and a riveting personal saga."
—Debra Ollivier, author of *Entre Nous* and
What French Women Know About Love and Sex

"Beautiful, painful, compelling. At times I didn't want to read on but I couldn't stop. A lyrical lesson in how the human spirit still shines through the shadowed shames of history."
—Beth Harbison, author of *Shoe Addicts Anonymous*

"A story of hearts broken, first by the past, then by family secrets, and the truth that begins to repair the pieces. A beautiful novel."
—Linda Francis Lee, bestselling author of *The Ex-Debutante*

With *Sarah's Key,* Tatiana de Rosnay has touched the hearts of Holocaust survivors

"The perusal of *Sarah's Key* evoked memories of my own experiences during the war in the Vichy zone of France. . . . Just like Sarah, I was forced to wear a yellow star. This was during my internment in the transit camp of Drancy. Just like Sarah's parents, I was deported from Drancy. Unlike her parents, I escaped from the train before it reached Auschwitz. Just like Sarah, I often walked through the rue de Saintonge in Paris. Interestingly, my aunt lived on that very street at number 62. . . . It is a page-turning read, and the reader is anxiously waiting throughout the book to learn the fate of Sarah's younger brother. The calamity of Vel' d'Hiv' is another thread in the tapestry of the French involvement in the Holocaust."

—Leo Bretholz, Holocaust survivor, scholar, and author of *Leap into Darkness*

"Once you open *Sarah's Key,* you will not want to put it down. Tatiana de Rosnay is an accomplished writer. You will follow her into every scene of then and now. You will be part of every event. You will be able to look at the story with the eyes of every actor. You will feel the entire range of their emotions. . . . By her skillful braiding of past and present . . . [she] has succeeded in bringing you back to the terrifying days of July 1942, the days of the Vel' d'Hiv' in Nazi-occupied Paris. She has also succeeded in bringing those days back from oblivion. . . . Some of us, Jewish children in Nazi-occupied France whose families had been 'amputated,' to use an expression of Pierre Vidal-Naquet, have long tried to understand. Microhistory has been my way. Seeking survivors and reuniting next of kin has been my passion. This is why I found the sensitivity of Tatiana de Rosnay so gripping and her sense of history so truthful."

—Isaac Levendel, Holocaust scholar and author of *Not the Germans Alone*

Sarah's Key

Sarah's Key

Tatiana de Rosnay

St. Martin's Griffin ❧ New York

This is a work of fiction. All of the characters, organizations, and events portrayed in this novel are either products of the author's imagination or are used fictitiously.

SARAH'S KEY. Copyright © 2007 by Tatiana de Rosnay. All rights reserved. Printed in the United States of America. For information, address St. Martin's Press, 175 Fifth Avenue, New York, N.Y. 10010.

www.stmartins.com

Nota bene: Pages 184 and 185 contain excerpts of Prime Minister Jean-Pierre Raffarin's speech during the 60th commemoration of the Vel' d'Hiv' roundup, on July 21, 2002.

Library of Congress Cataloging-in-Publication Data

Rosnay, Tatiana de, 1961–
    Sarah's Key / Tatiana de Rosnay.
        p. cm.
    ISBN-13: 978-0-312-35685-9
    ISBN-10: 0-312-35685-4
    1. Jews—France—Fiction. 2. World War, 1939–1945—France—Anniversaries, etc.—Fiction. 3. Americans—France—Fiction. 4. Women authors—Fiction. 5. Family secrets—Fiction. 6. France—History—German occupation, 1940–1945—Fiction. 7. Paris (France)—Fiction. I. Title.

PR9105.9.R66 S27 2007
823'.914—dc22

                                                                2006034536

First St. Martin's Griffin Edition: October 2008

10 9 8 7 6 5 4 3 2 1

✦

To Stella, my mother

To my beautiful, rebellious Charlotte

In memory of Natacha, my grandmother (1914–2005)

❧ *Author's Note* ❧

The characters in this novel are entirely fictitious. But several of the
events described are not, especially those that occurred in Occupied
France during summer of 1942, and in particular the great Vélodrome
d'Hiver roundup, which took place on July 16, 1942, in the heart of
Paris.

This is not a historical work and has no intention of being one. It is
my tribute to the children of the Vel' d'Hiv'. The children who never
came back. And the ones who survived to tell.

My God! What is this country doing to me? Because it
has rejected me, let us consider it coldly, let us watch it
lose its honor and its life.
                    —IRÈNE NÉMIROVSKY, *Suite Française* (1942)

Tyger! Tyger! burning bright
In the forests of the night,
What immortal hand or eye
Could frame thy fearful symmetry?
                    —WILLIAM BLAKE, *Songs of Experience*

*T*HE GIRL WAS THE first to hear the loud pounding on the door. Her room was closest to the entrance of the apartment. At first, dazed with sleep, she thought it was her father, coming up from his hiding place in the cellar. He'd forgotten his keys, and was impatient because nobody had heard his first, timid knock. But then came the voices, strong and brutal in the silence of the night. Nothing to do with her father. "Police! Open up! Now!"

The pounding took up again, louder. It echoed to the marrow of her bones. Her younger brother, asleep in the next bed, stirred. "Police! Open up! Open up!" What time was it? She peered through the curtains. It was still dark outside.

She was afraid. She remembered the recent, hushed conversations she had overheard, late at night, when her parents thought she was asleep. She had crept up to the living room door and she had listened and watched from a little crack through the panel. Her father's nervous voice. Her mother's anxious face. They spoke their native tongue, which the girl understood, although she was not as fluent as them. Her father had whispered that times ahead would be difficult. That they would have to be brave and very careful. He pronounced strange, unknown words: "camps," "roundup, a big roundup," "early morning arrests," and the girl wondered what all of it meant. Her father had murmured that only the men were in danger, not the women, not the children, and that he would hide in the cellar every night.

He had explained to the girl in the morning that it would be safer if he slept downstairs, for a little while. Till "things got safe." What "things," exactly? thought the girl. What was "safe"? When would things be "safe" again? She wanted to find out what he had meant by "camp" and "roundup," but she worried about admitting she had eavesdropped on her parents, several times. So she had not dared ask him.

"Open up! Police!"

Had the police found Papa in the cellar, she asked herself. Was that why they were here, had the police come to take Papa to the places he had mentioned during those hushed midnight talks: the "camps," far away, out of the city?

The girl padded fast on silent feet to her mother's room, down the corridor. Her mother awoke the minute she felt a hand on her shoulder.

"It's the police, Maman," the girl whispered. "They're banging on the door."

Her mother swept her legs from under the sheets, brushed her hair out of her eyes. The girl thought she looked tired, old, much older than her thirty years.

"Have they come to take Papa away?" pleaded the girl, her hands on her mother's arms. "Have they come for him?"

The mother did not answer. Again the loud voices down the hallway. The mother swiftly put a dressing gown over her night dress, then took the girl by the hand and went to the door. Her hand was hot and clammy, like a child's, the girl thought.

"Yes?" the mother said timidly, without opening the latch.

A man's voice. He shouted her name.

"Yes, Monsieur, that is me," she answered. Her accent came out strong, almost harsh.

"Open up. Immediately. Police."

The mother put a hand to her throat and the girl noticed how pale she was. She seemed drained, frozen. As if she could no longer move. The girl had never seen such fear on her mother's face. She felt her mouth go dry with anguish.

The men banged again. The mother opened the door with clumsy, trembling fingers. The girl winced, expecting to see green-gray suits.

Two men stood there. One was a policeman, wearing his dark blue knee-length cape and a high, round cap. The other man wore a beige raincoat. He had a list in his hand. Once again, he said the woman's name. And the father's name. He spoke perfect French. Then we are safe, thought the girl. If they are French, and not German, we are not in danger. If they are French, they will not harm us.

The mother pulled her daughter close to her. The girl could feel the woman's heart beating through her dressing gown. She wanted to push her mother away. She wanted her mother to stand up straight and look at the men boldly, to stop cowering, to prevent her heart from beating like that, like a frightened animal's. She wanted her mother to be brave.

"My husband is . . . not here," stuttered the mother. "I don't know where he is. I don't know."

The man with the beige raincoat shoved his way into the apartment.

"Hurry up, Madame. You have ten minutes. Pack some clothes. Enough for a couple of days."

The mother did not move. She stared at the policeman. He was standing on the landing, his back to the door. He seemed indifferent, bored. She put a hand on his navy sleeve.

"Monsieur, please—," she began.

The policeman turned, brushing her hand away. A hard, blank expression in his eyes.

"You heard me. You are coming with us. Your daughter, too. Just do as you are told."

Paris, May 2002

BERTRAND WAS LATE, AS usual. I tried not to mind, but I did. Zoë lolled back against the wall, bored. She looked so much like her father, it sometimes made me smile. But not today. I glanced up at the ancient, tall building. Mamé's place. Bertrand's grandmother's old apartment. And we were going to live there. We were going to leave the boulevard du Montparnasse, its noisy traffic, incessant ambulances due to three neighboring hospitals, its cafés and restaurants, for this quiet, narrow street on the right bank of the Seine.

The Marais was not an arrondissement I was familiar with, although I did admire its ancient, crumbling beauty. Was I happy about the move? I wasn't sure. Bertrand hadn't really asked my advice. We hadn't discussed it much at all, in fact. With his usual gusto, he had gone ahead with the whole affair. Without me.

"There he is," said Zoë. "Only half an hour late."

We watched Bertrand saunter up the street with his particular, sensual strut. Slim, dark, oozing sex appeal, the archetypal Frenchman. He was on the phone, as usual. Trailing behind him was his business associate, the bearded and pink-faced Antoine. Their offices were on the rue de l'Arcade, just behind the Madeleine. Bertrand had been part of an architectural firm for a long time, since before our marriage, but he had started out on his own, with Antoine, five years ago.

Bertrand waved to us, then pointed to the phone, lowering his eyebrows and scowling.

"Like he can't get that person off the phone," scoffed Zoë. "Sure."

Zoë was only eleven, but it sometimes felt like she was already a teenager. First, her height, which dwarfed all her girlfriends—as well as her feet, she would add grimly—and then a precocious lucidity that often made me catch my breath. There was something adult about her solemn, hazel gaze, the reflective way she lifted her chin. She had always been like that, even as a little child. Calm, mature, sometimes too mature for her age.

Antoine came to greet us while Bertrand went on with his conversation, just about loud enough for the entire street to hear, waving his hands in the air, making more faces, turning around from time to time to make sure we were hanging on to every word.

"A problem with another architect," explained Antoine with a discreet smile.

"A rival?" asked Zoë.

"Yes, a rival," replied Antoine.

Zoë sighed.

"Which means we could be here all day," she said.

I had an idea.

"Antoine, do you by any chance have the key to Madame Tézac's apartment?"

"I do have it, Julia," he said, beaming. Antoine always spoke English to my French. I suppose he did it to be friendly, but it secretly annoyed me. I felt like my French still wasn't any good after living here all these years.

Antoine flourished the key. We decided to go up, the three of us. Zoë punched out the *digicode* at the door with deft fingers. We walked through the leafy, cool courtyard to the elevator.

"I hate that elevator," said Zoë. "Papa should do something about it."

"Honey, he's only redoing your great-grandmother's place," I pointed out. "Not the whole building."

"Well, he should," she said.

As we waited for the elevator, my mobile phone chirped out the Darth Vader theme. I peered at the number flashing on my screen. It was Joshua, my boss.

I answered, "Yup?"

Joshua was to the point. As usual.

"Need you back by three. Closing July issues. Over and out."

"Gee whiz," I said pertly. I heard a chuckle on the other end of the line before he hung up. Joshua always seemed to like it when I said gee whiz. Maybe it reminded him of his youth. Antoine seemed amused by my old-fashioned Americanisms. I imagined him hoarding them up, then trying them out with his French accent.

The elevator was one of those inimitable Parisian contraptions with a diminutive cabin, hand-maneuvered iron screen, and double wooden doors that inevitably swung in your face. Squashed between Zoë and Antoine—a trifle heavy-handed with his Vétiver scent—I caught a glimpse of my face in the mirror as we glided up. I looked as eroded as the groaning lift. What had happened to the fresh-faced belle from Boston, Mass.? The woman who stared back at me was at that dreaded age between forty-five and fifty, that no-man's land of sag, oncoming wrinkle, and stealthy approach of menopause.

"I hate this elevator, too," I said grimly.

Zoë grinned and pinched my cheek.

"Mom, even Gwyneth Paltrow would look like hell in that mirror."

I had to smile. That was such a Zoë-like remark.

*T*HE MOTHER BEGAN TO sob, gently at first, then louder. The girl
looked at her, stunned. In all her ten years, she had never seen her
mother cry. Appalled, she watched the tears trickle down her mother's
white, crumpled face. She wanted to tell her mother to stop crying, she
could not bear the shame of seeing her mother snivel in front of these
strange men. But the men paid no attention to the mother's tears. They
told her to hurry up. There was no time to waste.

In the bedroom, the little boy slept on.

"But where are you taking us?" pleaded her mother. "My daughter is
French, she was born in Paris, why do you want her too? Where are you
taking us?"

The men spoke no more. They loomed over her, menacing, huge. The
mother's eyes were white with fear. She went to her room, sank down on
the bed. After a few seconds, she straightened her back and turned to the
girl. Her voice was a hiss, her face a tight mask.

"Wake your brother. Get dressed, both of you. Take some clothes, for
him and you. Hurry! Hurry, now!"

Her brother went speechless with terror when he peeped through
the door and saw the men. He watched his mother, disheveled, sobbing, trying to pack. He mustered all the strength he had in his four-
year-old body. He refused to move. The girl cajoled him. He would not
listen. He stood, motionless, his little arms folded over his chest.

The girl took off her night dress, grabbed a cotton blouse, a skirt. She slipped her feet into shoes. Her brother watched her. They could hear their mother crying from her room.

"I'm going to our secret place," he whispered.

"No!" she urged. "You're coming with us, you must."

She grabbed him, but he wriggled out of her grasp and slithered into the long, deep cupboard hidden in the surface of the wall of their bedroom. The one they played hide-and-seek in. They hid there all the time, locked themselves in, and it was like their own little house. Maman and Papa knew about it, but they always pretended they didn't. They'd call out their names. They'd say with loud, bright voices, "But *where* did those children go? How *strange*, they were here a minute ago!" And she and her brother would giggle away with glee.

They had a flashlight in there and some cushions and toys and books, even a flask of water that Maman would fill up every day. Her brother couldn't read yet, so the girl would read *Un Bon Petit Diable* out loud to him. He loved the tale of the orphan Charles and the terrifying Madame Mac'miche and how Charles got back at her for all her cruelty. She would read it to him over and over again.

The girl could see her brother's small face peeking out at her from the darkness. He had his favorite teddy bear clutched to him, he was not frightened anymore. Maybe he'd be safe there, after all. He had water and the flashlight. And he could look at the pictures in the Comtesse de Ségur book. His favorite was the one of Charles's magnificent revenge. Maybe she should leave him there for the moment. The men would never find him. She would come back to get him later in the day when they were allowed to go home again. And Papa, still in the cellar, would know where the boy was hiding, if ever he came up.

"Are you afraid in there?" she said softly, as the men called out for them.

"No," he said. "I'm not afraid. You lock me in. They won't get me."

She closed the door on the little white face, turned the key in the lock. Then she slipped the key into her pocket. The lock was hidden by a pivoting device shaped like a light switch. It was impossible to see the outline of the cupboard in the paneling of the wall. Yes, he'd be safe there. She was sure of it.

The girl murmured his name and laid her palm flat on the wooden panel.

"I'll come back for you later. I promise."

W E ENTERED THE APARTMENT, fumbled with light switches. Nothing happened. Antoine opened a couple of shutters. The sun poured in. The rooms were bare, dusty. Without furniture, the living room seemed immense. The golden rays slanted in through the long, grimy windowpanes, dappling the deep brown floorboards.

I looked around at the empty shelves, the darker squares on the walls where the beautiful paintings used to hang, the marble chimney where I remembered so many winter fires burning, and Mamé holding out her delicate, pale hands to the warmth of the flames.

I went to stand by one of the windows and looked down at the quiet, green courtyard. I was glad Mamé left before she ever got to see her empty apartment. It would have upset her. It upset me.

"Still smells of Mamé," said Zoë. "Shalimar."

"And of that awful Minette," I said, turning up my nose. Minette had been Mamé's last pet. An incontinent Siamese.

Antoine glanced at me, surprised.

"The cat," I explained. I said it in English this time. Or course I knew that *la chatte* was the feminine for "cat," but it could also mean "pussy." The last thing I wanted was having Antoine guffaw at some dubious double entendre.

Antoine appraised the place with a professional eye.

"The electrical system is ancient," he remarked, pointing at the old-fashioned, white porcelain fuses. "And the heating as well."

The oversized radiators were black with dirt, as scaly as a reptile.

"Wait till you see the kitchen and the bathrooms," I said.

"The bathtub has claws," said Zoë. "I'm going to miss those."

Antoine examined the walls, knocking on them.

"I suppose you and Bertrand want to redo it completely?" he asked, looking at me.

I shrugged.

"I don't know what he wants to do exactly. It was his idea, taking on this place. I wasn't so hot about coming here. I wanted something more . . . practical. Something new."

Antoine grinned.

"But it will be brand-new once we finish it."

"Maybe. But to me, it will always be Mamé's apartment."

The apartment still bore Mamé's imprint, even if she had moved to a nursing home nine months ago. My husband's grandmother had lived here for years. I remembered our first encounter, sixteen years back. I had been impressed by the old master paintings, the marble fireplace boasting family photos framed in ornate silver, the deceptively simple, elegant furniture, the numerous books lining the library shelves, the grand piano draped with lush red velvet. The sunny living room gave onto a peaceful inner courtyard with a thick thatch of ivy spreading out on the opposite wall. It was right here that I had met her for the first time, that I had held out my hand to her, awkwardly, not yet at ease with what my sister Charla dubbed "that kissy French thing."

You didn't shake a Parisian woman's hand, even if you were meeting her for the first time. You kissed her once on each cheek.

But I hadn't known that, yet.

*T*HE MAN WITH THE beige raincoat looked at his list again.

"Wait," he said, "there's a child missing. A boy."

He pronounced the boy's name.

The girl's heart skipped a beat. The mother glanced toward her daughter. The girl put a swift finger to her lips. A movement the men did not catch.

"Where is the boy?" demanded the man.

The girl stepped forward, wringing her hands.

"My brother is not here, Monsieur," she said with her perfect French, the French of a native. "He left at the beginning of the month with some friends. To the country."

The man in the raincoat looked at her thoughtfully. Then he made a quick gesture with his chin to the policeman.

"Search the place. Fast. Maybe the father is hiding, too."

The policeman lumbered through the rooms, clumsily opening doors, looking under beds, into cupboards.

While he made his noisy way through the apartment, the other man paced the room. When he had his back to them, the girl quickly showed her mother the key. Papa will come up and get him, Papa will come later, she mouthed. Her mother nodded. All right, she seemed to say, I understand where the boy is. But her mother started to frown, to make a key gesture with her hand as if to ask, where will you leave the key for Papa, how will he know where it is? The man turned around swiftly and watched them. The mother froze. The girl trembled with fear.

He stared at them for a while. Then he abruptly closed the window.

"Please," the mother said, "it's so hot in here."

The man smiled. The girl thought she had never seen an uglier smile.

"We keep it closed, Madame," he said. "Earlier this morning, a lady threw her child out of the window, then jumped. We wouldn't want that to happen again."

The mother said nothing, numb with horror. The girl glared at the man, hating him, hating every inch of him. She loathed his florid face, his glistening mouth. The cold, dead look in his eyes. The way he stood there, his legs spread, his felt hat tilted forward, his fat hands locked behind his back.

She hated him with all her might, like she had never hated anyone in her life, more than she hated that awful boy at school, Daniel, who had whispered horrible things to her under his breath, horrible things about her mother's accent, her father's accent.

She listened to the policeman continuing his clumsy search. He would not find the boy. The cupboard was too cleverly hidden. The boy would be safe. They would never find him. Never.

The policeman came back. He shrugged, shook his head.

"There is no one here," he said.

The man in the raincoat pushed the mother toward the door. He asked for the keys to the apartment. She handed them over, silently. They filed down the stairs, their progress slowed by the bags and bundles the mother carried. The girl was thinking fast, how could she get the key to her father? Where could she leave it? With the concierge? Would she be awake at this hour?

Strangely, the concierge was already awake and waiting behind her door. The girl noticed she had an odd, gloating expression on her face. Why did she look like that, the girl wondered, why did she not glance at her mother, or at her, but only at the men, as if she did not want to see her or her mother, as if she had never seen them. And yet her mother had always been kind to this woman. She had looked after the concierge's baby from time to time, little Suzanne, who often fretted because of stomach pains, and her mother had been so patient, had sung to Suzanne in her native tongue, endlessly, and the baby had loved it, had fallen asleep peacefully.

"Do you know where the father and the son are?" asked the policeman. He gave her the keys to the apartment.

The concierge shrugged. She still did not look at the girl, at her mother. She pocketed the keys with a swift, hungry movement the girl didn't like.

"No," she said to the policeman. "I haven't seen much of the husband lately. Maybe he's gone into hiding with the boy. You could look through the cellars or the service rooms on the top floor. I can show you."

The baby in the small loge began to whimper. The concierge looked back over her shoulder.

"We don't have time," said the man wearing the raincoat. "We need to move on. We'll come back later if we have to."

The concierge went to get the wailing baby and held it to her chest. She said she knew there were other families in the building next door. She pronounced their names with an expression of distaste, thought the girl, as if she was saying a swearword, one of those dirty words you were never supposed to utter.

B ERTRAND POCKETED HIS PHONE at last and turned his attention to me. He gave me one of his irresistible grins. Why did I have such an impossibly attractive husband? I wondered for the umpteenth time. When I first met him all those years ago, skiing at Courchevel in the French Alps, he had been the slim, boyish type. Now, at forty-seven, heavier, stronger, he exuded manliness, "Frenchiness," and class. He was like good wine, maturing with grace and power, whereas I felt certain I had lost my youth somewhere between the Charles River and the Seine and was certainly not blossoming in middle age. If silver hair and wrinkles seemed to highlight Bertrand's beauty, I felt sure they diminished mine.

"Well?" he said, cupping my ass with a careless, possessive hand, despite his associate and our daughter looking on. "Well, isn't this great?"

"Great," echoed Zoë. "Antoine has just told us everything needs to be redone, which means we probably won't move in for another year."

Bertrand laughed. An amazingly infectious laugh, a cross between a hyena and a saxophone. That was the problem with my husband. Intoxicating charm. And he loved turning it on full blast. I wondered whom he had inherited it from. His parents, Colette and Edouard? Wildly intelligent, refined, knowledgeable. But not charming. His sisters, Cécile and Laure? Well-bred, brilliant, perfect manners. But they only laughed when they felt they were obliged to. I guessed he probably got it from Mamé. Rebellious, belligerent Mamé.

"Antoine is such a pessimist," laughed Bertrand. "We'll be here soon enough. It will be a lot of work, but we'll get the best teams on it."

We followed him down the long corridor with creaking floorboards, visiting the bedrooms that gave onto the street.

"This wall needs to go," Bertrand declared, pointing, and Antoine nodded. "We need to bring the kitchen closer. Otherwise Miss Jarmond here wouldn't find it 'practical.'"

He said the word in English, looking at me with a naughty wink and drawing little quotation marks with his fingers in the air.

"It's quite a big apartment," remarked Antoine. "Rather grand."

"Now, yes. But it was a lot smaller in the old days, a lot humbler," said Bertrand. "Times were hard for my grandparents. My grandfather didn't make good money till the sixties. Then he bought the apartment across the hall and joined the two together."

"So when Grand-père was a kid, he lived in this small part?" Zoë asked.

"That's right," said Bertrand. "This part through here. That was his parents' room, and he slept here. It was a lot smaller."

Antoine tapped on the walls thoughtfully.

"Yes, I know what you're thinking." Bertrand smiled. "You want to bring these two rooms together, right?"

"Right!" admitted Antoine.

"Not a bad idea. Needs working on, though. There's a tricky bit of wall here, I'll show you later. Thick paneling. Pipes and stuff going through. Not as easy as it looks."

I looked at my watch. Two-thirty.

"I have to go," I said. "Meeting with Joshua."

"What do we do with Zoë?" asked Bertrand.

Zoë rolled her eyes.

"I can, like, take a bus back to Montparnasse."

"What about school?" said Bertrand.

Roll of eyes again.

"Papa! It's Wednesday. No school on Wednesday afternoons, remember?

Bertrand scratched his head.

"In my days it—"

"It was on Thursday, no school on Thursdays," chanted Zoë.

"Ridiculous French educational system," I sighed. "And school on Saturday mornings to boot!"

Antoine agreed with me. His sons attended a private school where there were no classes on Saturday mornings. But Bertrand—like his parents—was a staunch believer in the French public school system. I had wanted to put Zoë in a bilingual school. There were several of them in Paris, but the Tézac tribe would have none of that. Zoë was French, born in France. She would go to a French school. At present she attended the Lycée Montaigne, near the Luxembourg Garden. The Tézacs kept forgetting Zoë had an American mother. Luckily, Zoë's English was perfect. I had never spoken anything else to her, and she went often enough to Boston to visit my parents. She spent most summers on Long Island with my sister Charla and her family.

Bertrand turned to me. He had that little glint in his eye, the one I felt wary about, the one that meant he was going to be either very funny or very cruel, or both. Antoine obviously knew what it suggested as well, judging from the meek way he plunged into a studious survey of his patent-leather, tasseled loafers.

"Oh, yes indeed, we know what Miss Jarmond thinks of our schools, our hospitals, our endless strikes, our long vacations, our plumbing systems, our postal service, our TV, our politics, our dogshit on the sidewalks," said Bertrand, flashing his perfect teeth at me. "We have heard about it so many times, so many times, have we not? 'I like to be in America, everything's *clean* in America, everybody picks up dogshit in America!'"

"Papa, stop it, you're so rude!" Zoë said, taking my hand.

OUTSIDE, THE GIRL SAW a neighbor wearing pajamas leaning from his window. He was a nice man, a music teacher. He played the violin, and she liked listening to him. He often played for her and her brother from across the courtyard. Old French songs like "*Sur le pont d'Avignon*" and "*À la claire fontaine,*" and also songs from her parents' country, songs that always got her mother and father dancing gaily, her mother's slippers sliding across the floorboards, her father twirling her mother round and round, round and round till they all felt dizzy.

"What are you doing? Where are you taking them?" he called out.

His voice rang across the courtyard, covering the baby's yells. The man in the raincoat did not answer him.

"But you can't do this," said the neighbor. "They're honest, good people! You can't do this!"

At the sound of his voice, shutters began to open, faces peered out from behind curtains.

But the girl noticed that nobody moved, nobody said anything. They simply watched.

The mother stopped dead in her tracks, her back racked with sobs. The men shoved her on.

The neighbors watched silently. Even the music teacher remained silent.

Suddenly the mother turned and screamed at the top of her lungs. She screamed her husband's name, three times.

The men seized her by the arms, shook her roughly. She dropped her bags and bundles. The girl tried to stop them, but they pushed her aside.

A man appeared in the doorway, a thin man with crumpled clothes, an unshaven chin, and red, tired eyes. He walked through the courtyard, holding himself straight.

When he came up to the men, he told them who he was. His accent was thick, like the woman's.

"Take me with my family," he said.

The girl slipped her hand through her father's.

She was safe, she thought. She was safe, with her mother, with her father. This was not going to last long. This was the French police, not the Germans. No one was going to harm them.

Soon they'd be back in the apartment, and Maman would make breakfast. And the little boy would come out of the hiding place. And Papa would go to the warehouse down the road where he worked as a foreman and made belts and bags and wallets with all his fellow workers, and everything would be the same. And things would become safe again, soon.

Outside, it was daylight. The narrow street was empty. The girl looked back at her building, at the silent faces in the windows, at the concierge cuddling little Suzanne.

The music teacher raised his hand slowly in a gesture of farewell.

She waved back at him, smiling. Everything was going to be all right. She was coming back, they were all coming back.

But the man seemed stricken.

There were tears running down his face, silent tears of helplessness and shame that she could not understand.

R UDE? YOUR MOTHER ADORES it," chuckled Bertrand, winking at Antoine. "Don't you, my love? Don't you, *chérie?*"

He gyrated through to the living room, clicking his fingers to the *West Side Story* tune.

I felt silly, foolish, in front of Antoine. Why did Bertrand take such pleasure in making me out to be the snide, prejudiced American, ever critical of the French? And why did I just stand there and let him get away with it? It had been funny, at one point. In the beginning of our marriage, it had been a classic joke, the kind that made both our American and French friends roar with laughter. In the beginning.

I smiled, as usual. But my smile seemed a little tight today.

"Have you been to see Mamé lately?" I asked.

Bertrand was already busy measuring something.

"What?"

"Mamé," I repeated patiently. "I think she would like to see you. To talk about the apartment."

His eyes met mine.

"Don't have time, *amour*. You go?"

A pleading look.

"Bertrand, I go every week. You know that."

He sighed.

"She's *your* grandmother," I said.

"And she loves *you*, *l'Américaine*." He grinned. "And so do I, *bébé*."

He came over to kiss me softly on the lips.

The American.

"So you're the American," Mamé had stated all those years ago in this very room, looking me over with brooding, gray irises. *L'Américaine*. How American that had made me feel, with my layered locks, sneakers, and wholesome smile. And how quintessentially French this seventy-five-year-old woman was, with her straight back, patrician nose, impeccable coil of hair, and shrewd eyes. And yet, I liked Mamé from the start. Her startling, guttural laugh. Her dry sense of humor.

Even today, I had to admit I liked her more than Bertrand's parents, who still made me feel like "the American," although I had been living in Paris for twenty-five years, been married to their son for fifteen, and produced their first grandchild, Zoë.

On the way down, confronted once again with the unpleasant reflection in the elevator mirror, it suddenly occurred to me that I had put up with Bertrand's jabs for too long, and always with a good-natured shrug.

And today, for some obscure reason, for the first time, I felt I had had enough.

*T*HE GIRL KEPT CLOSE to her parents. They walked all the way down her street, the man in the beige raincoat telling them to hurry up. Where were they going? she wondered. Why did they have to rush so? They were told to go into a large garage. She recognized the road, which was not far from where she lived, from where her father worked.

In the garage, men were bent over engines, wearing blue overalls stained with oil. The men stared at them, silent. No one said anything. Then the girl saw a large group of people standing in the garage with bags and baskets at their feet. Mostly women and children, she noticed. Some of them she knew, a little. But no one dared wave or say hello to each other. After a while, two policemen appeared. They called out names. The girl's father put up his hand when their family name was heard.

The girl looked around her. She saw a boy she knew from school, Léon. He looked tired and scared. She smiled at him, she wanted to tell him that everything was fine, that they could all go home soon. This wouldn't last long, they would soon be sent back. But Léon stared at her like she was crazy. She glanced down at her feet, her cheeks crimson. Maybe she had got it all wrong. Her heart was pounding. Maybe things were not going to happen like she thought they would. She felt very naïve, silly, and young.

Her father bent down to her. His unshaven chin tickled her ear. He said her name. Where was her brother? She showed him the key. The little brother was safe in their secret cupboard, she whispered, proud of herself. He'd be safe there.

Her father's eyes went wide and strange. He grasped her arm. But it's all right, she said, he's going to be all right. It's a deep cupboard, there is enough air in there for him to breathe. And he has water and the flashlight. He'll be fine, Papa. You don't understand, said the father, you don't understand. And to her dismay, she saw that tears filled his eyes.

She pulled his sleeve. She couldn't bear to see her father cry.

"Papa," she said, "we are going back home, aren't we? We are going back after they've called out our names?"

Her father wiped his tears. He looked down at her. Awful, sad eyes she could not bear gazing back at.

"No," he said, "we are not going back. They won't let us go back."

She felt something cold and horrible seep through her. Once again she remembered what she had overheard, her parents' faces glimpsed from behind the door, their fear, their anguish in the middle of the night.

"What do you mean, Papa? Where are we going? Why aren't we going back home? You tell me! Tell me!"

She nearly screamed the last words.

Her father looked down at her. He said her name again, very softly. His eyes were still wet, his eyelashes spiked with tears. He put his hand on the back of her neck.

"Be brave, my sweet love. Be brave, as brave as you can."

She could not cry. Her fear was so great it seemed to engulf everything else, it seemed to suck up every single emotion within her, like a monstrous, powerful vacuum.

"But I promised him I'd come back, Papa. I promised him."

The girl saw that he had started to cry again, that he wasn't listening to her. He was wrapped up in his own grief, in his own fear.

They were all sent outside. The street was empty, save for buses lined up by the sidewalks. The kind of ordinary buses the girl used to take with her mother and her brother to get about town—ordinary, everyday green-and-white buses with platforms at the rear.

They were ordered to get on the buses and were pushed against each other. The girl looked again for green-gray uniforms, for the curt, guttural language she had grown to fear. But these were only policemen. French policemen.

Through the bus's dusty pane, she recognized one of them, the young red-haired one who had often helped her cross the street on her way home from school. She tapped on the glass to attract his attention. When his eyes locked onto hers, he quickly looked away. He seemed embarrassed, almost annoyed. She wondered why. As they were all pushed into the buses, a man protested and was shoved, violently by police. A policeman yelled that he'd shoot if anybody tried to get away.

Listlessly, the girl watched the buildings, the trees drift by. She could only think of her brother in the cupboard, in the empty house, waiting for her. She could only think of him. They crossed a bridge, she saw the Seine sparkle. Where were they going? Papa didn't know. Nobody knew. They were all afraid.

A loud clap of thunder startled everybody. The rain came pouring down so thickly the bus had to halt. The girl listened to the drops pounding on the bus's roof. It did not last long. Soon the bus resumed its route, wheels hissing on glistening cobblestones. The sun came out.

The bus stopped and they all got off, laden with bundles, suitcases, crying children. The girl did not know this street. She had never been here. She saw the elevated *métro* on one end of the road.

They were led to a great pale building. There was something written on it in huge dark letters, but she couldn't make it out. She saw that the entire street was full of families like hers, stepping out of buses, shouted at by the police. The French police, again.

Clutching her father's hand, she was pushed and shoved into an enormous covered arena. Crowds of people were massed there in the middle of the arena, as well as on the hard, iron seats in the galleries. How many people? She didn't know. Hundreds. And there were more pouring in. The girl looked up at the immense blue skylight, shaped like a dome. The merciless sun shone through.

Her father found a place for them to sit. The girl watched the steady trickle of people thicken the crowd. The noise grew louder and louder, a constant hum of thousands of voices, children whimpering, women moaning. The heat grew unbearable, more and more stifling as the sun rose higher in the sky. There was less and less room, they were all huddled against each other. She watched the men, the women, the children, their pinched faces, their frightened eyes.

"Papa," she said, "how long are we going to stay here?"

"I don't know, my sweet."

"Why are we here?"

She put her hand on the yellow star sewn on the front of her blouse. "It's because of this, isn't it?" she said. "Everybody here has one."

Her father smiled, a sad, pathetic smile.

"Yes," he said. "It's because of that."

The girl frowned.

"It's not fair, Papa," she hissed. "It's not fair!"

He hugged her, said her name tenderly.

"Yes, my darling one, you're right. It's not fair."

She sat against him, her cheek pressed against the star he wore on his jacket.

A month or so ago, her mother had sewn the stars on all her clothes. On all the family's clothes, except the little brother's. Before that their identity cards had been stamped with the words "Jew" or "Jewess." And then, there had been all the things they were suddenly no longer allowed to do. Like playing in the park. Like riding a bicycle, going to the cinema, the theater, the restaurant, the swimming pool. Like no longer being allowed to borrow books from the library.

She had seen the signs that seemed to be put up everywhere: JEWS FORBIDDEN. And on the door of the warehouse where her father worked, a big card read JEWISH FIRM. Maman had to shop after four o'clock in the afternoon, when there was nothing left in the shops because of the rationings. They had to ride in the last carriage of the *métro*. And they had to be home before curfew and not leave their house till morning. What were they still allowed to do? Nothing. Nothing, she thought.

Unfair. So unfair. Why? Why them? Why all this? It suddenly seemed that nobody could possibly explain it to her.

JOSHUA WAS ALREADY IN the meeting room, drinking the weak coffee he was fond of. I hurried in and sat between Bamber, the photo director, and Alessandra, the features editor.

The room looked out onto the busy rue Marbeuf, just a stone's throw away from the Champs-Élysées. It wasn't my favorite area of Paris—too crowded, too gaudy—but I was used to coming here every day and making my way down the avenue, along the large, dusty sidewalks packed with tourists at every hour of the day, no matter what the season was.

I had been writing for the weekly American magazine *Seine Scenes* for the past six years. We published a paper edition as well as an online version. I usually chronicled any event capable of interesting an American Paris-based audience. This included "local color," which ranged from social and cultural life—shows, movies, restaurants, books—to the upcoming French presidential elections.

It was actually hard work. The deadlines were tight. Joshua was a tyrant. I liked him, but he was a tyrant. He was the kind of boss that had little respect for private lives, marriages, and children. If somebody got pregnant, she became a nonentity. If somebody had a sick child, she was glared at. But he had a shrewd eye, excellent editorial skills, and an uncanny gift for perfect timing. We all bowed down to him. We complained about him every time his back was turned, but we wallowed no end. Fiftyish, a born and bred New Yorker who'd spent the past ten years in Paris, Joshua looked deceptively placid. He had a longish face and drooping eyes. But the minute he opened his mouth, he ruled. One listened to Joshua. And one never interrupted him.

Bamber was from London, nearly thirty. He soared over six feet, wore purple-tinted glasses, sported various body-piercings, and dyed his hair marmalade. He had a marvelous British sense of humor that I found irresistible, but that Joshua rarely understood. I had a soft spot for Bamber. He was a discreet, efficient colleague. He was also wonderful support when Joshua was going through a bad day and unleashing his temper on each of us. Bamber was a precious ally.

Alessandra was part Italian; smooth-skinned, and terrifyingly ambitious. A pretty girl with a head of glossy black curls and the kind of plump, moist mouth men grow stupid about. I could never quite make up my mind whether I liked her or not. She was half my age and already getting paid as much as I was, even if my name was above hers on the masthead.

Joshua went through the charts for upcoming issues. There was a hefty article coming up for the presidential elections, a big topic since Jean-Marie Le Pen's controversial victory in the first round. I wasn't too eager to write about it and was secretly glad when it was allotted to Alessandra.

"Julia," said Joshua, looking up at me over his glasses, "this is up your alley. Sixtieth commemoration of the Vel' d'Hiv'."

I cleared my throat. What had he said? It sounded like "the veldeef."

My mind went blank.

Alessandra looked at me patronizingly.

"July 16, 1942? Ring a bell?" she said. Sometimes I hated her whining Miss Know-All-ish voice. Like today.

Joshua continued.

"The great roundup at the Vélodrome d'Hiver. That's what Vel' d'Hiv' is short for. A famous indoor stadium where biking races were held. Thousands of Jewish families, locked up there for days, in appalling conditions. Then sent to Auschwitz. And gassed."

It did ring a bell. Only faintly.

"Yes," I said firmly, looking at Joshua. "OK, what then?"

He shrugged.

"Well, you could start with finding Vel' d'Hiv' survivors or witnesses. Then check up on the exact commemoration, who's organizing it, where, when. Finally, facts. What happened, exactly. It'll be delicate work, you know. The French aren't fond of talking about Vichy, Pétain, all that. Not something they're overly proud of."

"There's a man who could help you," said Alessandra, slightly less patronizingly. "Franck Lévy. He created one of the biggest associations to help Jewish people find their families after the Holocaust."

"I've heard of him," I said, jotting his name down. I had. Franck Lévy was a public figure. He gave conferences and wrote articles about stolen Jewish goods and the horrors of deportation.

Joshua gulped another coffee down.

"Nothing wishy-washy," he said. "No sentimentalism. Facts. Testimonies. And"—glancing at Bamber—"good, strong photos. Look up old material as well. There isn't much available, as you will discover, but maybe this Lévy guy could help you."

"I'll start by going to the Vel' d'Hiv'," said Bamber. "Check it out."

Joshua smiled wryly.

"The Vel' d'Hiv' doesn't exist anymore. Torn down in '59."

"Where was it?" I asked, glad that I wasn't the only ignoramus.

Alessandra answered once again.

"Rue Nélaton. In the fifteenth arrondissement."

"We could still go there," I said, looking at Bamber. "Maybe there are people living on the street who remember what happened."

Joshua raised his shoulders.

"You could give it a try," he said. "But I don't think you'll find many people willing to talk to you. As I told you, the French are touchy. This is highly sensitive subject matter. Don't forget, it's the French police who arrested all those Jewish families. Not the Nazis."

Listening to Joshua, I realized how little I knew about what happened in Paris in July 1942. I hadn't learned about it in class back in Boston. And since I had come to Paris twenty-five years ago, I had not read much about it. It was like a secret. Something buried in the past.

Something no one mentioned. I was itching to get in front of the computer and start searching the Internet.

As soon as the meeting was over, I went to my little cubbyhole of an office, overlooking the noisy rue Marbeuf. We had cramped working space. But I was used to it. It didn't bother me. I had no place to write at home. Bertrand had promised I'd have a large room to myself in the new apartment. My own private office. At last. It seemed too good to be true. The kind of luxury that would take some getting used to.

I turned on the computer, logged on to the Internet, then on to Google. I typed, *"vélodrome d'hiver vel' d'hiv'."* The listings were numerous. Most of them were in French. A lot of them were very detailed.

I read for the entire afternoon. I did nothing but read and store information and search for books about the Occupation and roundups. Many of the books, I noticed, were out of print. I wondered why. Because nobody wanted to read about the Vel' d'Hiv'? Because no one cared anymore? I called a couple of bookstores. I was told it was going to be tough getting hold of the books. Please try, I said.

When I turned the computer off, I felt overwhelmingly tired. My eyes ached. My head and heart were heavy with everything I'd learned.

There had been over four thousand Jewish children penned in the Vel' d'Hiv', aged between two and twelve. Most of the children were French, born in France.

None of them came back from Auschwitz.

THE DAY DRAGGED ON, endless, unbearable. Huddled against her mother, the girl watched the families around her slowly losing their sanity. There was nothing to drink, nothing to eat. The heat was stifling. The air was full of a dry, feathery dust that stung her eyes and her throat.

The great doors to the stadium were closed. Along each wall, sullen-faced policemen threatened them silently, hands on their guns. There was nowhere to go. Nothing to do. Except to sit here, and wait. Wait for what? What was going to happen to them, to her family, to this mass of people?

With her father, they had tried to find the restrooms at the other end of the arena. An unimaginable stench greeted them. There were too few toilets for such a crowd, and these were soon out of order. The girl had to squat against the wall to relieve herself, fighting against the overpowering urge to vomit, her hand clapped over her mouth. People were pissing and defecating wherever they could, ashamed, broken, cowering like animals near the filthy floor. She saw a dignified old woman hiding behind her husband's coat. Another woman was gasping with horror, clasping her hands over her mouth and nose, shaking her head.

The girl followed her father through the crowd, back to where they'd left her mother. They had to pick their way through the throng. The galleries were thick with bundles, bags, mattresses, cribs—the arena black with people. How many, she wondered, how many people here?

Children ran through the aisles, bedraggled, dirty, screaming for water. A pregnant woman, faint with heat and thirst, yelled at the top of her lungs that she was going to die, that she was going to die now. An old man collapsed suddenly, flat out on the dusty floor. His blue face contorted and twitched. Nobody moved.

The girl sat down next to her mother. The woman had gone quiet. She hardly spoke. The girl took her hand and squeezed it; her mother did not respond. The father got up to ask a policeman for water for his child and wife. The man replied curtly that there was no water for the moment. The father said that this was abominable, that they could not be treated like dogs. The policeman turned away.

The girl saw Léon again, the boy she had seen in the garage. He was wandering through the crowd, looking toward the great doors. She noticed he was not wearing his yellow star. It had been torn off. She got up, went to him. His face was grimy. There was a bruise on his left cheek, another on his collarbone. She wondered if she looked like that too, tired and battered.

"I'm getting out of here," he said in a low voice. "My parents have told me to. Now."

"But how?" she said. "The police will never let you through."

The boy looked at her. He was her age, ten, but he appeared much older. There was no longer anything boyish about him.

"I'll find a way," he said. "My parents told me to go. They took off the star. It's the only way. Otherwise, it's the end. The end for all of us."

Again she felt the cold fear surge through her. The end? Was this boy right? Was it really the end?

He gazed at her, slightly contemptuous.

"You don't believe me, do you? You should come with me. Take off your star, come with me now. We'll hide. I'll look after you. I know what to do."

She thought of her little brother in the cupboard, waiting. She fingered the smooth key in her pocket. She could go with this fast, clever boy. She could save her brother, and herself.

But she felt too small, too vulnerable to do anything like that alone. She was too frightened. And her parents . . . Her mother, her father . . .

What would happen to them? Was this boy telling the truth? Could she trust him?

He put a hand on her arm, sensing her reluctance.

"Come with me," he urged.

"I don't know," she muttered.

He backed away.

"I've made up my mind. I'm leaving. Good-bye."

She watched him edge toward the entrance. The police were letting more people in: old men on stretchers and in wheelchairs, endless groups of sniveling children, tearful women. She watched Léon glide through the crowd, waiting for the right moment.

At one point a policeman grabbed him by the collar and threw him back. Lithe and quick, he picked himself up, inching back toward the doors, like a swimmer adroitly fighting the current. The girl watched, fascinated.

A group of mothers stormed the entrance, angrily demanding water for the children. The police seemed momentarily confused, not knowing what to do. The girl saw the boy slip through the pandemonium easily, fast as lightning. Then he was gone.

She went back to her parents. The night began to fall, slowly, and with it the girl felt that her despair, and that of the thousands of people locked in here with her, began to grow, like something monstrous, out of control, a sheer, utter despair that filled her with panic.

She tried to shut her eyes, her nose, her ears, to block out the smell, the dust, the heat, the howls of anguish, the visions of adults crying, of children moaning, but she could not.

She could only watch, helpless, silent. From high up near the skylight, where people were sitting in little groups, she noticed a sudden commotion. A heart-wrenching yell, a flurry of clothes cascading over the balconies, and a thump on the hard floor of the arena. Then a gasp from the crowd.

"Papa, what was that?" she asked.

Her father tried to turn her face away.

"Nothing, darling, nothing. Just some clothes falling from up there."

But she had seen. She knew what it was. A young woman, her mother's age, and a small child. The woman had jumped, her child held close, from the highest railing.

From where the girl sat, she could see the dislocated body of the woman, the bloody skull of the child, sliced open like a ripe tomato.

The girl bent her head and cried.

WHEN I WAS A girl, living at 49 Hyslop Road in Brookline, Mass., I never imagined I'd move to France one day and marry a Frenchman. I figured I'd stay in the States all my life. At eleven, I had a crush on Evan Frost, the boy next door. A freckle-faced, Norman Rockwell kid with a retainer, whose dog Inky liked to romp on my father's beautiful flower beds.

My dad, Sean Jarmond, taught at MIT. A "mad professor" type, with unruly locks and owl-like glasses. He was popular, students liked him. My mom, Heather Carter Jarmond, was an ex–tennis champion from Miami, that kind of sporty, tanned, lean female that never seems to grow old. She was into yoga and health food.

On Sundays, my father and the neighbor, Mr. Frost, would have endless yelling matches over the hedge about Inky ruining my dad's tulips, while my mother made bran-and-honey cupcakes in the kitchen and sighed. She loathed conflict. Heedless of the pandemonium, my little sister Charla would be watching *Gilligan's Island* or *Speed Racer* in the TV room, ingurgitating yards of red liquorice. Upstairs, my best friend Katy Lacy and I would be peering out from behind my curtains at gorgeous Evan Frost frolicking with the object of my father's furor, a jet-black Labrador.

It was a happy, sheltered childhood. No outbursts, no scenes. Runkle School down the road. Quiet Thanksgivings. Cozy Christmases. Long lazy summers at Nahant. Peaceful weeks merging into peaceful months. The only thing that scared the hell out of me was when my fifth-grade teacher, the tow-headed Miss Sebold, read out "The Tell-Tale Heart" by Edgar Allan Poe. Thanks to her, I had nightmares for years.

It was during my adolescence that I felt the first yearnings for France, an insidious fascination that grew stronger with the passage of time. Why France? Why Paris? The French language had always attracted me. I found it softer, more sensual than German, Spanish, or Italian. I used to give excellent imitations of the Looney Tunes French skunk, Pepe Le Pew. But deep down I knew my ever-growing ardor for Paris had nothing to do with the typical American clichés of romance, sophistication, and sexiness. It went beyond that.

When I first discovered Paris, I was quickly drawn to its contrasts; its tawdry, rough neighborhoods appealed to me as much as the Haussmannian, majestic ones. I craved its paradoxes, its secrets, its surprises. It took me twenty-five years to blend in, but I did it. I learned to put up with impatient waiters and rude taxi drivers. I learned to drive around the Place de l'Étoile, impervious to the insults yelled at me by irate bus drivers, and—more surprisingly—by elegant, highlighted blondes in shiny black Minis. I learned how to tame arrogant concierges, snotty saleswomen, blasé telephone operators, and pompous doctors. I learned how Parisians consider themselves to be superior to the rest of the world, and specifically to all other French citizens living from Nice to Nancy, with a particular disdain toward the inhabitants of the City of Light's suburbs. I learned how the rest of France nicknamed Parisians "dog faces" with the rhyme "*Parisien, tête de chien.*" Clearly, they were not overly fond of Parisians. No one loved Paris better than a true Parisian. No one was prouder of his city than a true Parisian. No one was half so arrogant, so haughty, so conceited, and quite so irresistible. Why did I love Paris so? I wondered. Maybe because it never gave in to me. It hovered enticingly close, yet it let me know my place. The American. I'd always be the American. *L'Américaine.*

I knew I wanted to be a journalist when I was Zoë's age. I first started writing for the high-school newspaper and had never stopped since. I came to live in Paris when I was a little over twenty, after graduating from Boston University with an English major. My first job was as a junior assistant for an American fashion magazine I soon left. I was looking for meatier topics than skirt lengths or spring colors.

I took the first job that came up. Rewriting press releases for an American TV network. It wasn't fantastically paid, but it was enough for me to stay on, living in the eighteenth arrondissement, sharing a place with two French gay men, Hervé and Christophe, who became long-lasting friends.

That week I had a dinner date with them at the rue Berthe, where I'd lived before meeting Bertrand. Bertrand rarely accompanied me. I sometimes wondered why he was so uninterested in Hervé and Christophe. "Because your dear husband, like most French bourgeois, well-to-do gentlemen, prefers women to homosexuals, *cocotte!*" I could almost hear my friend Isabelle's languid voice, her sly chuckle. Yes, she was right. Bertrand was definitely into women. Big time, as Charla would say.

Hervé and Christophe still lived in the same place I had shared with them. Except that my small bedroom was now a walk-in closet. Christophe was a fashion victim and proud of it. I enjoyed their dinners; there was always an interesting mix of people—a famous model or singer, a controversial writer, a cute, gay neighbor, another American or Canadian journalist, or some young editor just starting out. Hervé worked as a lawyer for an international firm, and Christophe was a yoga teacher.

They were my true, dear friends. I did have other friends here, American expats—Holly, Susannah, and Jan—met through the magazine or the American college where I often went to put up ads for babysitters. I even had a couple of close French girlfriends—like Isabelle, garnered through Zoë's ballet class at the Salle Pleyel—but Hervé and Christophe were the ones I called at one in the morning when Bertrand had been difficult. The ones who came to the hospital when Zoë broke her ankle falling off her scooter. The ones who never forgot my birthday. The ones who knew which films to see, which records to buy. Their meals were invariably a delight, candlelit and exquisite.

I arrived with a chilled bottle of champagne. Christophe was still in the shower, explained Hervé, greeting me at the door. In his mid-forties, Hervé was slim, mustachioed, and genial. He smoked like a chimney. It was impossible to get him to stop. So we had all given up.

"That's a nice jacket," he commented, putting down his cigarette to open the champagne.

Hervé and Christophe always noticed what I was wearing, if I sported new perfume, new makeup, a new hair style. When I was with them, I never felt like *l'Américaine* desperately trying to keep up with Parisian chic. I felt myself. And I loved that about them.

"That blue-green suits you, goes divinely with your eyes. Where did you buy it?" Hervé asked.

"H&M, on the rue de Rennes."

"You look superb. So, how's the apartment coming along?" he asked, handing me a glass and some warm toast spread with pink tarama.

"There's a hell of a lot to be done," I sighed. "It will take months."

"And I imagine the architect of a husband is thrilled at the whole thing?"

I winced.

"You mean he's indefatigable."

"Ah," said Hervé. "And therefore a pain in the ass for you."

"You got it," I said, sipping champagne.

Hervé looked at me closely through his tiny, rimless glasses. He had pale gray eyes and ridiculously long eyelashes.

"Say, Juju," he said, "are you all right?"

I smiled brightly.

"Yes, I'm fine."

But fine was far from what I felt. My recent knowledge about the events of July 1942 had awakened a vulnerability within me, triggered something deep, unspoken, that haunted me, that burdened me. I had dragged that burden around with me all week, ever since I'd started to research the Vel' d'Hiv' roundup.

"You just don't look yourself," Hervé said, concerned. He came to sit next to me, putting his slim, white hand on my knee. "I know that face, Julia. That's your sad face. Now you tell me what's going on."

*T*HE ONLY WAY TO shut out the hell around her was to bury her head between her pointed knees, and cup her hands over her ears. She rocked back and forth, pressing her face down onto her legs. Think of nice things, think of all the things you like, of all the things that make you happy, of all those special, magical moments you remember. Her mother taking her to the hairdresser, and everyone complimenting her thick, honey-colored hair. You will be proud of that head of hair later on, *ma petite*!

Her father's hands working on the leather in the warehouse, how fast and strong they were, how she admired his skill. Her tenth birthday and the new watch, the beautiful blue box, the leather strap her father had made, its rich, intoxicating smell, and the discreet tick-tock of the watch that fascinated her. She had been so proud. But Maman had said not to wear it to school. She might break it or lose it. Only her best friend Armelle had seen it. And she had been so jealous!

Where was Armelle now? She lived just down the road, they went to the same school. But Armelle had left the city at the beginning of the school vacations. She had gone somewhere with her parents, somewhere south. There had been one letter, and that was all. Armelle was small and red-haired and very clever. She knew all her multiplication tables by heart, and she even mastered the trickiest grammar.

Armelle was never afraid, the girl admired that about her. Even when the sirens went off in the middle of class, howling like enraged wolves, making everyone jump, Armelle remained calm, in control, she would take the girl's hand and lead her down to the musty school cellar, impervious to all the other children's frightened whispers and Mademoiselle Dixsaut's quavering orders. And they would huddle together, shoulder to shoulder, in the dark dampness, candlelight flickering on pale faces, for what seemed hours, and listen to the drone of the planes far above their heads, while Mademoiselle Dixsaut read Jean de La Fontaine or Molière and tried to stop her hands from trembling. Look at her hands, Armelle would giggle, she's afraid, she can hardly read, look. And the girl would glance at Armelle with wonder and whisper, "Aren't you afraid? Not even the tiniest bit?" A contemptuous shake of glossy red curls. No, I'm not. I'm not afraid. And sometimes, when the shudder of the bombs seeped through the grimy floor, making Mademoiselle Dixsaut's voice falter and stop, Armelle would grab the girl's hand and hold it tight.

She missed Armelle, she wished Armelle could be here now, to hold her hand and tell her not to be afraid. She missed Armelle's freckles and her mischievous green eyes and her insolent grin. Think of the things you love, of the things that make you happy.

Last summer, or was it two summers ago, she couldn't remember, Papa had taken them to spend a couple of days in the countryside by a river. She couldn't remember the name of the river. But the water had felt so smooth and wonderful to her skin. Her father had tried to teach her to swim. After a few days, she managed an inelegant dog paddle that made everybody laugh. By the river, her brother had gone mad with joy and excitement. He was tiny then, a mere toddler. She had spent the day running after him as he slipped and shrieked along the muddy shore. And Maman and Papa had looked so peaceful, young, and in love, her mother's head against her father's shoulder. She remembered the little hotel by the water, where they had eaten simple, succulent meals beneath the cool, leafy bower, and when the *patronne* had asked her to help behind the counter, and there she was handing out coffee and feeling very grown up and proud, until she dropped coffee on someone's foot, but the *patronne* had been very nice about it.

The girl lifted her head, saw her mother talking to Eva, a young woman who lived near them. Eva had four young children, a bunch of rambunctious boys the girl wasn't overly fond of. Eva's face, like her mother's, looked haggard and old. How was it they looked so much older overnight, she wondered. Eva was Polish, too. Her French, like her mother's, was not good. Like the girl's mother and father, Eva had family back in Poland. Her parents, aunts, and uncles. The girl remembered the awful day—when was it?—not very long ago, when Eva had received a letter from Poland, and she had turned up at the apartment, her face streaming with tears, and she had broken down in her mother's arms. Her mother had tried to comfort Eva, but the girl could tell she was stricken as well. Nobody wanted to tell the girl exactly what had happened, but the girl understood, hung on to every Yiddish word she could make out between the sobs. Something terrible, back in Poland, entire families had been killed, houses burnt down, only ashes and ruins remained. She had asked her father if her grandparents were safe. Her mother's parents, the ones whose black-and-white photograph was on the marble mantelpiece in the living room. Her father had said that he did not know. There had been very bad news from Poland. But he wouldn't tell her what the news was.

As she looked at Eva and her mother, the girl wondered if her parents had been right to protect her from everything, if they had been right to keep disturbing, bad news away from her. If they had been right not to explain why so many things had changed for them since the beginning of the war. Like when Eva's husband never came back last year. He had disappeared. Where? Nobody would tell her. Nobody would explain. She hated being treated like a baby. She hated the voices being lowered when she entered the room.

If they had told her, if they had told her everything they knew, wouldn't that have made today easier?

I'M FINE, JUST TIRED, that's all. So who's coming tonight then?"

Before Hervé could answer, Christophe entered the room, a vision of Parisian chic, khaki and cream overtones, exuding expensive men's perfume. Christophe was a little younger than Hervé, tanned all year round, skinny, and wore his long salt-and-pepper hair tied back in a thick ponytail, à la Karl Lagerfeld.

Almost simultaneously, the doorbell rang.

"Aha," said Christophe, blowing me a kiss, "that must be Guillaume."

He rushed to the front door.

"Guillaume?" I mouthed at Hervé.

"Our new pal. Does something in advertising. Divorced. Bright boy. You'll like him. He's our only guest. Everyone else is out of town because of the long weekend."

The man who entered the room was tall, dark, in his late thirties. He was carrying a wrapped scented candle and roses.

"This is Julia Jarmond," said Christophe. "Our very dear journalist friend from a long, long time ago when we were young."

"Which was merely yesterday," murmured Guillaume, in true gallant French fashion.

I tried to keep an easy smile on my face, aware of Hervé's inquiring eyes moving to me from time to time. It was odd, because usually I would have confided in Hervé. I would have told him how strange I had been feeling for the past week. And the business with Bertrand. I had always put up with Bertrand's provocative, sometimes downright nasty sense of humor. It had never hurt me. It had never bothered me. Until now. I used to admire his wit, his sarcasm. It had made me love him all the more.

People laughed at his jokes. They were even a little afraid of him. Behind the irresistible laugh, the twinkling blue-gray eyes, the charming smile, was a tough, demanding man who was used to getting what he wanted. I had put up with it because he made up to me every time, every time he realized he had hurt me, he showered me with gifts, flowers, and passionate sex. In bed was probably the only place Bertrand and I truly communicated, the only place where nobody dominated the other. I remember Charla saying to me once, after witnessing a particularly sharp tirade delivered by my husband, "Is this creep ever *nice* to you?" And watching my face slowly redden, "Jesus. I get the picture. Pillow talk. Actions speak louder than words." And she had sighed and patted my hand. Why hadn't I opened up to Hervé tonight? Something held me back. Something sealed my lips.

Once seated around the octagonal marble table, Guillaume asked me what newspaper I worked for. When I told him, his face remained blank. I wasn't surprised. French people had never heard of *Seine Scenes*. It was mostly read by Americans living in Paris. That didn't bother me; I had never craved fame. I was content with a well-paid job that kept my hours relatively free, despite Joshua's occasional despotism.

"And what are you writing about at the present?" asked Guillaume politely, twisting green pasta around his fork.

"The Vel' d'Hiv'," I said. "The sixtieth commemoration is coming up."

"You mean that roundup during the war?" asked Christophe, his mouth full.

I was about to answer him when I noticed that Guillaume's fork had stopped halfway between his plate and his mouth.

"Yes, the big roundup at the Vélodrome d'Hiver," I said.

"Didn't that take place somewhere out of Paris?" Christophe went on, munching away.

Guillaume had put his fork down, quietly. Somehow his eyes had locked onto mine. He had dark eyes, a sensitive, fine mouth.

"It was the Nazis, I believe," said Hervé, pouring out more Chardonnay. Neither of them seemed to have noticed Guillaume's tight face. "The Nazis who arrested Jews during the Occupation."

"Actually, it wasn't the Germans—," I began.

"It was the French police," interrupted Guillaume. "And it happened in the middle of Paris. In a stadium which used to house famous bike races."

"Really?" asked Hervé. "I thought it was the Nazis, in the suburbs."

"I've been researching this for the past week," I said. "German orders, yes, but French police action. Weren't you taught this in school?"

"I can't remember. I don't think so," admitted Christophe.

Guillaume's eyes, looking at me again, as if he were drawing something out of me, probing me. I felt perturbed.

"It's quite amazing," said Guillaume, with an ironic smile, "the number of French people who still don't know what happened. What about the Americans? Did you know about it, Julia?"

I did not avert my eyes.

"No, I didn't know, and I wasn't told about it at school back in Boston in the seventies. But now I know a lot more. And what I have found out has overwhelmed me."

Hervé and Christophe remained silent. They seemed at a loss, not knowing what to say. Guillaume finally spoke.

"In July '95, Jacques Chirac was the first president ever to draw attention to the role of the French government during the Occupation. And toward this particular roundup. His speech made headlines. Do you remember it?"

I had read Chirac's speech during my recent research. He had certainly gone out on a limb. But I had not recalled it although I must have heard it on the news six years ago. And the boys—I couldn't help calling them that, I always had—obviously had not read or remembered Chirac's speech. They gazed at Guillaume, embarrassed. Hervé chain-smoked and Christophe bit his nails, which he always did when he felt nervous or ill at ease.

Silence fell upon us. It was odd, silence in this room. There had been so many joyful, noisy parties here, people roaring with laughter, endless jokes, loud music. So many games, birthday speeches, dancing till the small hours, despite irate neighbors banging from underneath with a broom.

The silence felt heavy and painful. When Guillaume started to speak again, his voice had changed. His face had changed too. He was pale, and he could not look at us any longer. He stared down at his plate of untouched pasta.

"My grandmother was fifteen the day of the roundup. She was told she was free because they were only taking small children between two and twelve with their parents. She was left behind. And they took all the others. Her little brothers, her little sister, her mother, her father, her aunt, her uncle. Her grandparents. It was the last time she ever saw them. No one came back. No one at all."

*T*HE GIRL'S EYES WERE glazed over with the ghastliness of the night. In the small hours, the pregnant woman had given birth to a premature, stillborn child. The girl had witnessed the screams, the tears. She saw the baby's head, mottled with blood, appear between the woman's legs. She knew she should be looking away, but she could not help staring, appalled, fascinated. She saw the dead baby, gray and waxen, like a shrunken doll, promptly hidden behind a dirty sheet. The woman moaned constantly. No one could silence her.

At dawn, her father had fished through the girl's pocket for the key to the secret cupboard. He took it and went to talk to a policeman. He brandished the key. He explained the situation. He was trying to remain calm, the girl could tell, but he was at the breaking point. He had to go and get his four-year-old son, he told the man. He would return here, he promised. He would fetch his son and come straight back. But the policeman laughed in his face and sniggered, "You think I am going to believe you, my poor man?" The father urged the man to come with him, to accompany him, he was just going to get the boy and come back, immediately. The policeman ordered him out of the way. The father returned to his place, his shoulders stooped. He was crying.

The girl took the key from his trembling hand and put it back into her pocket. How long could her brother survive, she wondered. He must still be waiting for her. He trusted her; he trusted her implicitly.

She couldn't bear the idea of him waiting in the dark. He must be hungry, thirsty. His water had probably run out. And the battery on the flashlight. But anything was better than here, she thought. Anything was better than this hell, the stink, the heat, the dust, the people screaming, the people dying.

She looked at her mother, crouched by herself, who hadn't uttered a whimper in the last couple of hours. She looked at her father, his face haggard, his eyes hollow. She looked around her, at Eva and her exhausted, pitiful boys, at all the other families, at all these unknown people, who, like her, had yellow stars on their chests. She looked at the thousands of children, running wild, hungry, thirsty, the little ones who could not understand, who thought it was some bizarre game that had gone on too long, and who wanted their homes, their beds, their teddy bears.

She tried to rest, putting her pointed chin back onto her knees. The heat came again with the rising sun. She didn't know how she was going to face another day here. She felt weak, tired. Her throat was parched. Her stomach ached with emptiness.

After a while, she dozed off. She dreamed she was back home, back in her little room overlooking the street, back in the living room where the sun used to shine through the windows and make patterns on the fireplace and on her Polish grandmother's photograph. And she would listen to the violin teacher play to her across the leafy courtyard. "*Sur le pont d'Avignon, on y danse, on y danse. Sur le pont d'Avignon, on y danse tout en rond.*" Her mother was making dinner, singing along, *Les beaux messieurs font comme ça, et puis encore comme ça.* Her brother was playing with his little red train down the long corridor, sliding it over the dark floorboards with a clatter and a bang. *Les belles dames font comme ça, et puis encore comme ça.* She could smell her home, its comforting scent of candle wax and spices, and all the tempting things cooking in the kitchen. She could hear her father's voice, reading to her mother. They were safe. They were happy.

She felt a cool hand on her forehead. She looked up to see a young woman wearing a blue veil branded with a cross.

The young woman smiled at her and handed her a cup of fresh water, which she drank avidly. Then the nurse gave her a papery biscuit and some canned fish.

"You must be brave," murmured the young nurse.

But the girl saw that she, too, like the girl's father, had tears in her eyes.

"I want to get out," whispered the girl. She wanted to go back to the dream, to the peace and safety she had felt.

The nurse nodded. She smiled a tiny sad smile.

"I understand. There is nothing I can do. I'm so sorry."

She got up, headed toward another family. The girl stopped her, grabbing her sleeve.

"Please, when are we going to leave?" she asked.

The nurse shook her head. She caressed the girl's cheek softly. Then she moved on to the next family.

The girl thought she was going to go crazy. She wanted to scream and kick and yell, she wanted to leave this dreadful, hideous place. She wanted to go back home, back to what her life had been before the yellow star, before the men had banged on their door.

Why was this happening to her? What had she done, or her parents done, to deserve this? Why was being Jewish so dreadful? Why were Jews being treated like this?

She remembered the first day she'd worn her star to school. That moment when she had walked into the class, and everybody's eyes had been drawn to it. A large yellow star the size of her father's palm on her small chest. And then she saw that there were other girls in the class who had the star too. Armelle wore one as well. It had made her feel a little better.

At recess, all the girls with the stars huddled together. They were pointed at by the other pupils, by all of those who used to be their friends. Mademoiselle Dixsaut had made a point of explaining that the stars should not change anything. All the pupils were to be treated the same way as before, star or no star.

But Mademoiselle Dixsaut's speech had not helped. From that day forward, most girls stopped speaking to the children with the stars. Or worse still, stared at them with disdain. She could not stand the disdain. And that boy, Daniel, had whispered to her and Armelle in the street, in front of the school, his mouth cruel and twisted, "Your parents are dirty Jews, you are dirty Jews." Why dirty? Why was being a Jew dirty? It made her feel ashamed, sad. It made her want to cry. Armelle had said nothing, biting her lip till the blood came. It was the first time she had seen Armelle look afraid.

The girl wanted to rip off the star, she told her parents she refused to go back to school with it. But her mother had said no, that she should be proud of it, she should be proud of her star. Her brother had thrown a fit because he, too, wanted a star. But he was under six, explained his mother patiently. He had to wait another couple of years. He had wailed all afternoon.

She thought of her brother in the dark, deep cupboard. She wanted to take his hot little body in her arms, to kiss his curly blond hair, his plump neck. She gripped the key as hard as she could in her pocket.

"I don't care what anybody says," she whispered to herself. "I'll find a way to go back and save him. I'll find a way."

A FTER DINNER, HERVÉ OFFERED US some *limoncello*, an ice-cold Italian liqueur made with lemon. It had a beautiful yellow color. Guillaume sipped his slowly. He had not said much during the meal. He seemed subdued. I did not dare bring the Vel' d'Hiv' up again. But it was he who turned to speak to me as the others listened.

"My grandmother is old now," he said. "She won't talk about it anymore. But she told me everything I need to know, she told me everything about that day. I think the worst thing for her was having to live on without the others. To have to continue without them. Her entire family."

I could not think of what to say. The boys were silent.

"After the war, my grandmother went to the Hotel Lutétia on the boulevard Raspail, every day," continued Guillaume. "That's where you had to go to find out if anyone had returned from the camps. There were lists and organizations. She went there every day and waited. But after a while, she stopped going. She began to hear about the camps. She began to understand that they were all dead. That no one would come back. Nobody had really known before. But then, with survivors returning and telling their stories, everybody knew."

Another silence.

"You know what I find most shocking about the Vel' d'Hiv'?" Guillaume said. "Its code name."

I knew the answer to that, thanks to my extensive reading.

"Operation Spring Breeze," I murmured.

"A sweet name, isn't it, for something so horrible?" he said. "The Gestapo had asked the French police to 'deliver' a certain number of Jews between sixteen and fifty years old. The police were so intent on deporting the maximum number of Jews that they decided to ameliorate the orders, so they arrested all those little children, the ones born in France. French children."

"The Gestapo hadn't asked for those children?" I said.

"No," he replied. "Not at first. Deporting children would have revealed the truth: it would have been obvious to all that Jews were not being sent to work camps, but to their deaths."

"So why were the children arrested?" I asked.

Guillaume took a sip of his *limoncello*.

"The police probably thought that children of Jews, even if they were born in France, were still Jews. In the end, France sent nearly eighty thousand Jews to the death camps. Only a couple of thousand made it back. And hardly any of the children did."

On the way home, I could not get Guillaume's dark sad eyes out of my mind. He had offered to show me photographs of his grandmother and her family, and I had given him my phone number. He had promised to call me soon.

Bertrand was watching television when I came in. He was lying flat out on the sofa, an arm under his head.

"So," he said, barely taking his eyes off the screen, "how were the boys? Up to their usual standards of refinement?"

I slipped off my sandals and sat on the sofa beside him, looking at his fine, elegant profile.

"A perfect meal. There was an interesting man. Guillaume."

"Aha," said Bertrand, looking at me, amused. "Gay?"

"No, I don't think so. But I never notice that anyway."

"And what was so interesting about this Guillaume guy?"

"He was telling us about his grandmother, who escaped the Vel' d'Hiv' roundup, back in 1942."

"Hmm," he answered, changing channels with the remote control.

"Bertrand," I said, "when you were at school, were you taught about the Vel' d'Hiv'?"

"No idea, *chérie.*"

"That's what I'm working on now for the magazine. The sixtieth anniversary is soon."

Bertrand picked up one of my bare feet and began to massage it with sure, warm fingers.

"Do you think your readers are going to be interested in the Vel' d'Hiv'?" he asked. "It's the past. It's not something most people want to read about."

"Because the French are ashamed, you mean?" I said. "So we should bury it and move on, like them?"

He took my foot off his knee and the glint in his eye appeared. I braced myself.

"My, my," he said with a devilish grin, "yet another chance to show your compatriots how devious we Frogs were, collaborating with the Nazis and sending those poor innocent families to their deaths. Little Miss Nahant bares the truth! What are you going to do, *amour,* rub our noses in it? Nobody cares anymore. Nobody remembers. Write about something else. Something funny, something cute. You know how to do that. Tell Joshua the Vel' d'Hiv' is a mistake. No one will read it. They'll yawn and turn to the next column."

I got up, exasperated.

"I think you're wrong," I seethed. "I think people don't know enough about it. Even Christophe didn't know much about it, and he's French."

Bertrand snorted.

"Oh, Christophe can hardly read! The only words he deciphers are Gucci and Prada."

I left the room in silence, went into the bathroom, and ran a bath. Why hadn't I told him to go to hell? Why did I put up with him, again and again? Because you're crazy about him, right? Ever since you met him, even if he's bossy, rude, and selfish? He's clever, he's handsome, he can be so funny, he's such a wonderful lover, isn't he? Memories of endless, sensual nights, kisses and caresses, crumpled sheets, his beautiful body, warm mouth, impish smile. Bertrand. So charming. So irresistible. So arduous. That's why you put up with him. Isn't it?

But for how long? A recent conversation with Isabelle came back to me. Julia, do you put up with Bertrand because you're afraid of losing him? We were sitting in a small café by the Salle Pleyel, while our daughters were attending ballet class, and Isabelle had lit up her umpteenth cigarette and looked me straight in the eye. No, I had said. I love him. I really love him. I love the way he is. She had whistled, impressed, but unconvinced. Well, lucky him then. But for God's sake, when he goes too far, tell him. Just tell him.

Lying in the bath, I remembered the first time I met Bertrand. In some quaint discothèque in Courchevel. He was with a group of loud, tipsy friends. I was with my then-boyfriend, Henry, whom I'd met a couple of months earlier at the TV network I worked for. We had a casual, easygoing relationship. Neither of us was deeply in love with the other. We were just two fellow Americans living it up in France.

Bertrand had asked me to dance. It hadn't seemed to bother him at all that I was sitting with another man. Galled, I had refused. He had been very insistent. "Just one dance, miss. Only one dance. But such a wonderful dance, I promise you." I had glanced at Henry. Henry had shrugged. "Go ahead," he had said, winking. So I got up and danced with the audacious Frenchman.

I was rather stunning at twenty-seven. And yes, I *had* been Miss Nahant when I was seventeen. I still had my rhinestone tiara tucked away somewhere. Zoë used to like playing with it when she was little. I've never been vain about my looks. But I had noticed that living in Paris, I got much more attention than on the other side of the Atlantic. I did also discover that French men were more daring, more overt, when it came to flirting. And I also understood that despite the fact I had nothing of the sophisticated Parisian—too tall, too blond, too toothy—my New England allure appeared to be just the flavor of the day. In my first months in Paris, I had been amazed at the way French men—and women—stare overtly at each other. Sizing each other up, constantly. Checking out figures, clothes, accessories. I remembered my first spring in Paris and walking down the boulevard Saint-Michel with Susannah from Oregon and Jan from Virginia. We weren't even dressed up to go out, we were wearing jeans, T-shirts, and flip-flops. But we were, all three of us, tall, athletic, blond, and definitely American-looking. Men came up to us constantly. *"Bonjour, Mesdemoiselles, vous êtes américaines, Mesdemoiselles?"* Young men, mature men, students, businessmen, endless men, demanding phone numbers, inviting us to dinner, to a drink, pleading, joking, some charming, others much less charming. This did not happen back home. American men did not tag after girls on the street and declare their flame. Jan, Susannah, and I had giggled helplessly, feeling both flattered and dismayed.

Bertrand says he fell in love with me during that first dance in the Courchevel nightclub. Right then and there. I don't believe that. I think, for him, it came a little later. Maybe the next morning, when he took me skiing. *"Merde alors,"* French girls don't ski like that, he had panted, staring at me with blatant admiration. Like what, I had asked. They don't go half as fast, he had laughed, and kissed me passionately. However, *I* had fallen for him on the spot. So much so that I had hardly given poor Henry a departing look as I left the discothèque on Bertrand's arm.

Bertrand talked almost immediately about getting married. It had never been my idea so soon, I was happy enough being his girlfriend for a while. But he had insisted, and he had been so charming, and so amorous, I had finally agreed to marry him. I believe he felt I was going to be the perfect wife, the perfect mother. I was bright, cultivated, well-schooled (summa cum laude from Boston University), and well-behaved—"for an American," I could almost hear him thinking. I was healthy and wholesome and strong. I didn't smoke, didn't take drugs, hardly drank, and believed in God. And so back in Paris, I met the Tézac family. How nervous I had been on that first day. Their impeccable, classic apartment on the rue de l'Université. Edouard's cold blue eyes, his dry smile. Colette and her careful makeup, her perfect clothes, trying to be friendly, handing me coffee and sugar with elegant, manicured fingers. And the two sisters. One was angular, blond, and pale: Laure. The other auburn, ruby-cheeked, and voluptuous: Cécile. Laure's fiancé, Thierry, was there. He hardly spoke to me. The sisters had both looked at me with apparent interest, baffled by the fact that their Casanova of a brother had picked out an unsophisticated American, when he had *le tout Paris* at his feet.

I knew Bertrand—and his family, too—were expecting me to have three or four children in rapid succession. But the complications started right after our wedding. Endless complications that we had not expected. A series of early miscarriages had left me distraught.

I managed to have Zoë after six difficult years. Bertrand hoped for a long time for number two. So did I. But we never talked about it anymore.

And then there was Amélie.

But I certainly did not want to think about Amélie tonight. I had done enough of that in the past.

The bathwater was lukewarm, so I got out, shivering. Bertrand was still watching TV. Usually, I would have gone back to him, and he would have held out his arms to me, and crooned, and kissed me, and I would have said he was just too rude, but I would have said it with a little girl voice, and a little girl pout. And we would have kissed, and he would have taken me back to our room and made love to me.

But tonight I did not go to him. I slipped into bed and read some more about the Vel' d'Hiv' children.

And the last thing I saw before I turned off the light was Guillaume's face when he had told us about his grandmother.

How long had they been here? The girl could not remember. She felt deadened, numbed. The days had mingled with the nights. At one point she had been sick, bringing up bile, moaning in pain. She had felt her father's hand upon her, comforting her. The only thing she had in mind was her brother. She could not stop thinking about him. She would take the key from her pocket and kiss it feverishly, as if kissing his plump little cheeks, his curly hair.

Some people had died here during the past days, and the girl had seen it all. She had seen women and men go mad in the stifling, stinking heat and be beaten down and tied to stretchers. She had seen heart attacks, and suicides, and high fever. The girl had watched the bodies being carried out. She had never seen such horror. Her mother had become a meek animal. She hardly spoke. She cried silently. She prayed.

One morning, curt orders were shouted through loudspeakers. They were to take their belongings and gather near the entrance. In silence. She got up, groggy and faint. Her legs felt weak, they could hardly carry her. She helped her father haul her mother to her feet. They picked up their bags. The crowd shuffled slowly to the doors. The girl noticed how everybody moved slowly, painfully. Even the children hobbled like old people, backs bent, heads down. The girl wondered where they were going. She wanted to ask her father, but his closed thin face meant she was not going to get an answer now. Could they be going home at last? Was this the end? Was it over? Would she be able to go home and free her brother?

They walked down the narrow street, the police ordering them on. The girl glanced at the strangers watching them from windows, balconies, doors, from the sidewalk. Most of them had empty, uncompassionate faces. They looked on, not saying a word. They don't care, thought the girl. They don't care what is being done to us, where we are being taken to. One man laughed, pointing at them. He was holding a child by the hand. The child was laughing, too. Why, thought the girl, why? Do we look funny, with our stinking, wretched clothes? Is that why they are laughing? What is so funny? How can they laugh, how can they be so cruel? She wanted to spit at them, to scream at them.

A middle-aged woman crossed the street and quickly pressed something into her hand. It was a small roll of soft bread. The woman was shooed off by a policeman. The girl just had enough time to see her return to the other side of the street. The woman had said, "You poor little girl. May God have pity." What was God doing, thought the girl, dully. Had God given up on them? Was he punishing them for something she did not know about? Her parents were not religious, although she knew they believed in God. They had not bought her up in the traditional religious fashion, like Armelle had been by her parents, respecting all the rites. The girl wondered whether this was not their punishment. Their punishment for not practicing their religion well enough.

She handed the bread to her father. He told her to eat it. She wolfed it down, too fast. It nearly choked her.

They were taken in the same town buses to a railway station overlooking the river. She didn't know which station it was. She had never been there before. She had rarely left Paris in all her ten years. When she saw the train, she felt panic overcome her. No, she couldn't leave, she had to stay, she had to stay because of her brother, she had promised to come back to save him. She tugged on her father's sleeve, whispering her brother's name. Her father looked down at her.

"There is nothing we can do," he said with helpless finality. "Nothing."

She thought of the clever boy who had escaped, the one who had gotten away. Anger swept through her. Why was her father being so weak, so gutless? Did he not care about his son? Did he not care about his little boy? Why didn't he have the courage to run away? How could he just stand there and be led into a train, like a sheep? How could he just stand there and not break away, and not run back to the apartment, and the boy, and to freedom? Why didn't he take the key from her and run away?

Her father looked at her, and she knew he read all the thoughts in her head. He told her very calmly that they were in great danger. He did not know where they were being taken. He did not know what was going to happen to them. But he did know that if he tried to escape now, he would be killed. Shot down, instantly, in front of her, in front of her mother. And if that happened, that would be the end. She and her mother would be alone. He had to stay with them, to protect them.

The girl listened. He had never used this voice with her before. It was the voice she had overheard during those worrying, secret conversations. She tried to understand. She tried not to let her face show her anguish. But her brother . . . It was her fault! She was the one who had told him to stay in the cupboard. It was all her fault. He could have been here with them now. He could have been here, holding her very hand, if it hadn't been for her.

She began to cry, burning tears that scalded her eyes, her cheeks. "I didn't know!" she sobbed. "Papa, I didn't know, I thought we were coming back, I thought he'd be safe." Then she looked up at him, fury and pain in her voice, and pummeled her little fists against his chest. "You never told me, Papa, you never explained, you never told me about the danger, never! Why? You thought I was too small to understand, didn't you? You wanted to protect me? Is that what you were trying to do?"

Her father's face. She could no longer look at it. He gazed down at her with such despair, such sadness. Her tears washed the image of his face away. She cried into her palms, alone. Her father did not touch her. In those awful, lonely minutes, the girl understood. She was no longer a happy little ten-year-old girl. She was someone much older. Nothing would ever be the same again. For her. For her family. For her brother.

She exploded one last time, tugging on her father's arm with a violence that was new to her.

"He is going to die! He will die!"

"We are all in danger," he replied at last. "You and me, your mother, your brother, Eva and her sons, and all these people. Everyone here. I am here with you. And we are with your brother. He is in our prayers, in our hearts."

Before she could answer, they were pushed into a train, a train that had no seats, just bare wagons. A covered cattle train. It smelled rank and dirty. Standing near the doors, the girl looked out to the gray, dusty station.

On a nearby platform, a family was waiting for another train. The father, the mother, and two children. The mother was pretty, her hair done up in a fancy bun. They were probably off on vacation. There was a girl, just her age. She had a pretty, lilac dress. Her hair was clean, her shoes shiny.

The two girls gazed at each other from across the platform. The pretty, fancy-haired mother was looking, too. The girl in the train knew her tearful face was black with filth, her hair greasy. But she did not bow her head with shame. She stood straight, her chin high. She wiped away the tears.

And when the doors were heaved closed, when the train gave a jolt, wheels clanging and groaning, she peered out through a tiny chink in the metal. She never stopped looking at the little girl. She watched until the figure in the lilac dress completely disappeared.

I HAD NEVER BEEN FOND of the fifteenth arrondissement. Probably because of the monstrous surge of high-rise modern buildings that disfigured the banks of the Seine just next to the Eiffel Tower, and that I had never been able to get used to, although they were built in the early seventies, a long while before I arrived in Paris. But when I turned up at the rue Nélaton with Bamber, where the Vélodrome d'Hiver once stood, I thought to myself I liked this area of Paris even less.

"God-awful street," muttered Bamber. He took a couple of shots with his camera.

The rue Nélaton was dark and silent. It obviously never got much sunshine. On one side, bourgeois stone buildings built in the late nineteenth century. On the other, where the Vélodrome d'Hiver used to be, a large brownish construction, typically early sixties, hideous in both color and proportion. MINISTÈRE DE L'INTERIEUR, read the sign above the revolving glass doors.

"Odd place to build governmental offices," remarked Bamber. "Don't you think?"

Bamber had only found a couple of existing photographs of the Vel' d'Hiv'. I held one of them in my hand. Big black lettering read: VEL' D'HIV' against a pale façade. A huge door. A cluster of buses parked along the sidewalk, and the tops of people's heads. Probably taken from a window across the street on the morning of the roundup.

We looked for a plaque, for something that mentioned what had happened here, but could not find it.

"I can't believe there is nothing," I said.

We finally found it on the boulevard de Grenelle, just around the corner. A smallish sign. Rather humble. I wondered if anyone ever glanced at it. It read:

> On July 16 and 17, 1942, 13,152 Jews were arrested in Paris and the suburbs, deported and assassinated at Auschwitz. In the Vélodrome d'Hiver that once stood on this spot, 1,129 men, 2,916 women, and 4,115 children were packed here in inhuman conditions by the government of the Vichy police, by order of the Nazi occupant. May those who tried to save them be thanked. Passerby, never forget!

"Interesting," mused Bamber. "Why so many children and women, and so few men?"

"Rumors of a big roundup had been circulating," I explained. "There had already been a couple before, especially in August of 1941. But so far, only men were arrested. And they hadn't been as vast, as minutely planned as this one. That's why this one is infamous. The night of July 16, most of the men went into hiding, thinking the women and the children would be safe. That's where they were wrong."

"How long had it been planned for?"

"For months," I answered. "The French government had been working on it intently since April '42, writing up all the lists of the Jews to arrest. Over six thousand Parisian policemen were commissioned to carry it out. At first, the initial chosen date was July 14. But that's the national *fête* here. So it was scheduled a little later."

We walked toward the *métro* station. It was a dismal street. Dismal and sad.

"And then what?" asked Bamber. "Where were all these families taken?"

"Penned in the Vel' d'Hiv' for a couple of days. A group of nurses and doctors were finally let in. They all described chaos and despair. Then the families were taken to Austerlitz Station, and then on to the camps around Paris. And then sent straight to Poland."

Bamber raised an eyebrow.

"Camps? You mean concentration camps in France?"

"Camps that are considered the French antechambers to Auschwitz. Drancy—that's the one closest to Paris—and Pithiviers, and Beaune-la-Rolande."

"I wonder what they look like today, these places," said Bamber. "We should go there and find out."

"We will," I said.

We stopped at the corner of the rue Nélaton for a coffee. I glanced at my watch. I had promised to go see Mamé today. I knew I wouldn't make it. Tomorrow, then. It was never a chore for me. She was the grandmother I had never had. Both of mine had passed away when I was a small child. I just wished Bertrand would make more of an effort, considering she doted upon him.

Bamber dragged me back to the Vel' d'Hiv'.

"Sure makes me glad I'm not French," he said.

Then he remembered.

"Oops, sorry. *You* are now, aren't you?"

"Yes," I said. "By marriage. I have dual nationality."

"Didn't mean what I said," he coughed. He looked embarrassed.

"Don't worry." I smiled. "You know, even after all these years my in-laws still call me the American."

Bamber grinned.

"Does that bother you?"

I shrugged.

"Sometimes. I've spent more than half of my life here. I really feel I belong here."

"How long have you been married?"

"It will soon be sixteen years. But I've been living here for twenty-five."

"Did you have one of those posh French weddings?"

I laughed.

"No, it was simple enough. In Burgundy, where my in-laws have a house, near Sens."

I fleetingly remembered that day. There had not been a great deal exchanged between Sean and Heather Jarmond, and Edouard and Colette Tézac. It seemed like the entire French side of the family had forgotten their English. But I hadn't cared. I was so happy. Brilliant sunshine. The quiet little country church. My simple ivory dress that my mother-in-law approved of. Bertrand, stunning in his gray morning coat. The dinner party at the Tézacs', beautifully done. Champagne, candles, and rose petals. Charla delivering a very funny speech in her terrible French, and that only I had laughed at. Laure and Cécile, simpering. My mother and her pale magenta suit, and her little whisper in my ear, "I do hope you'll be happy, angel pie." My father waltzing with the stiff-backed Colette. It seemed so long ago.

"Do you miss America?" Bamber asked.

"No. I miss my sister. But not America."

A young waiter came to bring us our coffees. He took one look at Bamber's flame-colored hair and smirked. Then he saw the impressive arrays of cameras and lenses.

"You tourists?" he asked. "Taking nice photos of Paris?"

"Not tourists. Just taking nice photos of what's left of the Vel' d'Hiv'," said Bamber in French, with his slow British accent.

The waiter seemed taken aback.

"Nobody asks about the Vel' d'Hiv' much," he said. "The Eiffel Tower, yes, but not the Vel' d'Hiv'."

"We're journalists," I said. "We work for an American magazine."

"Sometimes there are Jewish families who come in here," recalled the young man. "After one of the anniversary speeches at the memorial down by the river."

I had an idea.

"You wouldn't know of anybody, a neighbor on this street, who knows about the roundup, who could talk to us?" I asked. We had already spoken to several survivors; most of them had written books about their experience, but we were lacking witnesses. Parisians who had seen all this happen.

Then I felt silly; after all, the young man was barely twenty. His own father probably wasn't even born in '42.

"Yes, I do," he answered, to my surprise. "If you walk back up the street, you'll see a newspaper store on your left. The man in charge there, Xavier, he'll tell you. His mother knows, she's lived there all her life."

We left him a large tip.

*T*HERE HAD BEEN AN endless, dusty walk from the little train station, through a small town, where more people had stared and pointed. Her feet ached. Where were they going now? What was going to happen to them? Were they far from Paris? The train ride had been fast, barely a couple of hours. As always, she thought of her brother. Her heart sank lower with each mile they covered. How was she ever going to get back home? How was she going to make it? It made her feel sick to think he probably thought she'd forgotten him. That's what he believed, locked up in the dark cupboard. He thought she had abandoned him, that she didn't care, that she didn't love him. He had no water, no light, and he was afraid. She had let him down.

Where were they? She hadn't had time to look at the name of the station as they had pulled in. But she had noticed the first things a city child pays attention to: the lush countryside, the flat green meadows, the golden fields. The intoxicating smell of fresh air and summer. The hum of a bumble bee. Birds in the sky. Fluffy white clouds. After the stink and heat of the past few days, this was glorious, she felt. Maybe it wasn't going to be that bad, after all.

She followed her parents through barbed-wire gates, with stern looking guards on each side holding guns. And then she saw the rows of long dark barracks, the grimness of the place, and her spirits sank. She cowered against her mother. Policemen started to shout orders. The women and children were told to go to the sheds on the right, the men on the left. Helpless, holding on to her mother, she watched her father be pushed along with a group of men. She felt afraid without him by her side. But there was nothing she could do. The guns terrified her. Her mother did not move. Her eyes were dulled. Dead. Her face was white and sickly.

The girl took her mother's hand as they were shoved toward the barracks. The inside was bare and grimy. Planks and straw. Stench and dirt. The latrines were outside, planks of wood astride holes. They were ordered to sit there, in groups, to piss and defecate in view of all, like animals. It revolted her. She felt she could not go. She could not do this. She looked on as her mother straddled one of the holes. She bowed her head in shame. But she finally did what she was told, cringing, hoping no one was looking at her.

Just above the barbed wire, the girl could glimpse the village. The black spire of a church. A water tower. Roofs and chimneys. Trees. Over there, she thought, in those nearby houses, people had beds, sheets, blankets, food, and water. They were clean. They had clean clothes. Nobody screamed at them. Nobody treated them like cattle. And they were just there, just on the other side of the fence. In the clean little village where she could hear the church bell chime.

There were children on vacation over there, she thought. Children going on picnics, children playing hide-and-seek. Happy children, even if there was a war, and less to eat than usual, and maybe their Papa had gone away to fight. Happy, loved, cherished, children. She couldn't imagine why there was such a difference between those children and her. She couldn't imagine why she and all these people here with her had to be treated this way. Who had decided this, and what for?

They were given tepid cabbage soup. It was thin and sandy. Nothing else. Then she watched as rows of women stripped naked and fought to wash their dirty bodies under a trickle of water over rusty, iron washbasins. She found them ugly, grotesque. She hated the flabby ones, the skinny ones, the old ones, the young ones; she hated to have to see their nudity. She did not want to look at them. She hated having to see them.

She huddled against her mother's warmth and tried not to think of her brother. Her skin felt itchy, her scalp too. She wanted a bath, her bed, her brother. Dinner. She wondered if anything could be worse than what had been happening to her over the past few days. She thought of her friends, of the other little girls in her school who also wore stars. Dominique, Sophie, Agnès. What had happened to them? Had some been able to escape? Were some safe, hiding somewhere? Was Armelle hiding with her family? Would she ever see her again, see her other friends again? Would she go back to school in September?

That night, she couldn't sleep; she needed her father's reassuring touch. Her stomach hurt her, she felt it contract with pain. She knew they were not allowed to leave the barracks during the night. She clenched her teeth, wrapping her arms around her belly. But the pain grew worse. Slowly she got up, tiptoed through the rows of sleeping women and children, to the latrines outside the door.

Glaring spot lights swept the camp as she huddled over the planks. The girl peered in and saw thick pale worms writhing in the dark mass of shit. She was afraid a policeman up there in the watchtowers would see her bottom, and she pulled her skirt down over her loins. She quickly made her way back to the barrack.

Inside, the air was stuffy and foul. Some children whimpered in their sleep. She could hear a woman sobbing. She turned to her mother, gazing at the sunken, white face.

Gone was the happy, loving woman. Gone was the mother who used to sweep her into her arms and whisper love words, Yiddish nicknames. The woman with the glossy honey locks and the voluptuous figure, the one all the neighbors, all the shopkeepers would greet by her first name. The one who smelled a warm, comforting, motherly smell: delicious cooking, fresh soap, clean linen. The one with the infectious laugh. The one who said that even if there was a war, they'd pull through, because they were a strong, good family, a family full of love.

That woman had little by little disappeared. She had become gaunt, and pale, and she never smiled or laughed. She smelled rank, bitter. Her hair had become brittle and dry, streaked with gray.

The girl felt like her mother was already dead.

THE OLD WOMAN LOOKED at Bamber and me with rheumy, translucent eyes. She must be getting on toward a hundred, I thought. Her smile was toothless, like a baby's. Mamé was a teenager compared to her. She lived just above her son's shop, the newsdealer on the rue Nélaton. A poky apartment cluttered with dusty furniture, moth-eaten rugs, and withered plants. The old lady sat in a sagging armchair by the window. She watched us walk in and introduce ourselves. She seemed pleased to be entertaining impromptu visitors.

"American journalists, so," she quavered, appraising us.

"American and British," corrected Bamber.

"Journalists that are interested in the Vel' d'Hiv'?" she asked.

I got my pen and pad of paper out and balanced them on my knee.

"Do you remember anything about the roundup, Madame?" I asked her. "Could you tell us something, even the smallest detail?"

She let out a cackle.

"You think I don't remember, young lady? You think I have forgotten, maybe?"

"Well," I said, "it was a while ago, after all."

"How old are you?" she asked bluntly.

I felt my face redden. Bamber hid a smile behind his camera.

"Forty-five," I said.

"I am going to be ninety-five years old," she said, flaunting decayed gums. "On July 16, 1942, I was thirty-five. Ten years younger than you are now. And I remember. I remember everything."

She paused. Her dimmed eyes looked outside, onto the street.

"I remember being woken very early by the rumbling of buses. Buses just outside my window. I looked outside and I saw the buses arrive. More and more buses. Our own city buses, the buses I used every day. Green and white. So many of them. I wondered why on earth they were here. Then I saw the people come out. And all the children. So many children. You see, it's hard to forget the children."

I scribbled away as Bamber slowly clicked his camera.

"After a while I got dressed and went down with my boys, who were small then. We wanted to know what was going on, we were curious. Our neighbors came, too, and the concierge. Then we saw the yellow stars, and we understood. The Jews. They were rounding up the Jews."

"Did you have any idea of what was going to happen to these people?" I asked.

She shrugged her old shoulders.

"No," she said. "We had no idea. How could we? It was after the war that we found out. We thought they were being sent to work somewhere. We did not think anything bad was going on. I remember someone said, 'It's the French police, no one will harm them.' So we did not worry. And the next day, even when this had happened in the middle of Paris, there was nothing in the papers, nothing on the radio. No one seemed preoccupied. So we weren't either. Until I saw the children."

She paused.

"The children?" I repeated.

"A few days later, the Jews were taken away again by bus," she continued. "I was standing on the sidewalk, and I saw the families come out of the *vélodrome*, all these dirty, crying children. They looked frightened, filthy. I was appalled. I realized that in the *vélodrome*, they hadn't had much to eat or drink. I felt helpless and angry. I tried to throw them bread and fruit, but the police would not let me."

She paused again, for a long time. She seemed tired all of a sudden, weary. Bamber quietly put his camera away. We waited. We did not move. I wondered if she was going to speak again.

"After all these years," she said finally, her voice subdued, almost a whisper, "after all these years, I still see the children, you know. I see them climbing onto the buses and being driven away. I did not know where they were going, but I had this feeling. This horrible feeling. Most of the people around me were indifferent. They felt like this was normal. It was normal for them that the Jews were being taken away."

"Why do you think they felt that way?" I asked.

Another cackle.

"We French had been told for years that Jews were the enemies of our country, that's why! In '41 or '42, there was an exhibit, at the Palais Berlitz, if I remember correctly, on the boulevard des Italiens, called 'The Jew and France.' The Germans made sure it went on for months. A big success with the Parisian population. And what was it? A shocking display of anti-Semitism."

Her gnarled old fingers smoothed out her skirt.

"I remember the policemen, you know. Our own good Parisian policemen. Our own good honest gendarmes. Pushing the children onto the buses. Shouting. Using their batons."

She bent her chin to her chest. She mumbled something I did not catch. It sounded like, "Shame on us all for not having stopped it."

"You didn't know," I said softly, touched by her suddenly watery eyes. "What could you have done?"

"Nobody remembers the Vel' d'Hiv' children, you know. Nobody is interested."

"Maybe this year, they will," I said. "Maybe this year, it will be different."

She pursed her shrunken lips.

"No. You'll see. Nothing has changed. Nobody remembers. Why should they? Those were the darkest days of our country."

S HE WONDERED WHERE HER father was. Somewhere in the same camp, in one of the sheds, surely, but she only saw him once or twice. She had no notion of the days slipping by. The only thing that haunted her was her brother. She woke at night, trembling, thinking of him in the cupboard. She took out the key and stared at it with pain and horror. Maybe he was dead by now. Maybe he had died of thirst, of hunger. She tried to count the days since that black Thursday the men had come to get them. A week? Ten days? She didn't know. She felt lost, confused. It had been a whirlwind of terror, starvation, and death. More children had died at the camp. Their little bodies had been taken away amid tears and cries.

One morning, she noticed a number of women talking with anima- tion. They looked worried, upset. She asked her mother what was going on, but her mother said she didn't know. Not to be deterred, the girl asked a woman who had a little boy her brother's age, and who had slept next to them for the past few days. The woman's face was reddish, as if she had a fever. She said there were rumors, rumors going around the camp. The parents were going to be sent East, to work. They were to prepare for the arrival of the children, who were to come later, in a cou- ple of days. The girl listened, shocked. She repeated the conversation to her mother. Her mother's eyes seemed to click open. She shook her head vehemently. She said no, that couldn't possibly happen. They couldn't possibly do that. They couldn't separate the children from the parents.

In that sheltered, gentle life that seemed far away, the girl would have believed her mother. She used to believe everything her mother said. But in this harsh new world, the girl felt she had grown up. She felt older than her mother. She knew the other women were saying the truth. She knew the rumors were true. She did not know how to explain this to her mother. Her mother had become like a child.

When the men came into the barracks, she did not feel afraid. She felt she had been hardened. She felt a thick wall had grown around her. She took her mother's hand and held it tight. She wanted her mother to be brave, to be strong. They were ordered outside. They had to file into another shed, by small groups. She waited in line patiently with her mother. She kept looking around her to catch a glimpse of her father. He was nowhere to be seen.

When it was their turn to step into the shed, she saw a couple of policemen sitting behind a table. There were two women standing next to the men, wearing ordinary clothes. Women from the village, looking at the lines of people with cold, hard faces. She heard them ordering the old woman in front of her in the line to hand over money and jewelry. She watched the old woman fumble with her wedding ring, her watch. A little girl of six or seven stood next to her, shivering with fear. A policeman pointed to the tiny gold rings the little girl wore in her ears. She was too frightened to take them off herself. The grandmother bent down to unclasp them. The policeman let out a sigh of exasperation. This was going far too slowly. They'd be here all night at this rate.

One of the village women went over to the small girl and with a quick gesture yanked the rings through her ears, tearing the tiny lobes. The little girl screamed, her hands creeping to her bloody neck. The old woman screamed, too. A policeman hit her in the face. They were pulled outside. A murmur of fear went through the line. The policemen waved their guns. There was silence.

The girl and her mother had nothing to hand over. Just the mother's wedding band. A florid-faced village woman tore open the mother's dress from collarbone to navel, revealing her pale skin and faded underclothes. Her hands groped through the folds of the dress, to the underclothes, to the openings of the mother's body. The mother flinched, but said nothing. The girl watched, fear rising through her. She hated the way the men eyed her mother's body, hated the way the village woman touched her, handling her like a piece of meat. Were they going to do that to her, too, she wondered. Would they tear her clothes as well? Maybe they would take her key. She clenched it in her pocket with all her might. No, they couldn't take that. She wouldn't let them. She wouldn't let them take the key to the secret cupboard. Never.

But the policemen were not interested in what was in her pockets. Before she and her mother stepped aside, she had one last look at the growing piles on the desk: necklaces, bracelets, brooches, rings, watches, money. What were they going to do with all that? she thought. Sell them? Use them? What did they need these things for?

Back outside, they were lined up again. It was a hot and dusty day. The girl was thirsty, her throat felt prickly and dry. They stood around for a long time, under the policemen's silent glare. What was going on? Where was her father? Why were they all standing there? The girl could hear incessant whispers behind her. Nobody knew. Nobody could answer. But she knew. She felt it. And when it happened, she was expecting it.

The policemen fell upon them like a swarm of large, dark birds. They dragged the women to one side of the camp, the children to the other. Even the tiniest children were separated from their mothers. The girl watched it all, as if she was in another world. She heard the screams, the yells, she saw the women hurling themselves to the ground, their hands pulling at their children's clothes, their children's hair. She watched the policemen raise their truncheons and bludgeon the women's heads, their faces. She saw a woman collapse, her nose a bloody pulp.

Her own mother stood next to her, frozen. She could hear the woman breathing in short, sharp gasps. She held on to her mother's cold hand. She felt the policemen wrench them apart, she heard her mother shriek, and then saw her dive back toward her, her dress gaping open, her hair wild, her mouth contorted, screaming her daughter's name. She tried to grab her mother's hands, but the men shoved her aside, sending her to her knees. Her mother fought like a mad creature, overpowering the policemen for a couple of seconds, and at that precise moment, the girl saw her real mother emerge, the strong, passionate woman she missed and admired. She felt her mother's arms hold her once more, felt the thick bushy hair caress her face. Suddenly torrents of cold water blinded her. Spluttering, gasping for breath, she opened her eyes to see the men drag her mother away by the collar of her sopping dress.

It seemed to her that it took hours. Tearful, lost children. Buckets of water thrown in their faces. Struggling, broken women. Sharp thuds of the blows. But she knew it had happened very fast.

Silence. It was done. At last, the crowd of children stood on one side, the women on the other. Between them, a sturdy row of policemen. The policemen kept repeating that the mothers and children over twelve were preceding the others, that the younger ones would leave next week, to join them. The fathers has already left, they were told. Everybody was to cooperate and obey.

She saw her mother stand with the other women. Her mother looked back at her daughter with a tiny, brave smile. She seemed to say, "You see, darling, we'll be all right, the police said so. You'll be coming to join us in a few days. Don't worry, my sweet."

The girl looked around her at the crowd of children. So many children. She looked at the toddlers, their faces crumpled with grief and fright. She saw the little girl with the bleeding ear lobes, palms outstretched to her mother. What was going to happen to all these children, to her? she thought. Where were their parents being taken?

The women were led away, out through the camp gates. She saw her mother head right and walk down the long road that led through the village to the station. Her mother's face turned to her one last time.

Then she was gone.

WE'RE HAVING ONE OF our 'good' days today, Madame Tézac,"
said Véronique, beaming at me as I walked into the sunny,
white room. She was part of the staff that looked after Mamé at the
clean, cheerful nursing home in the seventeenth arrondissement, not
far from the Parc Monceau.

"Don't call her Madame Tézac," barked Bertrand's grandmother.
"She hates it. Call her Miss Jarmond."

I couldn't help smiling. Véronique seemed crestfallen.

"And anyway, Madame Tézac, that's *me*," said the old lady with a
touch of haughtiness, and total disdain for the other Madame Tézac,
her daughter-in-law Colette, Bertrand's mother. So typical of Mamé,
I thought. So feisty, even at her age. Her first name was Marcelle. She
loathed it. No one ever called her Marcelle.

"I'm sorry," said Véronique humbly.

I put a hand on her arm.

"Please don't worry about it," I said. "I don't use my married name."

"It's an American thing," said Mamé. "Miss Jarmond is American."

"Yes, I had noticed that," said Véronique, in better spirits.

Noticed what? I felt like asking. My accent, my clothes, my shoes?

"So, you've been having a good day then, Mamé?" I sat down next
to her and covered her hand with mine.

Compared to the old lady on the rue Nélaton, Mamé looked fresh-
faced. Her skin was hardly wrinkled. Her gray eyes were bright. But
the old lady of the rue Nélaton, despite her decrepit appearance, had

a clear head, and Mamé, at ninety, had Alzheimer's. Some days, she simply could not remember who she was.

Bertrand's parents had decided to move her to the nursing home when they realized she was incapable of living alone. She would turn on a gas burner and let it burn all day. She would let her bath run over. Or she would regularly lock herself out of the apartment and be found wandering in the rue de Saintonge in her dressing gown. She had put up a fight, of course. She hadn't wanted to come to the nursing home at all. But she had settled in nicely enough, despite occasional outbursts of temper.

"I'm having a 'good' day." She grinned as Véronique left us.

"Oh, I see," I said, "terrorizing the entire place, as usual?"

"As usual," she said. Then she turned to me. Her affectionate gray eyes roamed over my face. "Where's that good-for-nothing husband of yours? He never comes, you know. And don't give me any of that 'he's too busy' business."

I sighed.

"Well, at least you're here," she said gruffly. "You look tired. Everything all right?"

"Fine," I said.

I knew I looked tired. There wasn't much I could do about it. Go on vacation, I guess. But that wasn't planned till the summer.

"And the apartment?"

I had just been to see the work being done before coming to the nursing home. A hive of activity. Bertrand supervising everything with his usual energy. Antoine looking drained.

"It's going to be wonderful," I said. "When it's finished."

"I miss it," said Mamé. "I miss living there."

"I'm sure you do," I said.

She shrugged.

"You get attached to places, you know. Like people, I suppose. I wonder if André ever misses it."

André was her late husband. I had not known him. He had passed away when Bertrand was a teenager. I was used to Mamé speaking of him in the present tense. I never corrected her, never reminded her that he died years ago of lung cancer. She loved talking about him. When I first met her, long before she started to lose her memory, she would show me her photo albums every time I came to see her at the rue de Saintonge. I felt I knew André Tézac's face by heart. The same gray-blue eyes that Edouard had. A rounder nose. A warmer smile, maybe.

Mamé had told me lengthily how they had met, how they had fallen in love, and how everything had become difficult during the war. The Tézacs were originally from Burgundy, but when André had inherited a family wine business from his own father, he had not been able to make ends meet. So he had moved to Paris and started a small antique shop on the rue de Turenne, near the Place des Vosges. It had taken him a while to establish his reputation, for the business to flourish. Edouard had taken over the reins after his father's death and moved the shop to the rue du Bac in the seventh arrondissement, where the most prestigious antique shops in Paris were found. Cécile, Bertrand's younger sister, was now running the place and doing very well.

Mamé's doctor—the mournful but efficient Docteur Roche—once told me it was excellent therapy to ask Mamé about the past. According to him, she probably had a better perception of what went on thirty years ago than that very morning.

It was like a little game. During each of my visits, I would ask her questions. I did it naturally, not making a big thing out of it. She knew perfectly well what I was driving at, but pretended to ignore it.

It had been amusing finding out about Bertrand as a young boy. Mamé came up with the most interesting tidbits. He had been a gawky adolescent, not the cool dude I had heard of. He was a reluctant scholar, not the brilliant student his parents had raved about. At fourteen, there had been a memorable fight with his father about the neighbor's daughter, a promiscuous bottle-blonde who smoked marijuana.

Sometimes, though, it wasn't fun delving into Mamé's faulty memory. Often, there were grim, long blanks. She could not remember anything. On "bad" days, she shut up like a clam. She would glower at the television and set her mouth so that her chin jutted out.

One morning, she couldn't figure out who Zoë was. She kept asking, "Who is this child? What is she doing here?" Zoë, as ever, had been adult about it. But later on that night I had heard her crying in bed. When I gently asked her what was the matter, she admitted she couldn't bear seeing her great-grandmother growing older.

"Mamé," I said, "when did you and André move into the rue de Saintonge apartment?"

I expected her to screw up her face, looking like a wise old monkey, and come up with an "Oh, I can't remember at all . . ."

But the answer was like a whiplash.

"July 1942."

I sat up straight, staring at her.

"July 1942?" I repeated.

"That's right," she said.

"And how did you find the apartment? There was a war going on. It must have been difficult, surely?"

"Not at all," she said breezily. "It had been suddenly vacated. We heard about it through the concierge, Madame Royer, who was friendly with our old concierge. We used to live on the rue de Turenne, just above André's shop, a cramped, poky little apartment with only one bedroom. So we moved in, with Edouard who was ten or twelve at the time. We were thrilled to have a bigger place. And it was a cheap rent, I remember. In those days, that *quartier* was not half as fashionable as it is now."

I watched her carefully and cleared my throat.

"Mamé, do you remember if this was the beginning of July? Or the end?"

She smiled, pleased to be doing so well.

"I remember perfectly. It was the end of July."

"And do you remember why the place was vacated so suddenly?"

Another beaming smile.

"Of course. There had been a big roundup. People were arrested, you know. There were lots of places that were suddenly vacant."

I stared at her. Her eyes gazed back at mine. They clouded over when she saw the expression on my face.

"But how did it happen? How did you move in?"

She fussed with her sleeves, working her mouth.

"Madame Royer told our concierge that an empty three-roomed apartment was free on the rue de Saintonge. That's how it happened. That's all."

Silence. She stopped moving her hands and folded them in her lap.

"But Mamé," I whispered, "didn't you think these people might ever come back?"

Her face had sobered, and there was something tight, painful, about her lips.

"We knew nothing," she said finally. "Nothing at all."

And she looked down at her hands and did not speak again.

*T*HIS WAS THE WORST night. The worst night ever, for all of the children and for her, thought the girl. The sheds had been entirely looted. Nothing was left, no clothes, no blankets, nothing. Eiderdowns had been ripped in two, white feathers covering the ground like fake snow.

Children crying, children screaming, children hiccuping with terror. The little ones could not understand, kept moaning for their mothers. They wet their clothes, rolled on the ground, shrieked with despair. The older ones, like her, sat on the dirty floor, their heads in their hands.

No one looked at them. No one took care of them. They were rarely fed. They were so hungry, they nibbled dry grass, bits of straw. No one comforted them. The girl wondered: These policemen . . . didn't they have families, too? Didn't they have children? Children they went home to? How could they treat children this way? Were they told to do so, or did they act this way naturally? Were they in fact machines, not human beings? She looked closely at them. They seemed of flesh and bone. They were men. She couldn't understand.

The next day, the girl noticed a handful of people watching them through the barbed wire. Women, with packages and food. They were trying to push the food through the fences. But the policemen ordered them to leave. Nobody came to look at them again.

The girl felt like she had become someone else. Someone hard, and rude, and wild. Sometimes she fought with the older children, the ones et-

who tried to grab the old stale bread she had found. She swore at them. She hit them. She felt dangerous, savage.

At first, she had not looked at the smaller children. They reminded her too much of her brother. But now, she felt she had to help them. They were vulnerable, small. So pathetic. So dirty. A lot of them had diarrhea. Their clothes were caked with shit. There was no one to wash them, no one to feed them.

Little by little, she came to know their names, their ages, but some of them were so small they could hardly answer her. They were thankful for a warm voice, for a smile, a kiss, and they followed her around the camp, dozens of them, trailing after her like bedraggled sparrows.

She would tell them the stories she used to tell her brother, before his bedtime. At night, lying on the lice-infested straw, where rats made rustling noises, she would whisper the stories, making them even longer than they usually were. The older children gathered around, too. Some of them pretended not to listen, but she knew they did.

There was an eleven-year-old girl, a tall black-haired creature called Rachel, who often looked at her with a touch of contempt. But night after night, she listened to the stories, creeping closer to the girl, so that she wouldn't miss one word. And once, when most of the little children were at last asleep, she spoke to the girl.

She said in a deep, hoarse voice, "We should leave. We should escape."

The girl shook her head.

"There is no way out. The police have guns. We can't escape."

Rachel shrugged her bony shoulders.

"I am going to escape."

"What about your mother? She will be waiting for you in the other camp, like mine."

Rachel smiled.

"You believed all that? You believed what they said?"

The girl hated Rachel's knowing smile.

"No," she said firmly. "I didn't believe them. I don't believe anything anymore."

"Neither do I," said Rachel. "I saw what they did. They didn't even write down the little children's names properly. They tied on those small tags that got mixed up when most of the children took them off again. They don't care. They lied to all of us. To us and to our mothers."

And to the girl's surprise, Rachel reached out and took her hand. She held it tight, the way Armelle used to. Then she got to her feet and disappeared.

The next morning, they were woken very early. The policemen came into the barracks, pushing at them with their truncheons. The smaller children, hardly awake, started to scream. The girl tried to calm the ones nearest to her, but they were terrified. They were led into a shed. The girl held two toddlers by the hand. She saw a policeman holding an instrument in his hand. It had a strange shape. She didn't know what it was. The toddlers gasped with fear, backed away. They were slapped and kicked by the policemen, then dragged toward the man with the instrument. The girl watched, horrified. Then she understood. Their hair was being shaved off. All the children were to be shaved.

She looked on as Rachel's thick black hair fell to the floor. Her naked skull was white and pointed, like an egg. Rachel gazed at the men with hatred and contempt. She spat on their shoes. One of the gendarmes knocked her aside brutally.

The little ones were frantic. They had to be held down by two or three men. When it was her turn, the girl did not struggle. She bent her head. She felt the cold pressure of the machine and closed her eyes, unable to bear the sight of the long, golden strands falling to her feet. Her hair. Her beautiful hair that everyone admired. She felt sobs welling up in her throat but she forced herself not to cry. Never cry in front of these men. Never cry. Ever. It's only hair. Hair will grow back.

It was nearly over. She opened her eyes again. The policeman holding her had fat pink hands. She looked up at him while the other man shaved off the last locks.

It was the red-haired, friendly policeman from her neighborhood. The one her mother used to chat with. The one who always had a wink for her on her way to school. The one she had waved to the day of the roundup, the one who had looked away. He was too close now to look away.

She held his gaze, not glancing down once. His eyes were a strange, yellowish color, like gold. His face was red with embarrassment, and she thought she felt him tremble. She said nothing, staring at him with all the contempt she could muster.

He could only look back at her, motionless. The girl smiled, a bitter smile for a child of ten, and brushed off his heavy hands.

I LEFT THE NURSING HOME in a sort of daze. I was due at the office, where Bambei was waiting for me, but I found myself heading back to the rue de Saintonge. There were so many questions going around my head that I felt swamped. Was Mamé telling the truth or had she gotten mixed up, confused, due to her illness? Had there really been a Jewish family living here? How could the Tézacs have moved in and not known anything, as Mamé had stated?

I walked slowly through the courtyard. The concierge's loge would have been here, I thought. It had been transformed years ago into a small apartment. A row of metal mailboxes lined the hallway; there was no longer a concierge who brought mail up every day to each door. Madame Royer, that was her name, Mamé had said. I had read much about concierges and their particular role during the arrests. Most of them had complied with police orders, and some had even gone further, showing the police where certain Jewish families had gone into hiding. Others had plundered vacant apartments and hoarded goods right after the roundup. Only a few, I read, had protected the Jewish families the best they could. I wondered what sort of role Madame Royer had played here. I thought fleetingly of my concierge on the boulevard du Montparnasse; she was my age, and from Portugal, she had not known the war.

I ignored the elevator and walked up the four flights. The workmen were out on their lunch hour. The building was silent. As I opened the front door, I felt something strange engulf me, an unknown sensation of despair and emptiness. I walked to the older part of the apartment, the bit that Bertrand had shown us the other day. This is where it had happened. This is where the men came knocking on that hot July morning, just before dawn.

It seemed to me that everything I had read in the past weeks, everything I had learned about the Vel' d'Hiv' came to a head here, in the very place I was about to live in. All the testimonies I had pored over, all the books I had studied, all the survivors and witnesses I had interviewed made me understand, made me see, with an almost unreal clarity, what had happened between the walls that I now touched.

The article I had started to write a couple of days ago was nearly finished. My deadline was coming up. I still had to visit the Loiret camps outside Paris, and Drancy, and I had a meeting scheduled with Franck Lévy, whose association was organizing most of the commemorations for the sixtieth anniversary of the roundup. Soon, my investigation would be over, and I'd be writing about something else.

But now that I knew what had happened here, so close to me, so intimately linked to me, to my life, I felt I had to find out more. My search wasn't over. I felt I had to know everything. What had happened to the Jewish family living in this place? What were their names? Were there any children? Had anybody come back from the death camps? Was everybody dead?

I wandered through the empty apartment. In one room, the wall was being torn down. Lost in the rubble, I noticed a long deep opening, cleverly hidden behind a panel. It was now partly revealed. It would have made a good hiding place. If these walls could talk. . . . But I didn't need them to talk. I knew what had happened here. I could see it. The survivors had told me about the hot, still night, the bangs on the doors, the brisk orders, the bus ride through Paris. They had told me about the stinking hell of Vel' d'Hiv'. The ones who told me were the ones who lived. The ones who got away. The ones who tore off their stars and escaped.

I wondered suddenly if I could cope with this knowledge, if I could live here knowing that in my apartment a family had been arrested and sent on to their probable deaths. How had the Tézacs lived with that? I wondered.

I pulled out my cell phone and called Bertrand. When he saw my number show up, he mumbled, "Meeting." That was our code for "I'm busy."

"It's urgent," I said.

I heard him murmur something, then his voice came across clearly. "What's up, *amour*?" he said. "Make it quick, I've got someone waiting."

I took a deep breath.

"Bertrand," I said, "do you know how your grandparents got the rue de Saintonge apartment?"

"No," he said. "Why?"

"I've just been to see Mamé. She told me they moved in during July of '42. She said the place had been emptied because of a Jewish family arrested during the Vel' d'Hiv' roundup."

Silence.

"So?" asked Bertrand, finally.

I felt my face go hot. My voice echoed out through the empty apartment.

"But doesn't it bother you that your family moved in, knowing the Jewish people had been arrested? Did they ever tell you about it?"

I could almost hear him shrug in that typical French fashion, the downturn of the mouth, the arched eyebrows.

"No, it doesn't bother me. I didn't know, they never told me, but it still doesn't bother me. I'm sure a lot of Parisians moved into empty apartments in July of '42, after the roundup. Surely that doesn't make my family collaborationists, does it?"

His laugh hurt my ears.

"I never said that, Bertrand."

"You're getting too heated up about all this, Julia," he said with a gentler tone. "This happened sixty years ago, you know. There was a world war going on, remember. Tough times for everybody."

I sighed.

"I just want to know how it happened. I just don't understand."

"It's simple, *mon ange*. My grandparents had a hard time during the war. The antique shop wasn't doing well. They were probably relieved to move into a bigger, better place. After all, they had a child. They were young. They were glad to find a roof over their heads. They probably didn't think twice about the Jewish family."

"Oh, Bertrand," I whispered. "How could they *not* think about that family? How could they not?"

He blew kisses down the phone.

"They didn't know, I guess. I've got to go, *amour*. See you tonight."

And he hung up.

I stayed in the apartment for a while, walking down the long corridor, standing in the empty living room, running my palm along the smooth marble mantelpiece, trying to understand, trying not to let my emotions overwhelm me.

*W*ITH RACHEL, SHE HAD made up her mind. They were going to escape. They were going to leave this place. It was that, or die. She knew it. She knew that if she stayed here with the other children, it would be the end. Many of the children were ill. Half a dozen had already died. Once, she had seen a nurse, like the one in the stadium, a woman with a blue veil. One nurse, for so many sick, starving children.

Escaping was their secret. They had not told any of the other children. No one was to guess anything. They were going to escape in broad daylight. They had noticed that during the day, at most times, the policemen hardly paid attention to them. It could be easy and fast. Down behind the sheds, toward the water tower, where the village women had tried to push food through the barbed wire, they had found a small gap in the rolls of wire. Small, but maybe big enough for a child to crawl through.

Some children had already left the camp, surrounded by policemen. She had watched them leave, frail, thin creatures with their shorn heads and ragged clothes. Where were they being taken? Far away? To the mothers and fathers? She didn't believe that. Rachel didn't either. If they were all to be taken to the same place, why had the police separated the parents from the children in the first place? Why so much pain, so much suffering, thought the girl. "It's because they hate us," Rachel had told her with her deep, hoarse voice. "They hate Jews." Such hate, thought the girl. Why such hate? She had never hated anyone in her life, except perhaps a teacher, once. A teacher who had severely punished her because she had not learned her lesson. Had she ever wished that woman dead? she pondered. Yes, she had. So maybe that's how it worked. That's how all this had happened. Hating people so much that you wanted to kill them. Hating them because they wore a yellow star. It made her shiver. She felt as if all the evil, all the hatred in the world was concentrated right here, stocked up all around her, in the policemen's hard faces, in their indifference, their disdain. And outside the camp, did everybody hate Jews, too? Is this what her life was going to be about from now on?

She remembered, last June, overhearing neighbors in the stairway on her way home from school. Feminine voices, lowered to whispers. She had paused on the stairs, her ears cocked like a puppy's. "And do you know, his jacket opened, and there it was, the star. I never would have thought he was a Jew." She heard the other woman's sharp intake of breath. "Him, a Jew! Such a proper gentleman, too. What a surprise."

She had asked her mother why some of the neighbors didn't like Jewish people. Her mother had shrugged, had sighed, bending her head over her ironing. But she had not answered the girl. So the girl had gone to see her father. What was wrong with being a Jew? Why did some people hate Jews? Her father had scratched his head, had looked down at her with a quizzical smile. He had said, hesitatingly, "Because they think we are different. So they are frightened of us." But what was different? thought the girl. What was so different?

Her mother. Her father. Her brother. She missed them so much she felt physically ill. She felt as if she had fallen into a bottomless hole. Escaping was the only way for her to have some sort of grip on her life, on this new life she could not understand. Maybe her parents had managed to escape as well? Maybe they were all able to make their way back home? Maybe. . . . Maybe. . . .

She thought of the empty apartment, the unmade beds, the food slowly rotting in the kitchen. And her brother in that silence. In the dead silence of the place.

Rachel touched her arm, making her jump.

"Now," she whispered. "Let's try, now."

The camp was silent, almost deserted. Since the adults had been taken away, there were fewer policemen, they had noticed. And the policemen hardly talked to the children. They left them alone.

The heat pounded down on the sheds, unbearable. Inside, feeble, sick children lay on damp straw. The girls could hear male voices and laughs from farther on. The men were probably in one of the barracks, keeping out of the sun.

The only policeman they could see was sitting in the shade, his rifle at his feet. His head was tilted back against the wall, and he seemed fast asleep, his mouth open. They crept toward the fences, like quick, small animals. They could glimpse green meadows and fields stretching before them.

Silence, still. Heat and silence. Had anybody seen them? They crouched in the grass, hearts pounding. They peered back over their shoulders. No movement. No noise. Was it that easy, thought the girl. No, it couldn't be. Nothing was ever easy, not anymore.

Rachel was clutching a bundle of clothes in her arms. She urged the girl to put them on, the extra layers would protect their skin against the barbs, she said. The girl shuddered as she struggled into a dirty, ragged sweater, a tight, tattered pair of trousers. Who had these clothes belonged to, she wondered, some poor dead child whose mother had gone, and who had been left here to die alone?

Still crouching, they drew near the small gap in the rolls of wire. There was a policeman standing a little way off. They could not make out his face, just the sharp outline of his high round cap. Rachel pointed to the opening in the wire. They would have to hurry now. No time to waste. They got down on their stomachs, snaked their way to the hole. It seemed so small, thought the girl. How could they possibly wriggle through, not cut themselves on the barbed wire despite the extra clothes? How did they ever think they were going to make it? That nobody was going to see them? That they'd get away with it? They were crazy, she thought. Crazy.

The grass tickled her nose. It smelled delicious. She wanted to bury her face in it and breathe in the green, tangy scent. She saw that Rachel had already reached the gap and was gingerly pushing her head through it.

Suddenly the girl heard heavy thuds on the grass. Her heart stopped. She looked up to a huge shape looming over her. A policeman. He dragged her up by the frayed collar of her blouse, shook her. She felt herself go limp with terror.

"What the hell do you think you're doing?"

His voice hissing in her ear.

Rachel was halfway through the rolls. The man, still holding the girl by the scruff of her neck, reached down and seized Rachel's ankle. She fought and kicked, but he was too strong, pulling her back through the barbed wire, her face and hands bleeding.

They stood in front of him, Rachel sobbing, the girl straight-backed, her chin up. Inside she was trembling, but she had decided she would not show her fear. At least she was going to try.

And then she looked at him and gasped.

It was the red-haired policeman. He recognized her instantly. She saw his Adam's apple bob, felt the thick hand on her collar quiver.

"You can't escape," he said gruffly. "You must stay here, you understand?"

He was young, just over twenty, massive, and pink-skinned. The girl noticed he was sweating under the thick dark uniform. His forehead was glistening with moisture, his upper lip, too. His eyes blinked, he shifted from foot to foot.

She realized she was not afraid of him. She felt a sort of strange pity for him, which puzzled her. She put her hand on his arm. He looked down at it with surprise and embarrassment.

She said, "You remember me, don't you."

It was not a question. It was a fact.

He nodded, dabbing at the moist patch under his nose. She took the key from her pocket and showed it to him. Her hand did not waver.

"You remember my little brother," she said. "The little blond boy with the curly hair?"

He nodded again.

"You must let me go, Monsieur. My little brother, Monsieur. He is in Paris. Alone. I locked him in the cupboard because I thought—" Her voice broke. "I thought he'd be safe there! I must go back! Let me go through this hole. You can pretend you never saw me, Monsieur."

The man glanced back over his shoulder, toward the sheds, as if he was afraid someone might come, someone might see them or hear them.

He put a finger to his lips. He looked back at the girl. He screwed up his face, shook his head.

"I can't do that," he said, his voice low. "I have orders."

She pressed her hand down on his chest.

"Please, Monsieur," she said, quietly.

Next to her, Rachel sniffed, her face clotted with blood and tears. The man glanced over his shoulder once more. He seemed deeply perturbed. She again noticed that strange expression on his face, the one she had glimpsed the day of the roundup. A mixture of pity, shame, and anger.

The girl felt the minutes go by, leaden, heavy. Endless. She felt the sobs, the tears growing within her again, the panic. What was she going to do if he sent her and Rachel back to the barracks? How was she going to go on? How? She would try to escape again, she thought fiercely, yes, she would do it over and over again. Over and over again.

Suddenly, he said her name. He took her hand. His palm felt hot and clammy.

"Go," he said between clenched teeth, the sweat trickling down the sides of his pasty face. "Go, now! Fast."

Bewildered, she looked up to the golden eyes. He pushed her toward the hole, forcing her down with his hand. He held up the wire, shoved her through violently. The barbed wire stung her forehead. Then it was over. She scrambled to her feet. She was free, standing on the other side.

Rachel stared, motionless.

"I want to go, too," Rachel said.

The policeman clamped a hand on the back of her neck.

"No, you are staying," he said.

Rachel wailed.

"That's not fair! Why her, and not me? Why?"

He silenced her, raising his other hand. Behind the fence, the girl stood frozen to the spot. Why couldn't Rachel come with her? Why did Rachel have to stay?

"Please let her come," said the girl. "Please, Monsieur."

She spoke with a calm, quiet voice. The voice of a young woman.

The man seemed ill at ease, restless. But he didn't hesitate long.

"Go then," he said, pushing Rachel away. "Quickly."

He held the wire as Rachel crawled through. She stood next to the girl, breathless.

The man fumbled in his pockets, pulled something out, and handed it to the girl, through the fence.

"Take this," he ordered.

The girl looked at the thick wad of money in her hand. She put it in her pocket, next to the key.

The man looked back toward the barracks, his brow furrowed.

"For God's sake, run! Run now, quick, both of you. If they see you. . . . Take off your stars. Try to find help. Be careful! Good luck!"

She wanted to thank him, for his help, for the money, she wanted to hold her hand out to him, but Rachel grabbed her by the arm and took off, they ran as fast as they could though the high golden wheat, straight ahead, lungs bursting, legs and arms helter-skelter, far away from the camp, as far away as possible.

As I got home, I realized I had been feeling nauseous for the past couple of days. I hadn't bothered about it, caught up in researching the Vel' d'Hiv' article. Then, last week, there had been the revelation concerning Mamé's apartment. But it was the soreness, the tenderness of my breasts that made me pay attention to my queasiness for the first time. I checked my cycle. Yes, I was late. But that had happened, too, in the past years. I finally went down to the *pharmacie* on the boulevard to buy a pregnancy test. Just to be sure.

And there it was. A little blue line. I was pregnant. Pregnant. I couldn't believe it.

I sat down in the kitchen and hardly dared breathe.

The last pregnancy, five years ago, after two miscarriages, had been a nightmare. Early pain and bleeding, then the discovery that the egg was developing outside the womb, in one of my tubes. There had been a difficult operation. And a messy aftermath, both mentally and physically. It had taken me a long time to get over it. One of my ovaries had been removed. The surgeon had said he was dubious about another pregnancy. And, by then, I was already forty. The disappointment, the sadness in Bertrand's face. He never spoke about it, but I felt it. I knew it. The fact that he did not want to talk about his feelings, ever, made it worse. He kept it bottled up, away from me. The words that were never spoken grew like a tangible being between us. I had only talked about it to my psychiatrist. And with my very close friends.

I remembered a recent weekend in Burgundy, when we had invited Isabelle and her husband and children to stay. Their daughter Mathilde was Zoë's age, and then there was little Matthieu. And the way Bertrand had looked at that little boy, a delightful little fellow of four or five. Bertrand's eyes following him, Bertrand playing with him, carrying him around on his shoulders, smiling, but something sad and wistful in his eyes. It had been unbearable to me. Isabelle had found me crying alone in the kitchen while everybody was finishing their quiche Lorraine outside. She had hugged me hard, then poured out a hefty glass of wine and turned on the CD player, and deafened me with old Diana Ross hits. "It's not your fault, *ma cocotte*, it's not your fault. Remember that."

I had felt incompetent for a long time. The Tézac family had been kind and discreet about the whole thing, but I still felt like I had not been able to provide Bertrand with what he wanted most badly, a second child. And, most importantly, a son. Bertrand had two sisters and no brothers. The name would die out if there was no heir to carry it on. I had not realized how important that factor was for this particular family.

When I had made it clear that despite being Bertrand's wife, I was still to be called Julia Jarmond, I was greeted with surprised silence. My mother-in-law, Colette, had explained to me with a wooden smile that in France that sort of attitude was modern. Too modern. A feminist stance that did not go down well here at all. A French woman was to be known by her husband's name. I was to be, for the rest of my life, Madame Bertrand Tézac. I remember smiling my toothy white smile back at her, and telling her glibly I was going to stick to Jarmond. She had said nothing, and from then on, she and Edouard, my father-in-law, always introduced me as "Bertrand's wife."

I looked down at the blue line. A baby. A baby! A feeling of joy, of utter happiness, took over. I was going to have a baby. I glanced around the all-too-familiar kitchen. I went to stand by the window and looked down at the dark, grimy courtyard the kitchen gave onto. Boy or girl, it didn't matter. I knew Bertrand would hope it was a son.

But he would love a girl, too, I knew that. A second child. The child we'd been waiting for, for so long. The one we had stopped hoping for. The sister or brother Zoë had given up mentioning. That Mamé had stopped being so curious about.

How was I going to tell Bertrand? I couldn't just call him and blurt it out on the phone. We had to be together, just the two of us. Privacy, intimacy, was needed. And we had to be careful after that, not letting anyone know until I was at least three months pregnant. I longed to call Hervé and Christophe, Isabelle, my sister, my parents, but I refrained. My husband was to be the first to know. Then my daughter. An idea came to me.

I grabbed the phone and dialed Elsa, the babysitter. I asked her if she was free tonight to watch Zoë. She was. Then I made reservations at our favorite restaurant, a brasserie on the rue Saint-Dominique we had been to regularly since the beginning of our marriage. Finally, I called Bertrand, got his voice mail, and told him to meet me at Thoumieux at twenty-one hours sharp.

I heard the click of Zoë's key in the front door. The door slammed, then she walked into the kitchen, her heavy backpack in her hand.

"Hi, Mom," she said. "Good day?"

I smiled. As ever, like every time I laid eyes on Zoë, I was struck by her beauty, her slender height, her lucid hazel eyes.

"Come here, you," I said, engulfing her in a wolfish embrace.

She pulled back and gazed at me.

"This has been a good day, hasn't it?" she asked. "I can feel it in your hug."

"You're right," I said, longing to tell her. "It has been a very good day."

She looked at me.

"I'm glad. You've been weird lately. I thought it was because of those kids."

"Those kids?" I said, brushing her sleek brown hair from her face.

"You know, the children," she said. "The Vel' d'Hiv' children. The ones who never came home."

"You're right," I said. "It made me sad. It still does."

Zoë took my hand in hers, twisting my wedding band round and round, a trick she had since she was small.

"And then I heard you talking on the phone last week," she said, not looking at me.

"Well?"

"You thought I was asleep."

"Oh," I said.

"I wasn't. It was late. You were talking to Hervé, I think. You were talking about what Mamé had told you."

"About the apartment?" I asked.

"Yes," she said, looking at me at last. "About the family who lived there. And what had happened to that family. And how Mamé lived there all those years and didn't seem to care much about it."

"You heard all that," I said.

She nodded.

"Do you know anything about that family, Mom? Do you know who they were? What happened?"

I shook my head.

"No, honey, I don't."

"Is it true that Mamé didn't care?"

I had to be careful.

"Sweetie, I'm sure she did care. I don't think she really knew what happened."

Zoë twisted the band around again, faster this time.

"Mom, are you going to find out about them?"

I clasped the nervous fingers pulling at my ring.

"Yes, Zoë. That's exactly what I'm going to do," I said.

"Papa won't like it," she said. "I heard Papa telling you to stop thinking about it. To stop bothering about it. He sounded mad."

I pulled her close, laying my chin on her shoulder. I thought of the wonderful secret I carried within me. I thought of tonight at Thoumieux. Bertrand's incredulous face, his gasp of joy.

"Honey," I said, "Papa won't mind. I promise."

*E*XHAUSTED, THE CHILDREN AT last stopped running, ducking behind a large bush. They were thirsty, out of breath. The girl had a sharp pain in her side. If only she could drink some water. Rest a bit. Get her strength back. But she knew she couldn't stay here. She had to move on; she had to get back to Paris. Somehow.

"Take off the stars," the man had said. They wriggled out of the extra clothes, torn and tattered by the barbs. The girl looked down at her chest. There it was, the star, on her shirt. She pulled at it. Rachel, following her glance, picked at her own star with her nails. Hers came off easily. But the girl's was too tightly sewn on. She slipped out of the shirt, held the star up to her face. Tiny, perfect stitches. She remembered her mother, bent over the pile of handiwork, sewing on each star patiently, one after the other. The memory brought tears to her eyes. She cried into the blouse with a despair she had never known.

She felt Rachel's arms come around her, her bloody hands stroking her, holding her close. Rachel said, "Is it true, about your little brother? Is he really in the cupboard?" The girl nodded. Rachel held her harder, stroked her head clumsily. Where was her mother now? the girl wondered. And her father. Where had they been taken? Were they together? Were they safe? If they could see her at this very moment . . . If they could see her crying behind the bush, dirty, lost, hungry . . .

She drew herself up, doing her best to smile at Rachel through her wet lashes. Yes, dirty, lost, hungry, perhaps, but not afraid. She wiped her tears away with grimy fingers. She had grown up too much to be afraid anymore. She was no longer a baby. Her parents would be proud of her. That's what she wanted them to be. Proud because she had escaped from that camp. Proud because she was going to Paris, to save her brother. Proud, because she wasn't afraid.

She fell upon the star with her teeth, gnawing at her mother's minute stitches. Finally, the yellow piece of cloth fell away from the blouse. She looked at it. Big black letters. JEW. She rolled it up in her hand.

"Doesn't it look small, all of a sudden?" she said to Rachel.

"What are going to do with them?" said Rachel. "If we keep them in our pockets, and if we are searched, that's the end of us."

They decided to bury their stars beneath the bush with the clothes they had used for their escape. The earth was soft and dry. Rachel dug a hole, put the stars and clothes inside, then covered them up with the brown soil.

"There," she said, exulting. "I'm burying the stars. They're dead. In their grave. Forever and ever."

The girl laughed with Rachel. Then she felt ashamed. Her mother had told her to be proud of her star. Proud of being a Jew.

She didn't want to think about all that now. Things were different. Everything was different. They had to find water, food, and shelter, and she had to get home. How? She didn't know. She didn't even know where they were. But she had money. The man's money. He had not been that bad after all, that policeman. Maybe that meant there were other good people who could help them, too. People who did not hate them. People who did not think they were "different."

They weren't far from the village. They could see a signpost from behind the bush.

"Beaune-la-Rolande," read Rachel out loud.

Their instinct told them not to go into the village. They would not find help there. The villagers knew about the camp, yet nobody had come to help, except those women, once. And besides, the village was too close to the camp. They might meet a person who would send them right back there. They turned their backs on Beaune-la-Rolande and walked away, keeping close to the tall grass by the side of the road. If only they could drink something, thought the girl. She felt faint with thirst, with hunger.

They walked for a long time, pausing and hiding when they heard an occasional car, a farmer taking his cows home. Were they going in the right direction? To Paris? She didn't know. But at least, she knew they were heading farther and farther away from the camp. She looked at her shoes. They were falling apart. Yet they had been her second best pair, the pair for special occasions, like birthdays and the cinema and visiting friends. She had bought them last year with her mother, near the Place de la République. It seemed so long ago. Like another life. The shoes were too small now, they pinched her toes.

In the late afternoon, they came to a forest, a long, cool stretch of green leafiness. It smelled sweet and humid. They left the road, hoping they might find wild strawberries or blueberries. After a while, they came upon an entire thicket of fruit. Rachel uttered a cry of delight. They sat down and gobbled. The girl remembered picking fruit with her father, when they had spent those lovely days by the river, such a long time ago.

Her stomach, unused to such lavishness, heaved. She retched, holding her abdomen. She brought up a mass of undigested fruit. Her mouth tasted foul. She told Rachel they had to find water. She forced herself up, and they headed deeper into the forest, a mysterious emerald world dappled with golden sunlight. She saw a roe deer canter through the bracken and held her breath with awe. She wasn't used to nature, she was a true city child.

They came to a small, clear pond farther into the forest. It was cool and fresh to their touch. The girl drank for a long time, rinsed out her mouth, washed away the blueberry stains, then glided her legs into the still water. She had not gone swimming since that river escapade, and didn't dare enter the pond completely. Rachel knew, and told her to come in, she'd hold her. The girl slipped in, grasping Rachel's shoulders. Rachel held her under her stomach and her chin, the way her father used to. The water felt wonderful to her skin, a soothing, velvety caress. She wet her shaved head, where the hair had started to grow back, a golden fuzz, rough like the stubble on her father's chin.

All of a sudden, the girl felt drained. She wanted to lie down on the soft green moss and sleep. Only for a little while. Only for a quick rest. Rachel agreed. They could have a short rest. It was safe here.

They cuddled close to each other, reveling in the smell of fresh moss, so different from the stinking straw of the barracks.

The girl fell asleep quickly. It was a deep and untroubled sleep, the kind she hadn't had for a long time.

I T WAS OUR USUAL table. The one in the corner, on the right, as you
came in, past the old-fashioned bistro zinc bar and its tinted mir-
rors. The red velour banquette formed an L. I sat down and watched
the waiters bustling about in their long, white aprons. One of them
brought me a Kir royal. Busy night. Bertrand had taken me here on
our first date, years ago. It had not changed since. The same low ceiling, ivory walls, pale globe lights, starched tablecloths. The same
hearty food from Corrèze and Gascogne, Bertrand's favorite. When I
met him, he used to live on the nearby rue Malar, in a quaint rooftop
apartment that was to me unbearable during summer. As an American raised on permanent air-conditioning, I had wondered how he put
up with it. At that point, I still lived on rue Berthe with the boys, and
my dark, cool little room seemed like heaven during the stuffy Parisian summers. Bertrand and his sisters had been raised in this area of
Paris, the genteel and aristocratic seventh arrondissement, where his
parents had lived for years on the long, curving rue de l'Université,
and where the family antique shop flourished on the rue du Bac.

Our usual table. That's where we had been sitting when Bertrand
had asked me to marry him. That's where I'd told him I was pregnant
with Zoë. That's where I told him I had found out about Amélie.

Amélie.

Not tonight. Not now. Amélie was over. Was she, though? Was she
really? I had to admit I was not sure. But for now, I did not want to
know. I did not want to see. There was going to be a new baby. Amélie

could not fight against that. I smiled, a little bitterly. Closing my eyes. Wasn't that the typical French attitude, "closing your eyes" on your husband's wanderings? Was I capable of that? I wondered.

I had put up such a fight when I had first discovered he was being unfaithful ten years ago. We had been sitting right here, I mused. And I had decided to tell him then and there. He had not denied anything. He had remained calm, cool, had listened to me with his fingers crossed under his chin. Credit card slips. Hôtel de la Perle, rue des Canettes. Hôtel Lenox, rue Delambre. Le Relais Christine, rue Christine. One hotel receipt after the other.

He had not been particularly careful. Neither about the receipts, nor about her perfume, which would cling to him, his clothes, his hair, the passenger seat belt in his Audi station wagon and which was the first clue, the first sign, I recalled. L'Heure Bleue. The heaviest, most powerful, cloying scent by Guerlain. It wasn't difficult finding out who she was. In fact I already knew her. He had introduced her to me right after our marriage.

Divorced. Three teenage children. Fortyish, with silvery brown hair. The image of Parisian perfection. Small, slender, perfectly dressed. The right handbag and the right shoes. An excellent job. A spacious apartment overlooking the Trocadéro. A magnificent, old French name that sounded like a famous wine. A signet ring on her left hand.

Amélie. Bertrand's old girlfriend from the Lycée Victor Duruy, from all those years ago. The one he had never stopped seeing. The one he had never stopped fucking, despite marriages, children, and the years going by. "We are friends now," he had promised. "Just friends. Good friends."

After the meal, in the car, I had transformed myself into a lioness, fangs bared, claws drawn. He had been flattered, I suppose. He had promised, he had sworn. There was me, and only me. She was not important, she was just a *passade*, a passing thing. And for a long while, I had believed him.

And, recently, I had begun to wonder. Odd, flitting doubts. Nothing concrete, just doubts. Did I still believe him?

"You're crazy to believe him," said Hervé, said Christophe. "Maybe you should ask him outright," said Isabelle. "You're out of your mind to believe him," said Charla, said my mother, said Holly, Susannah, Jan.

No Amélie tonight, I decided firmly. Just Bertrand and me, and the wonderful news. I nursed my drink. The waiters smiled at me. I felt good. I felt strong. To hell with Amélie. Bertrand was *my* husband. I was going to have *his* baby.

The restaurant was full. I looked around at the busy tables. An old couple eating side by side, one glass of wine each, studiously bent over their meal. A group of young women in their thirties, collapsing with helpless giggles as a stern woman dining alone nearby looked on and frowned. Businessmen in their gray suits, lighting up cigars. American tourists, trying to decipher the menu. A family and their teenage children. The noise level was high. The smoke level, too. But it didn't bother me. I was used to it.

Bertrand would be late, as usual. It didn't matter. I had had time to change, to have my hair done. I wore my chocolate brown slacks, the ones I knew he liked, and a simple clinging fauve top. Pearl earrings from Agatha and my Hermès wristwatch. I glanced in the mirror on my left. My eyes seemed wider and bluer than usual, my skin glowed. Pretty damn good for a middle-aged pregnant female, I thought. And the way the waiters beamed at me made me think they thought so as well.

I took my agenda from my bag. Tomorrow morning, first thing, I had to call my gynecologist. Appointments needed to be made, fast. I probably had to go through tests. An amniocentesis, no doubt. No longer was I a "young" mother. Zoë's birth seemed so far away.

All of sudden, panic hit me. Was I going to be able to go through all this, eleven years later? The pregnancy, the birth, the sleepless nights, the bottles, the crying, the diapers? Well, of course I was, I scoffed. I had been longing for this for the past decade. Of course I was ready. And so was Bertrand.

But as I sat waiting for him, anxiety grew. I tried to ignore it. I opened my notebook and read the recent Vel' d'Hiv' notes I'd taken earlier on. Soon, I was lost in my work. I no longer heard the hubbub of the restaurant around me, people laughing, waiters moving swiftly through the tables, chair legs scraping the floor.

I looked up to see my husband sitting in front of me, observing me.

"Hey, how long have you been there?" I asked.

He smiled. He covered my hand with his.

"Long enough. You look beautiful."

He was wearing his dark blue corduroy jacket and a crisp, white shirt.

"*You* look beautiful," I said.

I nearly blurted it out, right then. But no, this was too soon. Too fast. I held back with difficulty. The waiter brought a Kir royal for Bertrand.

"Well?" he said. "Why are we here, *amour*? Something special? A surprise?"

"Yes," I said, raising my glass. "A very special surprise. Drink up! Here's to the surprise."

Our glasses clicked.

"Am I supposed to guess what it is?" he asked.

I felt impish, like a little girl.

"You'll never guess! Never."

He laughed, amused.

"You look like Zoë! Does she know what the special surprise is?"

I shook my head, feeling more and more excited.

"Nope. No one knows. No one except . . . me."

I reached out and took one of his hands. Smooth, tanned skin.

"Bertrand—," I said.

The waiter hovered above us. We decided to order. It was done in a minute, *confit de canard* for me and *cassoulet* for Bertrand. Asparagus for starters.

I watched the waiter's back retreat toward the kitchens, then I said it. Very fast.

"I'm going to have a baby."

I scrutinized his face. I waited for the mouth to tilt upward, the eyes to open wide with delight. But each muscle of his face remained motionless, like a mask. His eyes flickered back at me.

"A baby?" he echoed.

I pressed his hand.

"Isn't it wonderful? Bertrand, isn't it wonderful?"

He said nothing. I couldn't understand.

"How pregnant are you?" he asked, finally.

"I just found out," I murmured, worried by his stoniness.

He rubbed his eyes, something he always did when he was tired, or upset. He said nothing, I didn't either.

The silence stretched out between us like mist. I could almost feel it with my fingers.

The waiter came to bring the first course. Neither of us touched our asparagus.

"What's wrong?" I said, unable to bear it any longer.

He sighed, shook his head, rubbed his eyes again.

"I thought you'd be happy, thrilled," I continued, tears welling.

He rested his chin on his hand, looked at me.

"Julia, I had given up."

"But so had I! Completely given up."

His eyes were grave. I did not like the finality in them.

"What do you mean," I said, "just because you had given up, then you can't . . . ?"

"Julia. I'm going to be fifty in less than three years."

"So what?" I said, cheeks burning.

"I don't want to be an old father," he said quietly.

"Oh, for God's sake," I said.

Silence.

"We can't keep this baby, Julia," he said, gently. "We have another life now. Zoë will soon be a teenager. You are forty-five. Our life is not the same. A baby would not fit into our life."

The tears came now, splashing down my face, into my food.

"Are you trying to tell me," I choked, "are you trying to tell me that I have to get an abortion?"

The family at the next table stared overtly. I did not give a damn.

As usual, in times of crisis, I had reverted back to my maternal tongue. No French was possible at a moment like this.

"An abortion, after three miscarriages?" I said, shaking.

His face was sad. Tender and sad. I wanted to slap it, to kick it.

But I could not. I could only cry into my napkin. He stroked my hair, murmured over and over again that he loved me.

I shut his voice out.

WHEN THE CHILDREN AWOKE, the night had fallen. The forest was no longer the peaceful, leafy place they had wandered through that afternoon. It was large, stark, full of strange noises. Slowly, they made their way through the bracken, hand in hand, pausing at every sound. It seemed to them the night grew blacker and blacker. Deeper and deeper. They walked on. The girl thought she was going to drop with exhaustion. But Rachel's warm hand encouraged her.

They at last came to a wide path weaving across flat meadows. The forest loomed away. They looked up at a somber, moonless sky.

"Look," said Rachel, pointing ahead of her. "A car."

They saw headlights shine through the night. Headlights that were darkened with black paint, only letting a strip of light through. They heard the noisy engine approaching.

"What shall we do?" said Rachel. "Shall we stop it?"

The girl saw another pair of overshadowed headlights, then another. It was a long line of cars coming closer.

"Get down," she whispered, pulling at Rachel's skirt. "Quick!"

There were no bushes to hide behind. She lay flat out on her stomach, her chin in the dirt.

"Why? What are you doing?" asked Rachel.

Then she, too, understood.

Soldiers. German soldiers. Patrolling in the night.

Rachel scrambled down next to the girl.

The cars drew near, powerful engines rumbling. The girls could make out the shiny, round helmets of the men in the muted light of the head-lights. They are going to see us, thought the girl. We cannot hide. There is no place to hide, they are going to see us.

The first jeep rolled by, followed by the others. Thick, white dust blew into the girls' eyes. They tried not to cough, not to move. The girl lay face down in the dirt, her hands over her ears. The line of cars seemed endless. Would the men see their dark shapes by the side of the dirt road? She braced herself for the shouts, the cars stopping, doors slamming, fast footsteps and rough hands on their shoulders.

But the last cars went by, droning in the night. Silence returned. They looked up. The dirt road was empty, save for clouds of billowing white dust. They waited a moment, then crept down the path, going in the opposite direction. A light shimmered through trees. A white beck-oning light. They drew nearer, keeping to the sides of the road. They opened a gate, walked stealthily up to a house. It looked like a farm, thought the girl. Through the open window, they saw a woman reading by the fireplace, a man smoking a pipe. A rich smell of food wafted by their nostrils.

Without hesitating, Rachel knocked on the door. A cotton curtain was pulled back. The woman who looked at them through the glass pane had a long, bony face. She stared at the girls, pulled the curtain back again. She did not open the door. Rachel knocked again.

"Please, Madame, we would like some food, some water."

The curtain did not move. The girls went to stand in front of the open window. The man with the pipe got up from his chair.

"Go away," he said, his voice low and threatening. "Get away from here."

Behind him, the bony-faced woman looked on, silent.

"Please, some water," said the girl.

The window was slammed shut.

The girl felt like crying. How could these farmers be so cruel? There was bread on the table, she had seen it. There was a pitcher of water, too. Rachel dragged her on. They went back to the winding dirt road. There were more farm houses. Each time, the same thing happened. They were sent away. Each time, they fled.

It was late now. They were tired, hungry, they could hardly walk. They came to a large, old house, a little off the dirt road, lit by a high lamppost, shining down on them. Its façade was covered with ivy. They didn't dare knock. In front of the house, they noticed a large empty dog shed. They crept inside. It was clean and warm. It had a comforting, dog-like smell. There was a bowl of water and an old bone. They lapped up the water, one after the other. The girl was frightened the dog might come back and bite them. She whispered this to Rachel. But Rachel had already fallen asleep, curled up like a little animal. The girl looked down at her exhausted face, the thin cheeks, the hollow eye sockets. Rachel looked like an old woman.

The girl dozed fitfully, leaning against Rachel. She had a strange and horrible dream. She dreamed of her brother, dead in the closet. She dreamed of her parents being hit by the police. She moaned in her sleep.

Furious barks startled her awake. She nudged Rachel, hard. They heard a man's voice, steps coming closer. The gravel crunched. It was too late to slip out. They could only hold on to each other in despair. Now we are dead, thought the girl. Now we are going to be killed.

The dog was held back by its master. She felt a hand grope inside, grasp her arm, Rachel's arm. They slithered out.

The man was small, wizened, with a bald head and a silver mustache.

"Now what do we have here?" he murmured, peering at them in the glare of the lamppost.

The girl felt Rachel stiffen, guessed she was going to take off, fast, like a rabbit.

"Are you lost?" asked the old man. His voice seemed concerned.

The children were startled. They had expected threats, blows, anything but kindness.

"Please, sir, we are very hungry," said Rachel.

The man nodded.

"I can see that."

He bent to silence the whining dog. Then he said, "Come in, children. Follow me."

Neither of the girls moved. Could they trust this old man?

"Nobody will hurt you here," he said.

They huddled together, fearful still.

The man smiled, a kind, gentle smile.

"Geneviève!" he called, twisting back to the house.

An elderly woman wearing a blue dressing gown appeared in the large doorway.

"What is that idiotic dog of yours barking at now, Jules?" she asked, annoyed. Then she saw the children. Her hands fluttered to her cheeks.

"Heavens above," she murmured.

She came nearer. She had a placid, round face and a thick, white braid. She gazed at the children with pity and dismay.

The girl's heart leaped. The old lady looked like the photograph of her grandmother from Poland. The same light-colored eyes, white hair, the same comforting plumpness.

"Jules," the elderly lady whispered, "are they—"

The old man nodded.

"Yes, I think so."

The old lady said, firmly, "They must come in. They must be hidden at once."

She waddled down to the dirt road, peered both ways.

"Quick, children, come now," she said, holding out her hands. "You are safe here. You are safe with us."

THE NIGHT HAD BEEN dreadful. I woke up puffy faced with lack of sleep. I was glad Zoë had already left for school. I would have hated for her to see me now. Bertrand was kind, tender. He said we needed to talk it over some more. We could do so that evening, once Zoë was asleep. He said all this perfectly calmly, with great gentleness. I could tell he had made up his mind. Nothing or no one was going to make him want me to have this child.

I couldn't bring myself to talk about it yet to my friends or to my sister. Bertrand's choice had disturbed me to such an extent that I preferred to keep it to myself, at least for the time being.

It was difficult to get going this morning. Everything I did felt laborious. Every movement was an effort. I kept having flashbacks of last night. Of what he had said. There was no other solution but to throw myself into work. That afternoon, I was to meet Franck Lévy in his office. The Vel' d'Hiv' seemed far away all of a sudden. I felt like I had aged overnight. Nothing seemed to matter anymore, nothing except the child I carried and that my husband did not want.

I was on my way to the office when my cell phone rang. It was Guillaume. He had found a couple of those out-of-print books I needed concerning the Vel' d'Hiv', at his grandmother's place. He could lend them to me. Could I meet him later on in the day, or that evening, for a drink? His voice was cheerful, friendly. I said yes immediately. We agreed to meet at six o'clock, at the Select on the boulevard du Montparnasse, two minutes away from home. We said good-bye, and then my phone rang again.

It was my father-in-law this time. I was surprised. Edouard rarely called me. We got on, in that French polite way. We both excelled at mutual small talk. But I was never truly comfortable with him. I always felt as if he was holding something back, never showing his feelings, to me, or to anybody else for that matter.

The kind of man one listens to. The kind of man one looks up to. I could not imagine him showing any other emotion apart from anger, pride, and self-satisfaction. I never saw Edouard wearing jeans, even during those Burgundy weekends when he would sit in the garden under the oak tree reading Rousseau. I don't think I ever saw him without a tie, either. I remembered the first time I met him. He hadn't changed much in the last seventeen years. The same regal posture, silver hair, steely eyes. My father-in-law was overly fond of cooking, and was constantly shooing Colette away from the kitchen, turning out simple, delicious meals—pot-au-feu, onion soup, a savory ratatouille, or a truffle omelet. The only person allowed in the kitchen with him was Zoë. He had a soft spot for Zoë, although Cécile and Laure had both produced boys, Arnaud and Louis. He adored my daughter. I never knew what went on during their cooking sessions. Behind the closed door, I could hear Zoë's giggle, and vegetables being chopped, water bubbling, fat hissing in a pan, and Edouard's occasional deep rumble of a chuckle.

Edouard asked how Zoë was doing, how the apartment was coming along. And then he got to the point. He had been to see Mamé yesterday. It had been a "bad" day, he added. Mamé was in one of her sulks. He had been about to leave her pouting at her television, when all of a sudden, out of the blue, she had said something about me.

"And what was that?" I asked, curious.

Edouard cleared his throat.

"My mother said that you had been asking her all sorts of questions about the rue de Saintonge apartment."

I took a deep breath.

"Well, that's true, I did," I admitted. I wondered what he was getting at.

Silence.

"Julia, I prefer that you don't ask Mamé anything about the rue de Saintonge."

He spoke suddenly in English, as if he wanted to be perfectly sure I understood.

Stung, I replied in French.

"I'm sorry, Edouard. It's just that I'm researching the Vel' d'Hiv' roundup at the moment for the magazine. I was surprised at the coincidence."

Another silence.

"The coincidence?" he repeated, using French again.

"Well, yes," I said, "about the Jewish family who lived there just before your family moved in and who were arrested during the roundup. I think Mamé was upset when she told me about it. So I stopped asking her questions."

"Thank you, Julia," he said. He paused. "It *does* upset Mamé. Don't mention it to her again, please."

I halted in the middle of the sidewalk.

"Ok, I won't," I said, "but I didn't mean any harm, I only wanted to know how your family ended up in that apartment, and if Mamé knew anything about the Jewish family. Do you, Edouard? Do you know anything?"

"I'm sorry, I didn't catch that," he replied smoothly. "I must go, now. Good-bye, Julia."

The line went dead.

He had puzzled me to such an extent that for a brief moment, I forgot about Bertrand and last night. Had Mamé really complained to Edouard about my questioning her? I remembered how she had no longer wanted to answer me that day. How she had shut up, not opening her mouth once till I had left, baffled. Why had Mamé been so upset? Why were Mamé and Edouard so intent on me not asking questions about the apartment? What did they not want me to know?

Bertrand and the baby came back down on my shoulders with a heavy weight. All of a sudden, I couldn't face going to the office. Alessandra's curious gaze. She would be inquisitive, as usual, she would ask questions. Trying to be friendly, but failing. Bamber and Joshua glancing at my swollen face. Bamber, a true gentleman, would not say a thing, but would discreetly squeeze my shoulder. And Joshua. He would be the worst. "Well now, sugar plum, what's the drama? Ze French husband, again?" I could almost see his sardonic grin, handing me a cup of coffee. There was no way I could go to the office this morning.

I headed back up toward the Arc de Triomphe, picking my impatient but deft way through the hordes of tourists walking along at a sluggish pace, gazing up the arch and pausing for photos. I took my address book out and dialed Franck Lévy's association. I asked if I could come now, and not this afternoon. I was told there was no problem. Now was perfect. It wasn't far, just off the avenue Hoche. It only took me ten minutes to get there. Once off the engorged artery of the Champs-Élysées, the other avenues springing out from the Place de l'Étoile were surprisingly empty.

Franck Lévy was in his mid-sixties, I guessed. There was something profound, noble, and weary about his face. We went into his office, a high-ceilinged room filled with books, files, computers, photographs. I let my eyes linger over the black-and-white prints hung on the wall. Babies. Toddlers. Children wearing the star.

"Many of these are Vel' d'Hiv' children," he said, following my gaze. "But there are others, too. All part of the eleven thousand children deported from France."

We sat down at his desk. I had e-mailed him a couple of questions before our interview.

"You wanted to know about the Loiret camps?" he asked.

"Yes," I said. "Beaune-la-Rolande and Pithiviers. There's a lot more information available about Drancy, which is nearer to Paris. Much less on the other two."

Franck Lévy sighed.

"You're right. There's little to be found about the Loiret camps compared with Drancy. And you'll see, when you go there, there's not much there that explains exactly what happened. The people who live there don't want to remember either. They don't want to talk. Also, there were few survivors."

I looked again at the photos, at the rows of small, vulnerable faces.

"What were these camps in the first place?" I asked.

"They were standard military camps built in 1939 for imprisoning German soldiers. But under the Vichy government, Jews were sent there as from 1941. In '42, the first direct trains to Auschwitz left Beaune-la-Rolande and Pithiviers."

"Why weren't the Vel' d'Hiv' families sent to Drancy, in the Paris suburbs?"

Franck Lévy gave a bleak smile.

"The Jews without children were sent to Drancy after the roundup. Drancy is close to Paris. The other camps were more than an hour away. Lost in the middle of the quiet Loiret countryside. And it was there, in all discretion, that the French police separated the children from their parents. They could not have done that so easily in Paris. You have read about their brutality I suppose?"

"There is not much to read."

The bleak smile faded.

"You're right. Not much to read. But we know how it happened. I have a couple of books you're welcome to borrow. The children were torn from the mothers. Bludgeoned, beaten, drenched with cold water."

My eyes wandered once more over the little faces in the photos. I thought of Zoë, alone, torn from me and Bertrand. Alone and hungry and dirty. I shivered.

"Those four thousand Vel' d'Hiv' children were a severe headache for the French authorities," said Franck Lévy. "The Nazis had asked for the adults to be deported immediately. Not the children. The strict programming of the trains was not to be altered. Hence the brutal separation from the mothers in the beginning of August."

"And then, what happened to those children?" I asked.

"Their parents were deported from the Loiret camps straight to

Auschwitz. The children were left practically alone in horrifying sanitary conditions. Mid-August, the decision from Berlin came through. The children were to be deported as well. However, in order to avoid suspicion, the children were to be sent to Drancy, and then on to Poland, mixing with unknown adults from the Drancy camp, so that the public opinion would think these children were not alone, traveling east with their families to some Jewish work reserve."

Franck Lévy paused, looking as I did at the photographs hung along the wall.

"When those children arrived in Auschwitz, there was no 'selection' for them. No lining up with the men and the women. No checking to see who was strong, who was sick, who could work, who could not. They were sent directly to the gas chambers."

"By the French government, on French buses, on French trains," I added.

Maybe it was because I was pregnant, because my hormones had gone awry, or because I hadn't slept, but I suddenly felt devastated.

I stared at the photos, stricken.

Franck Lévy watched me in silence. Then he got up and put a hand on my shoulder.

*T*HE GIRL FELL UPON the food that was placed in front of her, cramming it into her mouth with slurping noises her mother would have detested. It was heaven. It seemed she had never tasted such savory, delicious soup. Such fresh, soft bread. Creamy, rich Brie cheese. Succulent, velvety peaches. Rachel ate more slowly. Glancing across at her, the girl saw that Rachel was pale. Her hands were trembling, her eyes feverish.

The elderly couple were bustling about the kitchen, pouring out more *potage*, filling glasses with fresh water. The girl heard their soft, gentle questions, but could not bring herself to answer them. It was only later, when Geneviève took her and Rachel upstairs for a bath, that she began to talk. She told her about the big place they were all taken to and locked in for days with hardly any water, any food, then the train ride through the countryside, the camp, and the horrible separation from her parents. And finally, the escape.

The old lady listened, nodded, deftly undressing the glassy-eyed Rachel. The girl watched as the bony body emerged, covered with angry red blisters. The old lady shook her head, appalled.

"What have they done to you?" she murmured.

Rachel's eyes barely flickered. The old woman helped Rachel slide into the warm soapy water. She washed her like the girl's mother used to bathe her little brother.

Then Rachel was wrapped up in a large towel and carried into a nearby bed.

"Your turn, now," said Geneviève, running a fresh bath. "What's your name, little one? You never told me."

"Sirka," said the girl.

"What a pretty name!" said Geneviève, handing her a clean sponge, and the soap. She noticed the girl was shy about being naked in front of her, so she turned around to let her undress and slip into the water. The girl washed herself carefully, reveling in the hot water, then she nimbly climbed out of the tub and wrapped herself in a deliciously soft lavender-scented towel.

Geneviève was busy washing the girls' filthy clothes in the large enamel sink. The girl watched her for a while, then she timidly put her hand on the old lady's plump, round arm.

"Madame, could you help me get back to Paris?"

The old lady, startled, turned to look at her.

"You want to go back to Paris, *petite*?"

The girl began to shake from head to foot. The old woman stared at her, concerned. She left the washing in the sink and toweled her hands dry.

"What is it, Sirka?"

The girl's lips began to tremble.

"My little brother, Michel. He is still in the apartment. In Paris. He is locked in a cupboard, in our special hiding place. He has been there since the day the police came to get us. I thought he'd be safe there. I promised to come back and save him."

Geneviève looked down at her with concern, tried to steady her by putting her hands on the bony little shoulders.

"Sirka, how long has your little brother been in the cupboard?"

"I don't know," the girl whispered dully. "I can't remember. I can't remember!"

All of a sudden, every ounce of hope she still harbored within her ran out. In the old lady's eyes she read what she most dreaded. Michel was dead. Dead in the cupboard. She knew. It was too late. She had waited too long. He had not survived. He had not made it. He had died there, all alone, in the dark, with no food and no water, just the bear and the storybook, and he had trusted her, he had waited, he had probably called out to her, screamed her name again and again, "Sirka, Sirka, where are you! Where are you?" He was dead, Michel was dead. He was four years old, and he was dead, because of her. If she had not locked him up that day, he could have been here, right now, she could be bathing him now, this instant. She should have watched over him, she should have brought him here to safety. It was her fault. It was all her fault.

The girl crumpled to the floor, a broken being. Wave after wave of despair washed over her. Never in her short life had she known such acute pain. She felt Geneviève gather her close, stroke her shorn head, murmur words of comfort. She let herself go, surrendered herself completely to the kind old arms that encircled her. Then she felt the sweet sensation of a soft mattress and clean sheets enveloping her. She fell into a strange, troubled slumber.

She awoke early, feeling lost, confused. She could not remember where she was. It had been strange, sleeping in a real bed after all those nights in the barracks. She went to the window. The shutters were slightly ajar, revealing a large, sweet-smelling garden. Hens roamed across the lawn, chased by the playful dog. On a wrought-iron bench, a plump ginger cat slowly licked its paws clean. The girl heard birds singing, a rooster crowing. A nearby cow mooing. It was a sunny, fresh morning. The girl thought she had never seen a lovelier, more peaceful place. The war, the hatred, the horror seemed far away. The garden and the flowers, and the trees, and all the animals, none of these things could ever be tainted by the evil she had witnessed in the past weeks.

She examined the clothes she was wearing. A white night dress, a little too long for her. She wondered who it belonged to. Maybe the elderly couple had children, or grandchildren. She looked around at the spacious room. It was simple but comfortable. There was a bookshelf near the door. She went to look at it. Her favorites were there, Jules Verne, the Comtesse de Ségur. On the flyleaves, a juvenile, scholarly handwriting: Nicolas Dufaure. She wondered who he was.

She went down the creaking, wooden stairs, following the murmur of voices she heard from the kitchen. The house was quiet and welcoming, in a shabby, unceremonious way. Her feet glided over square wine-red tiles. She glanced into a sunny living room that smelled of beeswax and lavender. A tall grandfather clock ticked solemnly away.

She tiptoed toward the kitchen, peeked around the door. There she saw the old couple sitting at the long table drinking from round blue bowls. They seemed concerned.

"I'm worried about Rachel," Geneviève was saying. "She's running a high fever and not keeping anything down. And her rash. It's nasty. Very nasty indeed." She sighed, deeply. "The state of these children, Jules. One of them even had lice in her eyelashes."

The girl walked into the room, hesitantly.

"I just wondered . . . ," she began.

The old couple looked up at her and smiled.

"Well," beamed the old man. "You are quite a different person this morning, Mademoiselle. There's a little pink in those cheeks."

"There was something in my pockets," said the girl.

Geneviève rose. She pointed to a shelf.

"A key and some money. Right over here."

The girl went to take the objects, cradling them.

"This is the key to the cupboard," she said in a low voice. "The cupboard Michel is in. Our special hiding place."

Jules and Geneviève exchanged glances.

"I know you think he's dead," said the girl, haltingly. "But I am going back there. I have to know. Maybe someone was able to help him, like you helped me! Maybe he is waiting for me. I must know, I must find out! I can use the money the policeman gave me."

"But how are you going to get to Paris, *petite*?" asked Jules.

"I will take the train. Surely Paris is not far from here?"

Another exchange of glances.

"Sirka, we live southeast of Orléans. You walked a very long way with Rachel. But you walked farther away from Paris."

The girl drew herself up. She would go back to Paris, go back to Michel, to see what had happened, no matter what was awaiting her.

"I need to leave," she said firmly. "There are trains from Orléans to Paris, surely. I will leave, today."

Geneviève came to her, grasped her hands.

"Sirka, here you are safe. You can stay for a while, with us. Because this is a farm, we have milk, meat, and eggs, we don't need rationing tickets. You can rest, and eat, and get better."

"Thank you," said the girl, "but I am already better. I need to go back to Paris. You don't have to come with me. I can manage on my own. Just tell me how to get to the station."

Before the old lady could answer, there was a long wail from upstairs. Rachel. They rushed up to her room. Rachel was twisting and turning in pain. Her sheets were drenched with something dark and putrid.

"It's what I feared," whispered Geneviève. "Dysentery. She needs a doctor. Fast."

Jules hobbled back down the stairs.

"I'll go to the village, see if Docteur Thévenin is around," he called over his shoulder.

He was back an hour later, puffing on his bicycle. The girl watched him from the kitchen window.

"Old boy's gone," he told his wife. "The house is empty. No one could tell me anything. So I went farther along, toward Orléans. I found a youngish fellow, got him to come, but he was a trifle arrogant, said he had more urgent things to look to first."

Geneviève bit her lip.

"I hope he comes. Soon."

The doctor did not turn up till later that afternoon. The girl hadn't dared mention Paris again. She sensed Rachel was very ill. Jules and Geneviève were too worried about Rachel to concentrate on her.

When they heard the doctor arrive, heralded by the dog's bark, Geneviève turned to the girl, told her to hide, fast, in the cellar. They didn't know this doctor, she explained quickly, he wasn't their usual one. They had to play it safe.

The girl slipped down through the trapdoor. She sat in the dark, listening to every word from above. She couldn't see the doctor's face, but she didn't like his voice; it was strident, nasal. He kept asking where Rachel was from. Where had they found her? He was insistent, stubborn. Jules's voice remained steady. The girl was the daughter of a neighbor who had gone to Paris for a couple of days.

But the girl could tell by the doctor's tone that he didn't believe a word of what Jules was saying. He had a nasty laugh. He kept talking about law and order. About the Maréchal Pétain and a new vision of France. About what the Kommandantur would think of this dark, thin little girl.

Finally, she heard the front door bang.

Then she heard Jules's voice again. It seemed aghast.

"Geneviève," he said. "What have we done?"

I WANTED TO ASK you something, Monsieur Lévy. Something that has nothing to do with my article."

He looked at me and went back to sit in his chair.

"Of course. Go ahead, please."

I leaned forward over the table.

"If I gave you an exact address, could you help me trace a family? A family that was arrested in Paris on July 16, 1942?"

"A Vel' d'Hiv' family," he said.

"Yes," I said. "It's important."

He looked at my tired face. My puffy eyes. I felt as if he could read within me, read the new grief I was carrying, read what I knew about the apartment. Read everything I was that morning, as I sat in front of him.

"For the past forty years, Miss Jarmond, I have been tracing every single Jewish person deported from this country between 1941 and 1944. A long and painful process. But a necessary process. Yes, it is possible for me to give you the name of that family. It is all in this computer, right here. We can have that name in a couple of seconds. But can you tell me why you want to know about this precise family? Is this merely a journalist's natural curiosity, or something else?"

I felt my cheeks heat up.

"It's personal," I said. "And not easy to explain."

"Try," he said.

Hesitating at first, I told him about the apartment on the rue de

Saintonge. About what Mamé had said. About what my father-in-law had said. Finally, with more fluidity, I told him I couldn't stop thinking about that Jewish family. About who they were, and what had happened to them. He listened to me, nodding from time to time.

Then he said, "Sometimes, Miss Jarmond, it's not easy to bring back the past. There are unpleasant surprises. The truth is harder than ignorance."

I nodded.

"I realize that," I said. "But I need to know."

He looked back at me, his eyes steady.

"I will give you the name. For you to know, and for you only. Not for your magazine. May I have your word?"

"Yes," I replied, struck by his solemnity.

He turned to the computer.

"Please, the address."

I complied.

His fingers flew over the keyboard. The computer gave a little crackle. I felt my heart pound. Then the printer whined, spat out a white sheet of paper. Franck Lévy handed it to me without a word. I read:

26, rue de Saintonge, 75003 Paris
STARZYNSKI
• Wladyslaw, born Warsaw, 1910. Arrested July 16, 1942. Garage, rue de Bretagne. Vel' d'Hiv'. Beaune-la-Rolande. Convoy number 15, August 5, 1942.
• Rywka, born Okuniew, 1912. Arrested July 16, 1942. Garage, rue de Bretagne. Vel' d'Hiv'. Beaune-la-Rolande. Convoy number 15, August 5, 1942.
• Sarah, born Paris 12th arrondissement, 1932. Arrested July 16, 1942. Garage, rue de Bretagne. Vel' d'Hiv'. Beaune-la-Rolande.

The printer emitted another whine.

"A photograph," said Franck Lévy. He looked at it before giving it to me.

It was of a ten-year-old girl. I read the caption: JUNE 1942. Taken at the school on the rue des Blancs-Manteaux. Right next to the rue de Saintonge.

The girl had slanted, light-colored eyes. They would have been blue or green, I thought. Shoulder-length pale hair with a bow in it, slightly crooked. A beautiful, shy smile. A heart-shaped face. She was sitting at her school desk, an open book in front of her. On her chest, the star.

Sarah Starzynski. A year younger than Zoë.

I looked back at the list of names. I didn't need to ask Franck Lévy where convoy number 15 leaving Beaune-la-Rolande had gone. I knew it was Auschwitz.

"What about the garage on the rue de Bretagne?" I asked.

"That's where most of the Jews living in the third arrondissement were gathered before being taken to the rue Nélaton and the *vélo-drome*."

I noticed that after Sarah's name, there was no mention of a convoy. I pointed this out to Franck Lévy.

"That means she was not on any of the trains that left for Poland. As far as we know."

"Could she have escaped?" I said.

"It's hard to say. A handful of children did escape from Beaune-la-Rolande and were saved by French farmers living nearby. Other children, who were much smaller than Sarah, were deported without their identities being clear. In that case, they were listed for example as "One boy, Pithiviers." Alas, I can't tell you what happened to Sarah Starzynski, Miss Jarmond. All I can tell you is that she apparently never arrived in Drancy with the other children from Beaune-la-Rolande and Pithiviers. She is not in the Drancy files."

I looked down at the beautiful, innocent face.

"What could have happened to her?" I murmured.

"The last trace of her we have is at Beaune-la-Rolande. She may have been saved by a neighboring family. She could have remained hidden during the war under another name."

"Did that happen a lot?"

"Yes, it did. A great number of Jewish children survived, thanks to the help and generosity of French families or religious institutions."

I looked at him.

"Do you think Sarah Starzynski was saved? That she survived?"

He looked down at the photograph of the lovely, smiling child.

"I hope she was. But now you know what you wanted. You know who lived in your apartment."

"Yes," I said. "Yes, thank you. But I still wonder how my husband's family could live there after the Starzysnkis' arrest. I can't understand that."

"You must not judge them so harshly," warned Franck Lévy. "There was indeed a considerable amount of Parisian indifference, but don't forget Paris was occupied. People feared for their lives. Those were very different times."

As I left Franck Lévy's office, I suddenly felt fragile, on the verge of tears. It had been a draining, taxing day. My world closed in around me, pressing down on me from every side. Bertrand. The baby. The impossible decision I was going to have to make. The talk I was going to have with my husband tonight.

And then, the mystery concerning the rue de Saintonge apartment. The Tézac family moving in, so quickly after the Starzynskis had been arrested. Mamé and Edouard not wanting to talk about it. Why? What had happened? What didn't they want me to know?

As I walked toward the rue Marbeuf, I felt like I was being swamped by something enormous, something I could not deal with.

Later on that evening, I met Guillaume at the Select. We sat near the bar, away from the noisy *terrasse*. He had a couple of books with him. I was delighted. They were the exact ones I just could not get my hands on. Particularly one concerning the Loiret camps. I thanked him warmly.

I had not planned to say anything about what I had discovered that afternoon, but it all came tumbling out. Guillaume listened to every word, intently. When I finished, he said that his grandmother had told him about Jewish apartments being plundered right after the roundup. Others had seals fixed on their doors by the police, seals that would be broken several months or years later when it was obvious that no one was coming back. According to Guillaume's grandmother, the police often worked closely with the concierges, who were able to find new tenants quickly by word of mouth. That's probably how it had happened for my in-laws.

"Why is this so important to you, Julia?" Guillaume asked, finally.

"I want to know what happened to that little girl."

He looked at me with dark, searching eyes.

"I understand. But be careful about questioning your husband's family."

"I know they are holding something back. I want to know what it is."

"Be careful, Julia," he repeated. He smiled, but his eyes remained serious. "You're playing with Pandora's box. Sometimes, it's better not to open it. Sometimes, it's better not to know."

Franck Lévy had said the same thing that very morning.

*F*OR TEN MINUTES, JULES and Geneviève had rushed about the house, like frantic animals, not speaking, wringing their hands. They seemed in agony. They tried to move Rachel, to carry her down the stairs, but she was too weak. They had finally kept her in bed. Jules did his best to calm Geneviève down, without much success; she kept collapsing on the nearest sofa or chair and bursting into tears.

The girl trailed after them like a worried puppy. They wouldn't answer any of her questions. She noticed Jules glancing again and again toward the entrance, peering through the window at the gates. The girl felt fear pluck at her heart.

At nightfall, Jules and Geneviève sat face to face in front of the fireplace. They appeared to have recovered. They seemed calm and composed. But the girl noticed Geneviève's hands trembling. They were both pale, they looked incessantly at the clock.

At one point, Jules turned to the girl. He spoke quietly. He told her to go back down into the cellar. There were large bags of potatoes. She would have to climb into one of them and hide there as best as she could. Did she understand? It was very important. If somebody went into the cellar, she would have to be invisible.

The girl froze. She said, "The Germans are coming!"

Before Jules or Geneviève could say a word, the dog barked, making them all jump. Jules signaled to the girl, pointing to the trapdoor. She obeyed instantly, slipping into the dark, musty cellar. She couldn't see, but she managed to find the potato bags, toward the back, feeling the rough material with her palms. There were several large sacks of them, piled one on top of the other. Quickly, she pulled them apart with her fingers and slithered between them. As she did so, one of the bags split open, and potatoes came tumbling around her, noisily, in a series of quick thumps. She hastily layered them around and over her.

Then she heard the steps. Loud and rhythmic. She had heard those steps before, in Paris, late at night, after the curfew. She knew what they meant. She had peered out of the window, and she had seen the men march by along the feebly lit street, with their round helmets and their precise movements.

Men marching. Marching right up to the house. The steps of a dozen men. A man's voice, muffled but still clear, came to her ears. He was speaking German.

The Germans were here. The Germans had come to get Rachel and her. She felt her bladder loosen.

Footsteps just above her head. The mumble of a conversation she did not catch. Then Jules's voice, "Yes, Lieutenant, there is a sick child here."

"A sick Aryan child, sir?" came the foreign, guttural voice.

"A child that is ill, Lieutenant."

"Where is the child?"

"Upstairs." Jules's voice, weary now.

She heard the heavy steps rock the ceiling. Then Rachel's thin scream all the way from the top of the house. Rachel torn from the bed by the Germans. Rachel moaning, too feeble to fight back.

The girl put her hands over her ears. She didn't want to hear. She could not hear. She felt protected by the sudden silence she had created.

As she lay under the potatoes, she saw a dim ray of light pierce the darkness. Somebody had opened the trapdoor. Somebody was coming down the cellar stairs. She took her hands off her ears.

"There is no one down there," she heard Jules say. "The girl was alone. We found her in our dog shed."

The girl heard Geneviève blowing her nose. Then her voice, tearful, spent.

"Please don't take the girl with you! She is too ill."

The guttural response was ironic.

"Madame, the child is a Jew. Probably escaped from one of the nearby camps. She has no reason to be in your house."

The girl watched the orange flicker of a flashlight creep along the stone cellar walls, edging closer, then, aghast, she saw the oversized black shadow of a soldier, cut out like a cartoon. He was coming for her. He was going to get her. She tried to make herself as small as possible, she stopped breathing. She felt as if her heart had stopped beating.

No, he would not find her! It would be too hideously unfair, too horrible if he found her. They already had poor Rachel. Wasn't that enough? Where had they taken Rachel? Was she outside in a truck with the soldiers? Had she fainted? Where were they taking her, she wondered, to a hospital? Or back to the camp? These bloodthirsty monsters. Monsters! She hated them. She wished them all dead. The bastards. She used all the swearwords she knew, all the words her mother had forbidden her ever to use. The dirty fucking bastards. She screamed the swearwords in her mind, as loud as she could in her mind, closing her eyes tight, away from the orange spot of light coming closer, running over the top of the sacks where she was hiding. He would not find her. Never. Bastards, dirty bastards.

Jules's voice, again.

"There is no one down there, Lieutenant. The girl was alone. She could hardly stand. We had to look after her."

The Lieutenant's voice droned down to the girl, "We are just checking. We are going to look around your cellar, then you will follow us back to the Kommandantur."

The girl tried not to move, not to sigh, not to breathe, as the flashlight roamed over her head.

"Follow you?" Jules's voice seemed stricken. "But why?"

A curt laugh: "A Jew in your house and you ask why?"

Then came Geneviève's voice, surprisingly calm. She sounded like she had stopped crying.

"You saw we were not hiding her, Lieutenant. We were helping her get better. That's all. We didn't know her name. She could not speak."

"Yes," continued Jules's voice, "we even called a doctor. We weren't hiding her in the least."

There was a pause. The girl heard the Lieutenant cough.

"That is indeed what Guillemin told us. You were not hiding the girl. He did say that, the good *Herr Doktor.*"

The girl felt potatoes being moved over her head. She remained as still as a statue, not breathing. Her nose tickled and she longed to sneeze.

She heard Geneviève's voice again, calm, bright, almost hard. A tone she had not heard Geneviève use.

"Would you gentlemen care for some wine?"

The potatoes stopped moving around her.

Upstairs the Lieutenant guffawed, "Some wine? *Jawohl!*"

"And some pâté, perhaps?" said Geneviève, with the same bright voice.

Steps retreated up the stairs, and the trapdoor slammed shut. The girl felt faint with relief. She hugged herself, tears streaming down her face. How long did they remain up there, glasses tinkling, feet shuffling, hearty laughs ringing out? It was endless. It seemed to her that the Lieutenant's bellow was jollier and jollier. She even caught a greasy belch. Of Jules and Geneviève, she heard nothing. Were they still up there? What was going on? She longed to know. But she knew she had to stay where she was until Jules or Geneviève came to fetch her. Her limbs had gone stiff, but still she dared not move.

At last, the house went silent. The dog barked once, then no more. The girl listened. Had the Germans taken Jules and Geneviève with them? Was she all alone in the house? Then she heard the stifled sound of sobs. The trapdoor opened with a groan and Jules's voice floated down to her.

"Sirka! Sirka!"

When she came up again, her legs aching, her eyes red with dust and her cheeks wet and grimy, she saw that Geneviève had broken down, her face in her hands. Jules was trying to comfort her. The girl looked on, helpless. The old woman glanced up. Her face had aged, had caved in. It frightened the girl.

"That child," she whispered, "taken away to her death. I don't know where, or how, but I know she will die. They wouldn't listen. We tried to make them drink, but they kept their heads clear. They let us be, but they took Rachel."

Geneviève's tears flowed down her wrinkled cheeks. She shook her head in despair, grasped Jules's hand, held it close.

"My God, what is our country coming to?"

Geneviève beckoned to the girl, clasped her small hand in her weathered old one. They saved me, the girl kept thinking. They saved me. They saved my life. Maybe somebody like them saved Michel, saved Papa and Maman. Maybe there is still hope.

"Little Sirka!" sighed Geneviève, squeezing her fingers. "You were so brave down there."

The girl smiled. A beautiful, courageous smile that touched the old couple right to their hearts.

"Please," she said, "don't call me Sirka anymore. That's my baby name."

"What should we call you then?" asked Jules.

The girl squared her shoulders and lifted her chin.

"My name is Sarah Starzynski."

ON MY WAY FROM the apartment, where I had checked on the work in progress with Antoine, I stopped by the rue de Bretagne. The garage was still there. And a plaque, too, reminding the passerby that Jewish families of the third arrondissement had been gathered here, the morning of July 16, 1942, before being taken to the Vel' d'Hiv' and deported to the death camps. This is where Sarah's odyssey had started, I thought. Where had it ended?

As I stood there, oblivious to the traffic, I felt I could almost see Sarah coming down the rue de Saintonge on that hot July morning, with her mother, and her father, and the policemen. Yes, I could see it all, I could see them being pushed into the garage, right here, where I now stood. I could see the sweet heart-shaped face, the incomprehension, the fear. The straight hair caught back in a bow, the slanted turquoise eyes. Sarah Starzynski. Was she still alive? She would be seventy today, I thought. No, she couldn't be alive. She had disappeared off the face of the earth, with the rest of the Vel' d'Hiv' children. She had never come back from Auschwitz. She was a handful of dust.

I left the rue de Bretagne and went back to my car. In true American style, I had never been able to drive a stick shift. My car was a small automatic Japanese model that Bertrand scoffed at. I never used it to drive around Paris. The bus and *métro* system were excellent. I felt I didn't need a car to get around the city. Bertrand scoffed at that, too.

Bamber and I were to visit Beaune-la-Rolande that afternoon. An hour's drive from Paris. I had been to Drancy this morning with Guillaume. It was very close to Paris, wedged in between the gray, shabby suburbs of Bobigny and Pantin. Over sixty trains had left from Drancy, situated smack in the heart of the French rail system, to Poland during the war. I had not realized, until we walked past a large, modern sculpture commemorating the place, that the camp was obviously lived in now. Women strolled by with baby carriages and dogs, children ran and shouted, curtains blew in the breeze, plants grew on windowsills. I was astounded. How could anyone live within these walls? I asked Guillaume if he knew of this. He nodded. I could tell by looking at his face that he was moved. His entire family had been deported from here. It was not easy for him to come to this place at all. But he had wanted to accompany me, he had insisted.

The curator of the Drancy Memorial Museum was a middle-aged, tired-looking man called Menetzky. He was waiting for us outside the minute museum that was only opened if one telephoned and made an appointment. We wandered around the small, plain room, gazing at photographs, articles, maps. There were some yellow stars, placed behind a glass panel. It was the first time I saw a real one. I felt impressed and sickened.

The camp had barely changed in the last sixty years. The huge U-shaped concrete construction, built in the late 1930s as an innovative residential project, and requisitioned in 1941 by the Vichy government for deporting Jews, now housed four hundred families in tiny apartments, and had been doing so since 1947. Drancy had the cheapest rents one could find in the vicinity.

I asked the sad Monsieur Menetzky if the residents of the Cité de la Muette—the name of the place, which oddly enough meant "City of the Mute"—had any idea where they were living. He shook his head. Most of the people here were young. They didn't know, and they didn't care, according to him. I then asked if many visitors came to this memorial. Schools sent their classes, he replied, and sometimes tourists came. We leafed through the visitors book. "To Paulette, my mother. I love you and will never forget you. I will come here every year to think of you. This is where you left for Auschwitz in 1944 and never came back. Your daughter, Danielle." I felt tears prick the back of my eyes.

We were then shown into the single cattle wagon that stood in the middle of the lawn, just outside the museum. It was locked, but the curator had the key. Guillaume helped me up, and we both stood in the small, bare space. I tried to imagine the wagon filled up with masses of people, squashed against each other, small children, grandparents, middle-aged parents, adolescents, on their way to death. Guillaume's face had gone white. He told me later he had never been into the wagon. He had never dared. I asked him if he felt all right. He nodded, but I could tell how disturbed he was.

As we walked away from the building, a stack of leaflets and books under my arm given to me by the curator, I could not help thinking of what I knew about Drancy. Its inhumanity during those years of terror. Endless trains of Jews shipped straight to Poland.

I could not help thinking of the heart-wrenching descriptions I had read about the four thousand Vel' d'Hiv' children arriving here at the end of summer of '42, parentless, stinking, sick, and ravenous. Had Sarah been with them after all? Had she left Drancy for Auschwitz, terrified and lonely in a cattle wagon full of strangers?

Bamber was waiting for me in front of our office. He folded his lanky frame into the passenger seat after having put his photo gear in the back. Then he looked at me. I could tell he was worried. He put a gentle hand on my forearm.

"Um, Julia, are you all right?"

The dark glasses didn't help, I guessed. My wretched night was written all over my face. The talk with Bertrand until the wee hours. The more he had talked, the more adamant he had become. No, he did not want this baby. It wasn't even a baby, for him, at this point. It wasn't even a human being. It was a little seed. It was nothing. He did not want it. He could not deal with it. It was too much for him. His voice had broken, to my stupefaction. His face had seemed ravaged, older. Where was my happy-go-lucky, cocksure, irreverent husband? I had stared at him in utter surprise. And if I decided to have it against his will, he had said hoarsely, that would be the end. The end of what? I had gazed at him, appalled. The end of us, he had said, with the awful, broken voice I did not recognize. The end of our marriage. We had remained silent, facing each other over the kitchen table. I had asked him why the birth of the baby terrified him to such an extent. He had turned away, had sighed, rubbing his eyes. He was getting old, he had said. He was approaching fifty. That in itself was already hideous. Growing old. The pressure in his job to keep up with younger jackals. Competing with them day after day. And then watching his looks fade. The face in the mirror he had such a hard time coming to terms with. I had never had this kind of talk with Bertrand before. I could never have fathomed aging had ever been such a problem for him. "I don't want to be seventy when this child is twenty," he muttered over and over again. "I can't. I won't. Julia, you have to get that into your head. If you have this child, it will kill me. Do you hear? It will kill me."

I took a deep breath. What could I tell Bamber? How could I ever begin? What could he understand, he was so young, so different. Yet I appreciated his sympathy, his concern. I squared my shoulders.

"Well, I'm not going to hide it from you, Bamber," I said, not looking at him and clenching the steering wheel with all my might. "I've had a hell of a night."

"Your husband?" he asked tentatively.

"My husband indeed," I quipped.

He nodded. Then he turned to me.

"If you want to talk about it, Julia, I am here," he said, with the same grave and forceful tone Churchill had used to utter, "We shall *never* surrender."

I couldn't help smiling.

"Thanks, Bamber. You rock."

He grinned.

"Um, how was Drancy?"

I groaned.

"Oh God, awful. The most depressing place you've ever seen. People are living in the building, can you believe it? I went there with a friend whose family was deported from there. You're not going to have fun taking those Drancy photos, believe me. It's ten times worse than the rue Nélaton."

I headed out of Paris, took the A6. Not that many people on the highway at this time of the day, thankfully. We drove in silence. I realized that I had to talk to someone, soon, about what was happening. About the baby. I couldn't go on keeping it to myself. Charla. Too early to call her. It was barely 6 A.M. in New York City, although her work day as a tough, successful lawyer was about to start. She had two small children who were the spitting image of her ex-husband, Ben. And there now was a new husband, Barry, who was charming and into computers, but I did not know him well, yet.

I yearned to hear Charla's voice, the soft, warm way she said "Hey!" on the phone when she knew it was me. Charla had never gotten along with Bertrand. They more or less put up with each other. It had been that way since the start. I knew what he thought of her: *Beautiful, brilliant, arrogant, American feminist.* And Charla, concerning him: *Chauvinistic, gorgeous, vain Frog.* I missed Charla. Her spirit, her laugh, her honesty. When I had left Boston for Paris, all those years ago, she was still in her teens. I had not missed her much, in the beginning. She was just my kid sister. It was now that I did. I missed her like hell

"Um," came Bamber's soft voice, "wasn't that our exit?"

It was.

"Shit!" I said.

"Never mind," said Bamber, fumbling with the map. "The next one's OK too."

"Sorry," I mumbled. "I'm a little tired."

He smiled in sympathy. And kept his mouth shut. I liked that about Bamber.

Beaune-la-Rolande drew near, a dreary little town lost in the middle of wheat fields. We parked in the center, by the church and the town hall. We walked around, Bamber taking an occasional photo. There were few people, I noticed. It was a sad, empty place.

I had read that the camp was situated in the northeast section and that a technical school had been built over it in the sixties. The camp used to be a couple of miles away from the station, exactly on the opposite side, which meant that the deported families had to walk through the heart of the town. There must be people here who remembered, I said to Bamber. People who saw the endless groups trudge by from their windows, their doorsteps.

The train station was no longer in use. It had been renovated and transformed into a day-care center. There was something ironic about that, I thought, peering through the windows at colorful drawings and stuffed animals. A group of small children were playing in a fenced-in area on the right of the building.

A woman in her late twenties carrying a toddler in her arms came out to ask me if I needed anything. I replied that I was a journalist, researching information about the old internment camp that used to be here in the forties. She had never heard of a camp in the area. I pointed to the sign nailed up just over the day-care center door.

> In memory of the thousands of Jewish children, women, and
> men, who between May 1941 and August 1943 passed through
> this station and the internment camp at Beaune-la-Rolande, before
> being deported to Auschwitz, the extermination camp, where they
> were assassinated. Never forget.

She shrugged, smiling at me apologetically. She didn't know. She was too young, anyway. This had happened long before her day. I asked her if people ever came to the station to look at the sign. She replied she had not noticed anyone since she started working there last year.

Bamber clicked away as I walked around the squat white building. The name of the town was etched out in black letters on either side of the station. I peered over the fence.

The old rails were grown over with weeds and grass, but still in place, with their ancient wooden planks and rusty steel. On those derelict rails, several trains had left directly for Auschwitz. I felt my heart tighten as I gazed at the planks. It was hard to breathe, all of a sudden.

Convoy number 15 of August 5, 1942, had carried Sarah Starzynski's parents straight to their deaths.

S ARAH SLEPT BADLY THAT night. She kept hearing Rachel scream, over and over again. Where was Rachel now? Was she all right? Was somebody looking after her, helping her get well again? Where had all those Jewish families been taken? And her mother, and her father? And the children back in the camp at Beaune-la-Rolande?

Sarah lay on her back in the bed and listened to the silence of the old house. So many questions. And no answers. Her father used to answer all her queries. Why the sky was blue, and what were clouds made of, and how babies came into the world. Why the sea had tides, and how flowers grew, and why people fell in love. He had always taken time to answer her, patiently, calmly, with clear, easy words and gestures. He had never told her he was too busy. He loved her incessant questions. He used to say she was such a bright little girl.

But recently, her father had not answered her questions the way he used to, she recalled. Her questions about the yellow star, about not being able to go the cinema, the public swimming pool. About the curfew. About that man, in Germany, who hated Jews, and whose very name made her shiver. No, he had not answered her questions properly. He had remained vague, silent. And when she had asked him, again, for the second or the third time, just before the men had come to get them on that black Thursday, what was it exactly about being a Jew that made others hate them—surely it couldn't be that they were afraid of Jews because Jews were "different"—he had looked away, as if he hadn't heard. But she knew that he had.

She didn't want to think about her father. It hurt too much. She couldn't even remember the last time she saw him. At the camp . . . but when exactly? She didn't know. With her mother, there had been that last time she had seen her mother's face turn to her, as she had walked away with the other sobbing women, up that long dusty road to the station. She had a clear image pasted in her mind, like a photograph. Her mother's pale face, the startling blue of her eyes. The ghost of a smile.

But there had been no last time with her father. No last image she could cling to, she could conjure. So she tried to remember him, to bring back his thin, dark face, his haunted eyes. The white teeth in the dark face. She had always heard she looked like her mother, and so did Michel. They had her fair, Slavic looks, the high, broad cheekbones, the slanted eyes. Her father used to complain that none of his children resembled him. She mentally pushed her father's smile away. It was too painful. Too deep.

Tomorrow she had to get to Paris. She had to get home. She had to find out what had happened to Michel. Maybe he was safe, too, like she was now. Maybe some good, generous people had been able to open up the door of the hiding place and free him. But who? she wondered. Who could have helped him? She had never trusted Madame Royer, the concierge. Sly eyes, thin smile. No, not her. Maybe the nice violin teacher, the one who had yelled out on that black Thursday morning, "Where are you taking them? They're honest, good people! You can't do this!" Yes, maybe he had been able to save Michel, maybe Michel was safe in the man's home, and the man was playing Polish tunes to him on his violin. Michel's laugh, his pink cheeks, Michel clapping his hands and dancing round and round. Maybe Michel was waiting for her, maybe he said to the violin teacher every morning, "Is Sirka coming today, when is Sirka coming? She promised she would come back and get me, she promised!"

When she was awoken at dawn by the call of a rooster, she realized her pillow was wet, sodden with her tears. She dressed quickly, slipping into the clothes that Geneviève had laid out for her. Clean, sturdy, old-fashioned boy clothes. She wondered who they belonged to. That Nicolas Dufaure who had painstakingly written his name out in all those books? She put the key and the money into her pocket.

Downstairs, the large, cool kitchen was empty. It was early still. The cat slept on, curled up in a chair. The girl nibbled on a soft loaf of bread, drank some milk. She kept feeling in her pocket for the wad of money and the key, making sure they were safe.

It was a hot, gray morning. There would be violent storms tonight, she knew. Those loud frightening storms that used to scare Michel so. She wondered how she was going to get to the station. Was Orléans far? She had no idea. How was she going to manage? How would she find her way? I got this far, she kept saying, I got this far, so I can't give up now, I'll find my way, I'll find a way. And she couldn't leave without saying good-bye to Jules and Geneviève. So she waited, throwing crumbs to the hens and chicks from the doorstep.

Geneviève came down half an hour later. Her face still carried the traces of last night's crisis. A few minutes later, Jules appeared, planting an affectionate kiss on Sarah's crew cut. The girl watched them prepare breakfast, with slow careful gestures. She had grown fond of them, she thought. More than fond of them. How was she going to tell them she was leaving today? They would be heartbroken, she was sure of that. But she had no choice. She had to get back to Paris.

When she did tell them, they had finished breakfast and were clearing up.

"Oh, but you can't do that," gasped the old lady, nearly dropping the cup she was drying. "The roads are patrolled, the trains are watched. You don't even have an identity card. You will be stopped and sent back to the camp."

"I have money," said Sarah.

"But that won't prevent the Germans from—"

Jules interrupted his wife with an uplifted hand. He tried to convince Sarah to stay a little longer. He spoke to her calmly, and firmly, like her father used to, she thought. She listened, nodding her head absently. But she had to make them understand. How could she explain her need to get home? How could she remain as calm and as firm as Jules?

Her words came out rushed and jumbled. She was fed up with trying to be adult. She stamped her foot in irritation.

"If you try and stop me," she said darkly, "if you stop me, I'll run away."

She stood up, headed to the door. They hadn't moved, they were staring at her, petrified.

"Wait!" said Jules at last. "Wait one minute."

"No. I am not waiting. I am going to the station," said Sarah, her hand on the handle.

"You don't even know where the station is," Jules said.

"I'll find out. I'll find my way."

She unlatched the door.

"Good-bye," she said to the old couple. "Good-bye, and thank you."

She turned and walked to the gates. It had been simple. It had been easy. But as she walked past the gates, bending to stroke the dog's head, she suddenly realized what she had done. She was on her own now. Completely on her own. She remembered Rachel's shrill scream. The loud, marching steps. The Lieutenant's chilling laugh. Her courage petered out. Against her will, she turned her head, looked back at the house.

Jules and Geneviève were still watching her through the windowpane, frozen. When they both moved, it was exactly at the same time. Jules grabbed his cap and Geneviève her purse. They hurried outside, locked the front door. When they caught up with her, Jules put a hand on her shoulder.

"Please don't stop me," mumbled Sarah, reddening. She was both happy and annoyed that they had followed her.

"Stop you?" Jules smiled. "We're not stopping you, you silly, stubborn girl. We're coming with you."

WE MADE OUR WAY to the cemetery under a hot, dry sun. I felt
queasy all of a sudden. I had to stop and breathe. Bamber
was concerned. I told him not to worry, it was just lack of sleep. Once
again, he looked dubious, but made no comment.

The graveyard was small, but we took a long time finding anything.
We had nearly given up when Bamber noticed pebbles on one of the
graves. A Jewish tradition. We came closer. On the flat white stone,
we read:

> The Jewish deported veterans had this monument established ten
> years after their internment in order to perpetuate the memory of
> their martyrs, victims of Hitlerian barbarity. May 1941–May 1951

"Hitlerian barbarity!" remarked Bamber dryly. "Makes the French
sound like they didn't have anything to do with the whole business."

There were several names and dates on the side of the tombstone.
I leaned forward for a closer look. Children. Barely two or three years
old. Children who had died at the camp, in July and August 1942. Vel'
d'Hiv' children.

I had always been acutely aware that everything I had read about
the roundup was true. And yet, on that hot spring day, as I stood looking at the grave, it hit me. The whole reality of it hit me.

And I knew that I would no longer rest, no longer be at peace, until I found out precisely what had become of Sarah Starzynski. And what the Tézacs knew and were so reluctant to tell me.

On our way back to the town center, we saw an old man shuffling along, carrying a bag of vegetables. He must have been in his eighties, with a round, red face and white hair. I asked him if he knew where the former Jewish camp used to be. He looked at us suspiciously.

"The camp?" he asked. "You want to know where the camp was?"

We nodded.

"Nobody asks about the camp," he mumbled. He picked at the leeks in his basket, avoiding our eyes.

"Do you know where it was?" I persisted.

He coughed.

"Of course I do. Lived here all my life. When I was a kid, I didn't know what that camp was. Nobody mentioned it. We acted as if it wasn't there. We knew it had something to do with Jews, but we didn't ask. We were too afraid. So we minded our own business."

"Do you remember anything specific about the camp?" I asked.

"I was about fifteen years old," he said. "I remember the summer of '42, crowds of Jews coming from the station, passing on this very street. Right here." His crooked finger pointed down the large street we were standing on. "Avenue de la Gare. Hordes of Jews. And one day, there was a noise. An awful noise. My parents used to live at a distance from the camp. But we still heard it. A roar that went through the entire town. Went on all day. I heard my parents talking to the neighbors. They were saying that the mothers had been separated from the children, back at the camp. What for? We didn't know. I saw a group of Jewish women walking to the station. No, they weren't walking. They were stumbling along the road, crying, bullied by the police."

His eyes looked back down the street, remembering. Then he picked up his basket with a grunt.

"One day," he said, "the camp was empty. I thought, the Jews have gone. I didn't know where. I stopped thinking about it. We all have. We don't talk about it. We don't want to remember. Some people here don't even know."

He turned and walked away. I scribbled it all down, feeling my stomach heave again. But this time I wasn't sure whether it was morning sickness, or what I deciphered in the old man's eyes, his indifference, his scorn.

We drove up the rue Roland from the Place du Marché and parked in front of the school. Bamber pointed out that the street was called rue des Déportés—Deportee Road. I was thankful for that. I don't think I could have stood it if it had been called avenue de la République.

The technical school was a grim, modern building with an old water tower looming over it. It was difficult to imagine the camp had been here, under thick cement and parking lots. Students were standing around the entrance, smoking. It was their lunch break. On an unkempt square of grass in front of the school, we noticed strange, curving sculptures with figures carved into them. On one of them, we read, "They must act with and for each other, in a spirit of fraternity." Nothing more. Bamber and I looked at each other, puzzled.

I asked one of the students if the sculptures had anything to do with the camp. He asked, "What camp?" A fellow student tittered. I explained the nature of the camp. It seemed to sober him up a little. Then the other student, a girl, said there was some sort of plaque, just a little farther down the road, heading back to the village. We hadn't noticed it on our drive up. I asked the girl if it was a memorial. She said she thought so.

The monument was in black marble with faded gold lettering. It had been erected in 1965 by the mayor of Beaune-la-Rolande. A gold star of David was etched out on its summit. And there were names. Endless names. I picked out two names that had become painfully, achingly familiar: "Starzynski, Wladyslaw. Starzynski, Rywka."

On the bottom of the marble post, I noticed a small, square urn. "Here are deposited the ashes of our martyrs from Auschwitz-Birkenau." A little farther up, beneath the list of names, I read another sentence: "To the 3,500 Jewish children torn from their parents, interned at Beaune-la-Rolande and Pithiviers, deported and exterminated at Auschwitz." Then Bamber read out loud, with his polished British accent: "Victims of the Nazis, buried at the graveyard of

Beaune-la-Rolande." Below, we discovered the same names engraved on the tomb in the cemetery. The Vel' d'Hiv' children who had died in the camp.

"'Victims of the Nazis' again," muttered Bamber. "Looks like a good case of amnesia to me."

He and I stood and looked on, in silence. Bamber had taken a few photographs, but now his camera was back in its case. On the black marble, there was no mention that the French police alone had been responsible for running the camp, and for what had happened behind the barbed wire.

I looked back toward the village, the sinister dark spire of the church on my left.

Sarah Starzynski had toiled up that very road. She had walked past where I was standing now, and she had turned left, into the camp. Several days later, her parents had come out again, to be taken to the station, on to their deaths. The children had been left alone for weeks, then sent to Drancy. And then to their solitary deaths, after the long trip to Poland.

What had happened to Sarah? Had she died here? There had been no sign of her name in the graveyard, on the memorial. Had she escaped? I looked beyond the water tower, standing at the edge of the village, heading north. Was she still alive?

My cell phone rang, making us both jump. It was my sister, Charla.

"Are you OK?" she asked, her voice surprisingly clear. It sounded like she was standing right next to me, and not thousands of miles away across the Atlantic. "I had a feeling I should call you."

My thoughts dragged away from Sarah Starzynski to the baby I was carrying. To what Bertrand had said last night: "The end of us."

Once again, I felt the sheer heaviness of the world around me.

*T*HE TRAIN STATION AT Orléans was a busy, noisy place, an anthill swarming with gray uniforms. Sarah pressed against the old couple. She did not want to show her fear. If she had made it all the way here, that meant there was hope left for her. Hope back in Paris. She had to be brave, she had to be strong.

"If anybody asks," whispered Jules, as they waited in the line to buy the tickets to Paris, "you are our granddaughter Stéphanie Dufaure. Your hair is shaved off because you caught lice at school."

Geneviève straightened Sarah's collar.

"There," she said, smiling. "You do look nice and clean. And pretty. Just like our granddaughter!"

"Do you really have a granddaughter?" asked Sarah. "Are these her clothes?"

Geneviève laughed.

"We have nothing but turbulent grandsons, Gaspard and Nicolas. And a son, Alain. He's in his forties. He lives in Orléans with Henriette, his wife. Those are Nicolas's clothes, he's a little older than you. Quite a handful, he is!"

Sarah admired the way the old couple pretended to be at ease, smiling at her, acting like this was a perfectly normal morning, a perfectly normal trip to Paris. But she noticed the quick way their eyes darted around constantly, always on the watch, always on the move. Her nervousness increased when she saw soldiers checking on all passengers boarding the trains. She craned her neck to observe them. German? No,

French. French soldiers. She had no identification on her. Nothing. Nothing except the key and the money. Silently, discreetly, she handed the thick wad of bills to Jules. He looked down at her, surprised. She pointed with her chin toward the soldiers barring the access to the trains.

"What do you want me to do with this, Sarah?" he whispered, puzzled.

"They are going to ask you for my identity card. I don't have one. This might help."

Jules observed the line of men standing in front of the train. He grew flustered. Geneviève gave him a dig with her elbow.

"Jules!" she hissed. "It could work. We must try. We don't have any other choice."

The old man drew himself up. He nodded to his wife. He seemed to have regained his composure. The tickets were bought, then they headed toward the train.

The platform was packed. Passengers pressed against them from all sides, women with squealing babies, stern-faced old men, impatient businessmen wearing suits. Sarah knew what she had to do. She remembered the boy who got away at the indoor stadium, the one who had slipped through the confusion. That was what she had to do now. Make the most of the pushing and squabbling, of the soldiers shouting orders, of the bustling crowd.

She let go of Jules's hand and ducked. It was like going under water, she thought. A tight, compact mass of skirts and trousers, shoes and ankles. She clambered past, pushing herself on with her fists, and then the train appeared, right in front of her.

As she climbed on, a hand grabbed her by the shoulder. She composed her face instantly, molding her mouth into an easy smile. The smile of a normal little girl. A normal little girl taking the train to Paris. A normal little girl like the one in the lilac dress, the one she had seen on the platform, when they had been taken to the camp, on that day that seemed so long ago.

"I'm with my granny," she said, flashing the innocent smile, pointing to the inside of the carriage. With a nod, the soldier let her go. Breathless, she squirmed her way onto the train, peering out of the window. Her heart was pounding. There were Jules and Geneviève emerging from the throng, looking up at her with amazement. She waved at them triumphantly. She felt proud of herself. She had gotten on the train all by herself, and the soldiers hadn't even stopped her.

Her smile vanished when she saw the number of German officers boarding the train. Their voices were loud and brutal as they made their way through the crowded corridor. People averted their faces, looked down, made themselves as small as possible.

Sarah stood in a corner of the carriage, half hidden by Jules and Geneviève. The only part that was visible was her face, peeping out between the old couple's shoulders. She watched the Germans draw nearer, gazed at them, fascinated. She couldn't keep her eyes off them. Jules whispered at her to look away. But she couldn't.

There was one man in particular that repelled her, tall, thin, his face white and angular. His eyes were such a pale shade of blue they seemed transparent under thick pink lids. As the group of officers passed them by, the tall thin man reached out with an endless, gray-swathed arm, and tweaked Sarah's ear. She shivered with shock.

"Well, boy," chuckled the officer, "no need to be afraid of me. One day, you too will be a soldier, right?"

Jules and Geneviève had painted, fixed smiles that did not waver on their faces. They held on to Sarah casually, but she could feel their hands trembling.

"Nice-looking grandson you have there." The officer grinned, rubbing his immense palm over Sarah's cropped head. "Blue eyes, blond hair, like the children back home, yes?"

A last appraising flicker of the pale, heavy-lidded eyes, then he turned and followed the group of men. He thought I was a boy, thought Sarah. And he didn't think I was Jewish. Was being Jewish something that one could immediately see? She wasn't sure. She had once asked Armelle. Armelle had said she didn't look Jewish because of her blond hair, her blue eyes. So my hair and my eyes have saved me today, she thought.

She spent most of the trip nestling close to the old couple's warm softness. Nobody spoke to them, nobody asked them anything. Staring out of the window, she thought of Paris edging nearer by the minute, bringing her closer to Michel. She watched the low gray clouds gather together, the first fat drops of rain splatter against the glass and trickle away, flattened by the wind.

The train stopped at the Austerlitz station. The station she had left from, with her parents, on that hot, dusty day. The girl followed the old couple out of the train, heading up the platform to the *métro*.

Jules's step faltered. They looked up. Directly ahead, they saw lines of policemen in their navy uniforms, stopping passengers, demanding identity cards. Geneviève said nothing, gently pushed them on. She walked at a firm pace, her round chin held high. Jules followed in her wake, clasping Sarah's hand.

Standing in the line, Sarah studied the policeman's face. A man in his forties, wearing a wedding band, a thick, gold one. He looked listless. But she noticed that his eyes darted back and forth from the paper in his hand to the person standing in front of him. He was doing his job, thoroughly.

Sarah let her mind go blank. She didn't want to think of what might happen. She did not feel strong enough to visualize it. She let her thoughts stray. She thought of the cat they used to have, a cat that made her sneeze. What was the cat's name? She couldn't remember. Something silly like Bonbon or Réglisse. They gave it away because it made her nose tickle and her eyes go red and swollen. She had been sad, and Michel had cried all day. Michel had said it was all her fault.

The man held out a blasé palm. Jules handed him the identity cards in an envelope. The man looked down, shuffled through it, eyes shooting up at Jules, then at Geneviève. Then he said:

"The child?"

Jules pointed to the cards.

"The child's card is there, Monsieur. With ours."

The man opened the envelope wider with a deft thumb. A large banknote folded into three appeared at the bottom of the envelope. The man did not budge.

He looked down again at the money, then at Sarah's face. She looked back at him. She did not cower or plead. She simply looked at him.

The moment seemed to drag on, endless, like that interminable minute when the man had finally let her go from the camp.

The man gave a curt nod. He handed the cards back to Jules and pocketed the envelope with a fluid gesture. Then he stood aside to let them pass.

"Thank you, Monsieur," he said. "Next person, please."

C HARLA'S VOICE ECHOED INTO my ear.

"Julia, are you serious? He can't have said that. He can't put you into that situation. He has no right."

It was the lawyer's voice I was hearing now, the tough, pushy Manhattan lawyer who wasn't afraid of anything, or anyone.

"He did say that," I replied, listless. "He said it would be the *end of us*. He said he would leave me if I kept the baby. He says he feels old, that he can't deal with another child, that he just doesn't want to be an old dad."

There was a pause.

"Does this have anything to do with the woman he had the affair with?" asked Charla. "I can't remember her name."

"No. Bertrand did not mention her once."

"Don't let him pressure you into anything, Julia. This is your child, too. Don't ever forget that, honey."

All day long, my sister's sentence had echoed within me. *"This is your child, too."* I had spoken to my doctor. She had not been surprised at Bertrand's decision. She had suggested that maybe he was going through a midlife crisis. That the responsibility of another child was too much for him to bear. That he was fragile. It happened to many men coming up to fifty.

Was Bertrand really going through a crisis? If that was the case, I had not seen it coming. How was that possible? I simply thought he was being selfish, that he was thinking of himself, as usual. I had told him that, during our talk. I had told him everything that was on my mind. How could he impose abortion after the numerous miscarriages I had gone through, after the pain, the crushed hope, the despair? Did he love me? I had asked, desperate. Did he truly love me? He had looked at me, nodding his head. Of course he loved me. How could I be so stupid? he had said. He loved me. And his broken voice came back to me, the stilted way he had admitted his fear of growing old. A midlife crisis. Maybe the doctor was right, after all. And maybe I hadn't realized it because I had so many things on my mind in the past few months. I felt totally lost. Incapable of dealing with Bertrand and his anxiety.

My doctor had informed me I did not have much time to make my mind up. I was already six weeks pregnant. If I was to abort, I would have to do it within the next two weeks. Tests had to be done, a clinic had to be found. She suggested we talk about it, Bertrand and I, with a marriage counselor. We had to discuss it, we had to bring it out into the open. "If you abort against your will," my doctor had pointed out, "you will never forgive him. And if you don't, he has admitted to you how much this is an intolerable situation for him. This all needs to be worked out, and fast."

She was right. But I could not bring myself to speed things up. Every minute I earned was sixty seconds more for this child. A child I already loved. It wasn't even bigger than a lima bean and I loved it as much as I loved Zoë.

I went to Isabelle's place. She lived in a small, colorful duplex on the rue de Tolbiac. I felt I just couldn't come home from the office and wait for my husband's return. I couldn't face it. I called Elsa, the babysitter, and asked her to take over. Isabelle made me some *crottin de chavignol* toasts and threw together a quick, delicate salad. Her husband was away on a business trip. "OK, *cocotte*," she said, sitting in front of me and smoking away from me, "try to visualize life without Bertrand. To imagine it. The divorce. The lawyers. The aftermath. What it would do to Zoë. What your lives will be like. Separate homes. Separate existences. Zoë going from you to him. From him to you. No longer a real family. No longer breakfast together, Christmas together, vacations together. Can you do this? Can you imagine this?"

I stared at her. It seemed unthinkable. Impossible. And yet, it happened so often. Zoë was practically the only child in her class with parents who'd been married for fifteen years. I told Isabelle I couldn't talk about it anymore. She offered me some chocolate mousse and we watched *Les Demoiselles de Rochefort* on her DVD player. When I got home, Bertrand was in the shower and Zoë in the land of Nod. I crawled into bed. My husband went to watch television in the living room. By the time he got to bed, I was fast asleep.

Today was "visiting Mamé" day. For the first time, I nearly telephoned to cancel. I felt drained. I wanted to stay in bed and sleep all morning. But I knew she would be waiting for me. I knew she would be wearing her best gray-and-lavender dress and her ruby lipstick and her Shalimar perfume. I couldn't let her down. When I turned up just before noon, I noticed my father-in-law's silver Mercedes parked in the courtyard of the nursing home. That unnerved me.

He was here because he wanted to see me. He never came to visit his mother at the same time as me. We all had our specific schedules. Laure and Cécile came on weekends, Colette on Monday afternoons, Edouard on Tuesdays and Fridays, I generally came on Wednesday afternoons with Zoë, and alone on Thursdays at midday. And we each stuck to our schedules.

Sure enough, there he was, sitting very straight, listening to his mother. She had just finished her lunch, always served ridiculously early. I felt nervous, all of a sudden, like a guilty schoolgirl. What did he want with me? Couldn't he just pick up his phone and call me if he wanted to see me? Why wait till now?

Masking all resentment and anxiety behind a warm smile, I kissed him on both cheeks and sat next to Mamé, taking her hand, as I always did. I half expected him to leave, but he stayed on, watching us with a genial expression. It was uncomfortable. I felt like my privacy had been invaded, that every single word I said to Mamé was listened to and judged.

After half an hour, he got up, glancing at his watch. He darted a strange smile at me.

"I need to talk to you, Julia, please," he murmured, lowering his voice so that Mamé's old ears wouldn't hear. I noticed he seemed nervous all of a sudden, shuffling his feet, glancing at me with impatience. So I kissed Mamé farewell and followed him to his car. He made a motion for me to get in. He sat down next to me, fingered the keys, but did not turn on the ignition. I waited, surprised by the anxious movement of his fingers. The silence thrived, full and heavy. I looked around us at the paved courtyard, watching nurses wheel helpless old people in and out of the premises.

Finally he spoke.

"How are you?" he asked, with the same forced smile.

"All right," I answered. "And you?"

"I am fine. And so is Colette."

Another silence.

"I spoke to Zoë last night while you were out," he said, not looking at me.

I studied his profile, the imperial nose, the regal chin.

"Yes?" I said, warily.

"She told me you'd been doing research—"

He halted, the keys jingling in his hands.

"Research about the apartment," he said, finally turning his eyes to mine.

I nodded.

"Yes, I found out who lived there before you moved in. Zoë probably told you that."

He sighed, and his chin sagged upon his chest, small folds of flesh covering his collar.

"Julia, I had warned you, remember?"

My blood began to pump faster.

"You told me to stop asking Mamé questions," I said, my voice blunt. "And that is what I did."

"Then why did you have to go on prying into the past?" he asked. His face had gone ashen. He was breathing painfully, as if it hurt him.

So it was out now. Now I knew why he had wanted to talk to me today.

"I found out who lived there," I went on heatedly, "and that's all. I had to know who they were. I don't know anything else. I don't know what your family had to do with the whole business—"

"Nothing!" he interrupted, nearly shouting. "We had nothing to do with that family's arrest."

I remained silent, staring at him. He was trembling, but I could not tell whether it was anger, or something else.

"We had nothing to do with that family's arrest," he repeated forcefully. "They were taken away during the Vel' d'Hiv' roundup. We never turned them in, did anything like that, do you understand?"

I looked back at him, shocked.

"Edouard, I never imagined such a thing. Never!"

He tried to recover his calm, smoothing his brow with nervous fingers.

"You were asking many questions, Julia. You were being very curious. Let me tell you how it happened. Listen to me. There was that concierge, Madame Royer. She was friendly with our concierge, when we lived on the rue de Turenne, not far from the rue de Saintonge. Madame Royer was fond of Mamé. Mamé was nice to her. She's the one who told my parents the apartment was free in the first place. The rent was good, cheap. It was bigger than our place on rue de Turenne. That's how it happened. That's how we moved in. That's all!"

I continued to stare at him and he continued to tremble. I had never seen him look so distraught, so lost. I touched his sleeve tentatively.

"Are you all right, Edouard?" I asked. His body shook beneath my hand. I wondered if he was sick.

"Yes, fine," he answered, but his voice was hoarse. I couldn't understand why he looked so agitated, so livid.

"Mamé doesn't know," he went on, lowering his voice. "Nobody knows. You understand? She mustn't know. She mustn't ever know."

I was puzzled.

"Know what?" I asked. "What are you talking about, Edouard?"

"Julia," he said, his eyes boring into mine, "you know who the family was, you saw their name."

"I don't understand," I murmured.

"You saw their name, didn't you?" he barked, making me jump. "You know what happened. Don't you?"

I must have looked completely lost because he sighed and buried his face in his hands.

I sat there, speechless. What on earth was he talking about? What had happened that nobody knew of?

"The girl," he said at last, looking up, his voice so low I could hardly hear. "What did you find out about the girl?"

"What do you mean?" I asked, petrified.

There was something about his voice, his eyes, that frightened me.

"The girl," he repeated, his voice muffled and strange, "she came back. A couple of weeks after we had moved in. She came back to the rue de Saintonge. I was twelve years old. I'll never forget. I'll never forget Sarah Starzynski."

To my horror, his face crumpled. Tears began to trickle down his face. I could not speak. I could only wait and listen. This was no longer my arrogant father-in-law.

This was somebody else. Somebody with a secret he had carried within him for years. For sixty years.

*I*T HAD BEEN A swift *métro* ride to the rue de Saintonge, only a couple of stops and a change at Bastille. As they turned into the rue de Bretagne, Sarah's heart started to beat faster. She was going home. In a few minutes, she would be home. Maybe while she had been away her mother or her father had been able to come back and maybe they were all waiting for her, with Michel, in the apartment, waiting for her to return. Was she crazy to think that? Was she out of her mind? Could she not hope, was that not allowed? She was ten years old and she wanted to hope, she wanted to believe, more than anything, more than life itself.

As she tugged on Jules's hand, urging him up the street, she felt hope grow, like a mad, wild plant she could no longer tame. A quiet, grave voice within her said, Sarah, don't hope, don't believe, try to prepare yourself, try to imagine that nobody is waiting for you, that Papa and Maman are not there, that the apartment is all dusty and dirty, and that Michel . . . Michel . . .

Number 26 appeared in front of them. Nothing had changed in the street, she noticed. It was still the same calm, narrow road she had always known. How was it possible that entire lives could change, could be destroyed, and that streets and buildings remained the same, she wondered.

Jules pushed the heavy door open. The courtyard was exactly the same, with its green leafiness, its musty smell of dust, of humidity. As they made their way through the courtyard, Madame Royer opened the door to her loge and poked her head out. Sarah let go of Jules's hand and dashed into the staircase. Quick now, she had to be quick, she was home at last, there was no time to lose.

She heard the concierge's inquisitive "Looking for anybody?" as she reached the first floor, already out of breath.

Jules's voice followed her up the steps: "We are looking for the Starzynski family."

Sarah caught Madame Royer's laugh, a disturbing, grating sound: "Gone, Monsieur! Vanished! Won't find them here, that's for sure."

Sarah paused on the second floor landing, peering out onto the courtyard. She could see Madame Royer standing there, in her dirty blue apron, with little Suzanne slung over her shoulder. Gone . . . Vanished. . . . What did the concierge mean? Vanished where? When?

No time to waste, no time to think about it now, thought the girl, another two flights to go before home. But the concierge's shrill voice floated up to her as she rapidly ascended the stairs: "The cops came to get them, Monsieur. Came to get all the Jews in the area. Took 'em away in a big bus. A lot of empty rooms here now, Monsieur. You looking for a place to rent? The Starzynskis' has been let out, but I might be able to help. There's a very nice place on the second floor, if you're interested. I can show you!"

Panting, Sarah reached the fourth floor. She was so out of breath, she had to lean against the wall and press her fist into her aching side.

She pounded on the door of her parents' apartment, quick, sharp blows with the palms of her hands. No answer. She pounded again, harder, with her fists.

Then she heard steps behind the door. It opened.

A young boy of twelve or thirteen appeared.

"Yes?" he asked.

Who was he? What was he doing in her apartment?

"I've come to get my brother," she stuttered. "Who are you? Where is Michel?"

"Your brother?" said the boy, slowly. "There is no Michel here."

She pushed him aside brutally, hardly noticing the new paintings on the entrance wall, an unknown bookshelf, a strange red and green carpet. The astonished boy shouted, but she did not stop, she rushed down the long familiar corridor and turned left, into her bedroom. She did not notice the new wallpaper, the new bed, the books, the belongings that had nothing to do with her.

The boy called out for his father, and there was a startled scuffle of footsteps in the next room.

Sarah whipped the key out of her pocket, pressed on the device with her palm. The hidden lock swung into view.

She heard the peal of the doorbell, a murmur of alarmed voices drawing near. Jules's voice, Geneviève's, and an unknown man's.

Fast now, she had to be fast. Over and over she mumbled, "Michel, Michel, Michel, it's me, Sirka." Her fingers were trembling so hard she dropped the key.

Behind her shoulder, the boy came running, out of breath.

"What are you doing?" he gasped. "What are you doing in my room?"

She ignored him, picked up the key, fumbled with the lock. She was too nervous, too impatient. It took her a moment to work it. Finally, the lock clicked, and she tugged the secret door open.

A rotten stench hit her like a fist. She drew away. The boy at her side recoiled, afraid. Sarah fell to her knees.

A tall man with salt-and-pepper hair burst into the room, followed by Jules and Geneviève.

Sarah could not speak, she could only quiver, her fingers covering her eyes, her nose, blocking out the smell.

Jules drew near, put a hand on her shoulder, glanced into the cupboard. She felt him wrap her in his arms, try to carry her away.

He murmured into her ear, "Come, Sarah, come with me."

She fought him with all her might, scratching, kicking, all teeth and nails, and managed to scramble back to the open cupboard door.

In the back of the cupboard, she glimpsed the small lump of a motionless, curled-up body, then she saw the beloved little face, blackened, unrecognizable.

She sank to her knees again, and she screamed at the top of her lungs, she screamed for her mother, for her father, screamed for Michel.

Edouard Tézac gripped the steering wheel with his hands till his knuckles turned white. I stared at them, mesmerized.

"I can still hear her scream," he whispered. "I cannot forget it. Ever."

I felt stunned with what I now knew. Sarah Starzynski had escaped from Beaune-la-Rolande. She had come back to the rue de Saintonge. She had made a hideous discovery.

I couldn't talk. I could only look at my father-in-law. He went on with a hoarse, low voice.

"There was a ghastly moment, when my father looked into the cupboard. I tried to look too. He pushed me away. I couldn't understand what was going on. There was this smell . . . The smell of something rotten, putrid. Then my father slowly pulled out the body of a dead boy. A child, not more than three or four. I had never seen a dead body in my life. It was the most heartbreaking sight. The boy had wavy blond hair. He was stiff, curled up, his face resting upon his hands. He had gone a horrible, green color."

He stopped, the words choking in his throat. I thought he was going to retch. I touched his elbow, tried to communicate my sympathy, my warmth. It was an unreal situation, me trying to comfort my proud, haughty father-in-law, reduced to tears, a quivering old man. He dabbed at his eyes with unsure fingertips. Then he went on.

"We all stood there, horrified. The girl fainted. She fell, right to the floor. My father picked her up, put her on my bed. She came around, saw his face, and backed away, screaming. I began to understand, listening to my father, to the couple who had come with her. The dead boy was her little brother. Our new apartment had been her home. The boy had been hidden there the day of the Vel' d'Hiv' roundup, on July 16. The girl thought she was going to be able to come back to free him, but she had been taken to a camp, outside Paris."

A new pause. It seemed endless to me.

"And then? What happened then?" I said, finding my voice at last.

"The old couple came from Orléans. The girl had escaped from a nearby camp and had ended up on their property. They had decided to help her, to bring her back to Paris, to her home. My father told them that our family had moved in at the end of July. He did not know about the cupboard, which was in my room. None of us knew. I *had* noticed a strong, bad smell, and my father thought there was something wrong with the drains, and we were expecting the plumber that week."

"What did your father do with . . . with the little boy?"

"I don't know. I remember he said he wanted to take care of everything. He was in shock, terribly unhappy. I think the old couple took the body away. I'm not sure. I don't remember."

"And then what?" I asked, breathless.

He glanced at me sardonically.

"And then what? And then what!" A bitter laugh. "Julia, can you imagine what we felt like when the girl left? The way she looked at us. She hated us. She loathed us. For her, we were responsible. We were criminals. Criminals of the worst sort. We had moved into her home. We had let her brother die. Her eyes . . . Such hatred, pain, despair. The eyes of a woman in the face of a ten-year-old girl."

I could see those eyes too. I shivered.

Edouard sighed, rubbed his tired, withered face with his palms.

"After they left, my father sat down and put his head in his hands. He cried. For a long time. I had never seen him cry. I never saw him cry again. My father was such a strong, rugged fellow. I was told that Tézac men never cry. Never show their emotions. It was a dreadful moment. He said that something monstrous had happened. Something that he and I would remember our entire lives. Then he began to tell me things he had never mentioned. He said I was old enough now to know. He said that he had not asked Madame Royer about who lived in the apartment before we moved in. He knew it had been a Jewish family, and that they had been arrested during that big roundup. But he had closed his eyes. He had closed his eyes, like so many other Parisians, during that terrible year of 1942. He had closed his eyes the day of the roundup, when he had seen all those people being driven away, packed on buses, taken God knows where. He hadn't even asked why the apartment was empty, what had happened to the family's belongings. He had acted like any other Parisian family, eager to move into a bigger, better place. He had closed his eyes. And now, this had happened. The girl had come back and the little boy was dead. He was probably already dead when we moved in. My father said that we could never forget. Never. And he was right, Julia. It has been there, within us. And it has been there for me, for the past sixty years."

He stopped, his chin still pressed down onto his chest. I tried to imagine what it must have been for him, to carry that secret for so long.

"And Mamé?" I asked, determined to push Edouard on, to drag the entire story out.

He shook his head slowly.

"Mamé was not there that afternoon. My father did not want her to find out what had happened. He felt overcome with guilt, he felt it was his fault, even if, of course, it wasn't. He couldn't bear the idea of her knowing. And perhaps judging him. He told me I was old enough to keep a secret. She must never know, he said. He seemed so desperate, so sad. So I agreed to keep the secret."

"And she still doesn't know?" I whispered.

He sighed again, deeply.

"I'm not sure, Julia. She knew about the roundup. We all knew about the roundup, it had happened right in front of us. When she came back that evening, my father and I were so strange, peculiar, that she sensed something had taken place. That night, and many nights after, I kept seeing the dead boy. I had nightmares. They lasted till well into my twenties. I was relieved to move out of that apartment. I think maybe my mother knew. I think maybe she knew what my father went through, how he must have felt. Maybe he ended up telling her, because it was too much for him to bear. But she never talked to me about it."

"And Bertrand? And your daughters? And Colette?"

"They know nothing."

"Why not?" I asked.

He put his hand on my wrist. It was frozen, its cold touch seeping through my skin like ice.

"Because I promised my father, on his deathbed, that I would not tell my children or my wife. He carried his guilt within him for the rest of his life. He could not share it. He could not speak to anyone about it. And I respected that. Do you understand?"

I nodded.

"Of course."

I paused.

"Edouard, what happened to Sarah?"

He shook his head.

"Between 1942 and the moment on his deathbed, my father never uttered her name. Sarah became a secret. A secret I never stopped thinking about. I don't think my father ever realized how much I thought of her. How his silence regarding her made me suffer. I longed to know how she was, where she was, what had happened to her. But every time I tried to question him, he would silence me. I could not believe that he no longer cared, that he had turned the page, that she no longer meant anything to him. It seemed like he had wanted to bury it all in the past."

"Did you resent him for that?"

He nodded.

"Yes, I did. I resented him. My admiration for him was tarnished, forever. But I could not tell him. I never did."

We sat in silence for a little moment. The nurses were probably beginning to wonder why Monsieur Tézac and his daughter-in-law were sitting in that car for so long.

"Edouard, don't you want to know what happened to Sarah Starzynski?"

He smiled for the first time.

"But I wouldn't know where to begin," he said.

I smiled, too.

"But that's my job. I can help you."

His face seemed less haggard, less ashen. His eyes were suddenly bright, full of a new light.

"Julia, there's one last thing. When my father died nearly thirty years ago, I was told by his attorney that a number of confidential papers were being held in the safe."

"Did you read them?" I asked, my pulse quickening.

He looked down.

"I glanced through them, briefly, just after my father's death."

"And?" I said, breathlessly.

"Just papers about the boutique, stuff concerning paintings, furniture, silverware."

"That's all?"

He smiled at my blatant disappointment.

"I believe so."

"What do you mean?" I asked, baffled.

"I never had another look. I went through the pile very fast, I remember being furious there was nothing there about Sarah. I resented my father all the more."

I bit my lip.

"So you're saying you're not sure there is nothing there."

"Yes. And I've never checked since."

"Why not?"

He pressed his lips together.

"Because I didn't want to be certain there was nothing there."

"And feel even worse about your father."

"Yes," he admitted.

"So you don't know what's in there for sure. You haven't known for thirty years."

"No," he said.

Our eyes met. It only took a couple of seconds.

He started the car. He drove like a bat of hell to where I assumed his bank was. I had never seen Edouard drive so fast. Drivers brandished furious fists. Pedestrians scooted aside with terror. We did not say a word as we hurtled along, but our silence was a warm, excited one. We were sharing this. We were sharing something for the first time. We kept looking at each other, and smiling.

But by the time we found a place to park on the avenue Bosquet and rushed to the bank, it was closed for lunch hour, another typically French custom that aggravated me, particularly today. I was so disappointed I could have cried.

Edouard kissed me on both cheeks, pushed me gently away.

"You go, Julia. I'll come back at two, when it opens. I'll call if there is something there."

I walked down the avenue and caught the 92 bus, which would take me straight to the office, over the Seine.

As the bus drove away, I turned around and saw Edouard waiting in front of the bank, a solitary, stiff figure in his dark-green coat.

I wondered how he would feel if there was nothing in the safe about Sarah, just masses of papers about old master paintings and porcelain.

And my heart went out to him.

"ARE YOU SURE ABOUT this, Miss Jarmond?" my doctor asked. She looked up at me from over her half-moon glasses.

"No," I replied truthfully. "But for the moment, I need to make those appointments."

She ran her eyes over my medical file.

"I'm happy to make the appointments for you, but I'm not certain you are entirely comfortable with what you have decided."

My thoughts ran back to last evening. Bertrand had been exceptionally tender, attentive. All night long, he had held me in his arms, told me again and again he loved me, he needed me, but that he couldn't face the prospect of having a child so late in life. He felt that growing older would bring us closer, that we would be able to travel often, while Zoë was becoming more independent. He had envisaged our fifties like a second honeymoon.

I had listened to him, tears running down my face in the dark. The irony of it all. He was saying everything, down to the very word, that I had always dreamed of hearing him say. It was all there, the gentleness, the commitment, the generosity. But the hitch was that I was carrying a baby he did not want. My last chance of being a mother. I kept thinking of what Charla had said: "This is your child, too."

For years, I had longed to give Bertrand another child. To prove myself. To be that perfect wife the Tézacs approved of, thought highly of. But now I realized I wanted this child for myself. My baby. My last child. I longed for its weight in my arms. I longed for the milky, sweet smell of its skin. My baby. Yes, Bertrand was the father, but this was my child. My flesh. My blood. I longed for the birth, for the sensation of the baby's head pressing down through me, for that unmistakable, pure, painful sensation of bringing a child into the world, albeit with pain, with tears. I wanted those tears, I wanted that pain. I did not want the pain of emptiness, the tears of a barren, scarred womb.

I left the doctor's office and headed toward Saint-Germain, where I was meeting Hervé and Christophe for a drink at the Café de Flore. I hadn't planned to reveal anything, but they took one look at my face and gasped with concern. So out it came. As usual, they had opposite opinions. Hervé believed I should abort, my marriage being the most important matter. Christophe insisted that the baby was the crucial point. There was no way I could not have that child. I would regret it for the rest of my life.

They became so heated that they forgot my presence and started to quarrel. I couldn't stand it. I stopped them by banging on the table with my clenched fist, making the glasses rattle. They looked at me with surprise. That wasn't my style. I excused myself, said I was too tired to go on discussing the matter, and left. They gawked at me, dismayed. Never mind, I thought, I'd make it up another time. They were my oldest friends. They'd understand.

I walked home through the Luxembourg Garden. No news from Edouard since yesterday. Did that mean he had been through his father's safe and found nothing concerning Sarah? I could imagine the resentment, all the bitterness resurfacing. The disappointment, too. I felt guilty, as if this was my fault. Rubbing salt on his old wound.

I walked slowly through the winding, flowery paths, avoiding joggers, strollers, elderly people, gardeners, tourists, lovers, tai-chi addicts, *pétanque* players, teenagers, readers, sunbathers. The usual Luxembourg throng. And so many babies. And of course, every single baby I saw made me think about the tiny being I carried within me.

Earlier on that day, before the doctor's appointment, I had talked to Isabelle. She had been particularly supportive, as usual. The choice was mine, she had pointed out, no matter how many shrinks or friends I could talk to, no matter whose side I was looking at, whose opinion I was examining. It was my choice, bottom line, and that was precisely what made it all the more painful.

There was one thing I did know: Zoë had to be kept out of this, at all costs. She would be on vacation in a couple of days, ready to spend part of the summer with Charla's children, Cooper and Alex, on Long Island, then with my parents, in Nahant. In a way, I was relieved. This meant the abortion would take place while she was away. If abortion was what I had finally agreed to.

When I got home, there was a large beige envelope on my desk. Zoë, on the phone with a friend, shouted from her room that the concierge had just brought it up.

No address, only my initials scrawled in blue ink. I opened it, pulled out a faded red file.

The name "Sarah" leaped out at me.

I knew instantly what the file was. Thank you, Edouard, I said to myself fervently, thank you, thank you, thank you.

Inside the file were a dozen letters, dating from September 1942 to April 1952. Thin blue paper. Neat round handwriting. I read them carefully. They were all from a certain Jules Dufaure, who lived near Orléans. Each brief letter was about Sarah. Her progress. Her schooling. Her health. Polite, short sentences. "Sarah is doing well. She is learning Latin this year. She had chicken pox last spring." "Sarah went to Brittany this summer with my grandsons and visited the Mont-Saint-Michel."

I assumed Jules Dufaure was the elderly gentleman who had hidden Sarah after her escape from Beaune-la-Rolande, and who had taken her back to Paris, the day of the horrible discovery in the cupboard. But why was Jules Dufaure writing to André Tézac about Sarah? And in such detail? I couldn't understand. Had André asked him to?

Then I found the explanation. A bank statement. Every month André Tézac had his bank send money to the Dufaures, for Sarah. A generous sum, I noticed. This had gone on for ten years.

For ten years, Edouard's father had tried to help Sarah, in his own way. I could not help thinking of Edouard's immense relief when he had discovered all this locked away in the safe. I imagined him reading these very letters, and making this discovery. Here was his father's redemption at long last.

I noticed that the letters from Jules Dufaure were not sent to the rue de Saintonge, but to André's old shop on the rue de Turenne. I wondered why. Probably because of Mamé, I supposed. André had not wanted her to know. And he had also not wanted Sarah to know that he was giving her this money on a regular basis. Jules Dufaure's neat script read: "As you have requested, your donations have not been revealed to Sarah."

At the back of the file, I came upon a wide manila envelope. I pulled out a couple of photographs. The familiar slanted eyes. The pale hair. How she had changed since that school portrait of June '42. There was a palpable sadness about her. The joy had gone out of her face. She was no longer a child. A tall, slim young woman of eighteen or so. The same sad eyes, despite the smile. A couple of young men of her age were with her on a beach. I turned the photo over. Jules's neat handwriting read: "1950, Trouville. Sarah, with Gaspard and Nicolas Dufaure."

I thought of all she had gone through. The Vel' d'Hiv'. Beaune-la-Rolande. Her parents. Her brother. Too much to bear for a child.

I was so wrapped up in Sarah Starzynski I didn't feel Zoë's hand brush my shoulder.

"Mom, who's that girl?"

I hastily covered the photos with the envelope, muttering something about a tight deadline.

"Well, who is it?" she asked.

"Nobody you know, honey," I said, hurriedly, pretending to tidy my desk.

She sighed, then said in a clipped, grown-up voice, "You're weird at the moment, Mom. You think I don't know, you think I don't see. But I see everything."

She turned and walked away. I felt guilt wash over me. I rose, caught her up in her bedroom.

"You're right, Zoë, I'm weird at the moment. I'm sorry. You don't deserve this."

I sat down on her bed, unable to face her wise, calm eyes.

"Mom, why don't you just talk to me? Just tell me what's wrong."

I felt a headache coming on. One of those powerful ones.

"You think I won't understand, because I'm only eleven, right?"

I nodded.

She shrugged.

"You don't trust me, do you?"

"Of course I trust you. But there are things I can't tell you because they are too sad, too difficult. I don't want you to be hurt by these things, the way they hurt me."

She touched my cheek gently, her eyes glistening.

"I don't want to be hurt. You're right, don't tell me. I won't sleep if I know. But promise me you'll be all right soon."

I took her in my arms, held her tight. My beautiful, brave girl. My beautiful daughter. I was lucky to have her. So lucky. Despite the headache's onslaught, my thoughts lurched back to the baby. Zoë's sister or brother. She knew nothing. Nothing of what I was going through. Biting my lip, I fought back tears. After a while, she slowly pushed me away and looked up at me.

"Tell me who that girl is. That girl in the black-and-white photos. The ones you were trying to hide from me."

"All right," I said. "But it's a secret, OK? Don't tell anyone. Promise?"

She nodded.

"Promise. Cross my heart and all that."

"Remember I told you I found out who lived in the rue de Saintonge apartment before Mamé moved in?"

She nodded again.

"You said a Polish family. A girl my age."

"Her name is Sarah Starzynski. Those were photos of her."

Zoë narrowed her eyes at me.

"But why is it a secret? I don't get it."

"It's a family secret. Something sad happened. Your grandfather doesn't want to talk about it. And your father doesn't know anything about her."

"Did something sad happen to Sarah?" she said carefully.

"Yes," I replied quietly. "Something very sad."

"Are you going to try and find her?" she asked, sobered by my tone.

"Yes."

"Why?"

"I want to tell her that our family is not what she thinks. I want to explain what happened. I don't think she knows what your great-grandfather did to help her. For ten years."

"How did he help her?"

"He sent her money, every month. But he asked that she not be told."

Zoë was silent for a moment.

"How are you going to find her?"

I sighed.

"I don't know, honey. I just hope I do. After 1952, there is no trace of her at all in this file. No more letters, no more photos. No address."

Zoë sat on my knees, pressing her slim back against me. I took a whiff of her thick, shiny hair, the familiar sugary Zoë-like smell that always reminded me of when she was a toddler, and smoothed a couple of unruly strands down with my palm.

I thought of Sarah Starzynski, who had been Zoë's age when horror came into her life.

I closed my eyes. But I could still see the moment when the policemen tore the children from the mothers at Beaune-la-Rolande. I could not get the image out of my mind.

I held Zoë close, so close she gasped.

O DD, THE WAY DATES go. Ironic, almost. Tuesday, July 16, 2002.
The Vel' d'Hiv' commemoration. And precisely the date of the
abortion. It was to take place in some clinic I had never been to,
somewhere in the seventeenth arrondissement, near Mamé's nursing
home. I had asked for another date, feeling July 16 was overloaded
with meaning, but it had not been possible.

Zoë, fresh out of school, was leaving for Long Island via New York
with her godmother, Alison, one of my old friends from Boston, who
often flew between Manhattan and Paris. I was to join my daughter
and Charla's family on the twenty-seventh. Bertrand did not take his
vacation till August. We usually spent a couple of weeks in Burgundy,
in the old Tézac house. I had never fully enjoyed my summers there.
My parents-in-law were anything but relaxed. Meals had to be eaten
on time, conversations kept mild, and children were seen and not
heard. I wondered why Bertrand always insisted that we spent time
there instead of going on a vacation, just the three of us. Luckily, Zoë
got on well with Laure and Cécile's boys, and Bertrand played endless
tennis matches with his brothers-in-law. And I felt left out, as usual.
Laure and Cécile kept their distance, year after year. They invited
their divorced girlfriends and spent hours by the pool tanning studiously. The thing was to have brown breasts. Even after fifteen years
I still could not get used to it. I never bared mine. And I felt I was
laughed at behind my back for being the *prude américaine*. So I spent
most of my days walking in the forest with Zoë, going on exhausting

bike rides till I felt I knew the area by heart, and showing off my impeccable butterfly stroke while the other ladies languidly smoked and tanned in their minimal Erès swimwear that never went in the pool.

"They're just jealous French cows. You look too damn good in a bikini," scoffed Christophe, whenever I complained of those painful summers. "They'd talk to you if you were riddled with cellulite and varicose veins." He made me guffaw, yet I could not quite believe him. But I did love the beauty of the place, the ancient quiet house that always felt cool even during the fiercest summers, the large rambling garden full of old oak trees and the view on the curvaceous river Yonne. And the nearby forest, where Zoë and I would go for long walks, when as a baby she had been entranced by the chirp of a bird, a twig with a strange shape, or the murky sparkle of hidden marsh.

The rue de Saintonge apartment, according to Bertrand and Antoine, would be ready in early September. Bertrand and his team had done a great job. But I had not yet envisaged living there. Living there now that I knew what had happened. The wall had been pulled down, but I remembered the secret deep cupboard. The cupboard where little Michel had waited for his sister to come back. In vain.

The story haunted me, relentlessly. I had to admit I was not looking forward to living in the apartment. I dreaded nights there. I dreaded bringing back the past, and I had no idea how to prevent myself from doing so.

It was hard not being able to talk to Bertrand about it. I needed his down-to-earth approach, longed to hear him say that despite the awfulness, we'd get over it, we'd find a way. I could not tell him. I had promised his father. What would Bertrand think of the whole story, I wondered. And his sisters? I tried to imagine their reaction. And Mamé's. It was impossible. The French were closed up, like clams. Nothing must be shown. Nothing must be revealed. Everything was to remain unruffled, undisturbed. That's how it was. How it had always been. And I found it increasingly tough to live with.

With Zoë gone to America, home felt empty. I spent more time at the office, working on a witty piece for the September issue about young French writers and the Parisian literary scene. Interesting and time consuming. Every evening, I found it harder and harder to leave the office, put off by the prospect of the silent rooms that awaited me. I took the long way home, reveling in what Zoë called "Mom's long shortcuts," enjoying the city's fiery beauty at sunset. Paris was beginning to take on that deliciously abandoned look it harbored from mid-July. Shops had rolled their iron grids down, with signs reading CLOSED FOR VACATION, OPENING UP SEPTEMBER 1. I had to walk for long stretches to find an open *pharmacie,* grocer's, *boulangerie,* or cleaner's. Parisians were taking off for their summer spree, leaving their city to indefatigable tourists. And as I walked home on those balmy July evenings, marching straight from the Champs-Élysées to Montparnasse, I felt Paris without its Parisians belonged to me at last.

Yes, I loved Paris, I had always loved it, but as I strolled at dusk along the Pont Alexandre III, with the golden dome of the Invalides gleaming like a huge jewel, I missed the States with such poignancy that the pain seared right to the pit of my gut. I missed home—what I had to call home, even if I had lived in France for more than half my life. I missed the casualness, the freedom, the space, the easiness, the language, the simplicity of being able to say "you" to each and every person, not the complicated *vous* and *tu* I had never perfectly mastered and which still threw me. I had to admit it. I missed my sister, my parents, I missed America. I missed it like I had never missed it before.

As I neared our neighborhood, beckoned by the tall brown grimness of the Tour Montparnasse that Parisians loved to hate (but that I was fond of because it allowed me to find my way back from any arrondissement), I suddenly wondered what Paris had been like under the Occupation. Sarah's Paris. Gray-green uniforms and round helmets. The implacability of curfew and *Ausweis.* German signs posted up in Gothic lettering. Huge swastikas plastered over the noble stone buildings.

And children wearing the yellow star.

THE CLINIC WAS A well-to-do, cushy place, with beaming nurses, obsequious receptionists and careful flower arrangements. The abortion was to take place the following morning, at seven. I had been asked to come in the night before, on July 15. Bertrand had gone to Brussels, to clinch an important business deal. I hadn't insisted for him to be there. I somehow felt better with him not around. It was easier to settle into the dainty apricot-colored room alone. At another moment, I would have wondered why Bertrand's presence seemed superfluous. How surprising, considering he was part and parcel of my everyday life. Yet here I was, going through the severest crisis of my life, without him, and relieved at his absence.

I moved like a robot, mechanically folding my clothes, putting my toothbrush on the shelf above the basin, staring through the window at the bourgeois façades of the quiet street. What the hell are you doing? whispered an inner voice I had tried to ignore all day. Are you crazy, are you really going to go through with this? I hadn't told anyone about my final decision. No one at all, apart from Bertrand. I did not want to think about his blissful smile when I told him I'd do it, the way he had pulled me close, kissing the top of my head with unrestrained fervor.

I sat on the narrow bed and took the Sarah file out of my bag. Sarah was the only person I could bear thinking about right now. Finding her felt like a sacred mission, felt like the only possible way to keep my head up, to dispel the sadness in which my life had become immersed. Finding her, yes, but how? There was no Sarah Dufaure or Sarah Starzynski in the phone book. That would have been too easy. The address on Jules Dufaure's letters was no longer in use. So I had decided to trace his children, or grandchildren, the young men in the Trouville photograph: Gaspard and Nicolas Dufaure, men who would be in their mid-sixties or early seventies, I guessed.

Unfortunately Dufaure was a common name. There were hundreds of them in the Orléans area. That meant phoning each one of them. I had worked at it hard in the past week, spent hours on the Internet, poring over phone books, making endless calls, and then facing disappointing dead ends.

And then, that very morning, I had spoken to a Nathalie Dufaure whose number had been listed in Paris. A young, joyful voice had answered me. I went into the usual routine, repeated what I had said over and over again to strangers on the other end of the line: "My name is Julia Jarmond, I'm a journalist, I'm trying to trace a Sarah Dufaure, born in 1932, the only names I have are Gaspard and Nicolas Dufaure—"

She interrupted me, Yes, Gaspard Dufaure was her grandfather. He lived in Aschères-le-Marché, just outside Orléans. He had an unlisted number. I held on to the receiver, breathless. I asked Nathalie if she remembered Sarah Dufaure at all. The young woman laughed. It was a nice laugh. She explained that she was born in 1982, and she didn't know much about her grandfather's childhood. No, she had not heard of Sarah Dufaure. At least, she didn't remember anything specific. She could call her grandfather if I liked. He was a gruff fellow, he didn't like the telephone, but she could do it and get back to me. She asked for my number. Then she said: "Are you American? I love your accent."

I had waited for her call all day. Nothing. I kept checking my mobile, making sure the batteries were charged, that it was turned on properly. Still nothing. Maybe Gaspard Dufaure was not interested in talking to a journalist about Sarah. Maybe I had not been persuasive enough. Maybe I had been too persuasive. Maybe I shouldn't have said I was a journalist. I should have said a friend of the family. But no, I couldn't say that. It wasn't true. I couldn't lie. I didn't want to.

Aschères-le-Marché. I had looked it up on a map. A small village halfway between Orléans and Pithiviers, the sister camp to Beaune-la-Rolande, not far away, either. It was not Jules and Geneviève's old address. So it had not been where Sarah had spent ten years of her life.

I grew impatient. Should I call Nathalie Dufaure back? As I was toying with the idea, the mobile rang. I grabbed it, breathed, *"Allô?"* It was my husband, calling from Brussels. I felt disappointment jab my nerves.

I realized I did not want to talk to Bertrand. What could I say to him?

THE NIGHT HAD BEEN brief and restless. At dawn, a matronly nurse had appeared, a folded blue paper gown in her arms. I would be needing it for "the operation." She smiled. There was also a blue paper bonnet and blue paper shoes. She would come back in half an hour, and I'd be wheeled straight to the operation room. She reminded me, still with the same hearty smile, that I was not allowed to drink or eat anything because of the anesthesia. She left, closing the door gently. I wondered how many women she was going to wake up this morning with that smile, how many pregnant women about to have a baby scraped out of their womb. Like me.

I put the gown on, docile. The paper felt itchy next to my skin. There was nothing else to do but wait. I turned the television on, zapped to LCI, the nonstop news channel. I watched, not concentrating. My mind felt numb. Blank. In an hour or so, it would be over. Was I ready for this? Could I cope with it? Was I strong enough? I felt incapable of answering those questions. I could only lie there in my paper dress and paper hat, and wait. Wait to be wheeled into the operating room. Wait to be put to sleep. Wait for the doctor to perform. I didn't want to think about the exact movements he was going to undertake within me, between my opened thighs. I blocked the thought out, fast, focused on a svelte blonde making professional, sweeping motions with manicured hands over a map of France dotted with sunny round faces. I remembered the last session with the therapist, a week ago. Bertrand's hand on my knee. "No, we do not want this child. We both agree." I had remained silent. The therapist had looked at me. Had I nodded? I couldn't remember. I remember feeling sedated, hypnotized. And then Bertrand, in the car: "That was the right thing to do, *amour*. You'll see. It will soon be over." And the way he had kissed me, passionate, heated.

The blonde vanished. An anchorman appeared, and the familiar jingle for the newsreel was heard. "Today, July 16, 2002, marks the sixtieth anniversary of the Vélodrome d'Hiver roundup, in which thousands of Jewish families were arrested by the French police. A black moment in France's past."

Quickly, I put up the sound. As the camera zoomed along the rue Nélaton, I thought of Sarah, wherever she was now. She would remember today. She didn't need to be reminded. Ever. For her, and for all those families who had lost loved ones, July 16 was not to be forgotten, and this morning, of all mornings, they would open eyelids heavy with pain. I wanted to tell her, tell them, tell all these people— how? I thought, feeling helpless, useless— I wanted to shout, to scream out to her, to them, that I knew, that I remembered, and that I could not forget.

Several survivors—some of whom I had already met and interviewed—were shown in front of the Vel' d'Hiv' plaque. I realized I had not yet seen this week's issue of *Seine Scenes* with my article in it. It was out today. I decided to leave a message on Bamber's mobile, asking him to have a copy sent to the clinic. I turned on my phone, eyes riveted to the television. Franck Lévy's grave face appeared. He talked about the commemoration. It was going to be more important than the previous years, he pointed out. The phone beeped, telling me I had voice mail. One message was from Bertrand, late last night, telling me he loved me.

The next one was from Nathalie Dufaure. She was sorry to be calling so late, she hadn't been able to phone before. She had good news: her grandfather was intent on meeting me, he had said he could tell me all about Sarah Dufaure. He had seemed so excited that Nathalie's curiosity had been aroused. Her animated voice drowned out Franck Lévy's level tones: "If you want, I could take you to Aschères tomorrow, Tuesday, I could drive you there, no problem. I really want to hear what Papy has to say. Please phone me, so we can meet somewhere."

My heart was beating fast, almost painfully. The anchorman was back on the screen, presenting another topic. It was too early to call Nathalie Dufaure now. I'd have to wait a couple of hours. My feet danced with anticipation in their paper slippers. ". . . tell me all about Sarah Dufaure." What did Gaspard Dufaure have to say? What would I learn?

A knock on the door startled me. The nurse's garish smile jolted me back to reality.

"Time to go, Madame," she said briskly, showing teeth and gums.

I heard the stretcher's rubbery wheels squeak outside the door.

All of a sudden, everything was perfectly clear. It had never been so clear, so easy.

I got up, faced her.

"I'm sorry," I said quietly. "I've changed my mind."

I pulled the paper bonnet off. She stared at me, unblinking.

"But Madame—," she began.

I tore the paper dress open. The nurse averted shocked eyes from my sudden nudity.

"The doctors are waiting," she said.

"I don't care," I said, firmly. "I'm not going to do this. I want to keep this baby."

Her mouth quivered with indignation.

"I will send the doctor to see you immediately."

She turned and walked away. I heard the click of her sandals along the linoleum, sharp with disapproval. I slipped a denim dress over my head, stepped into my shoes, seized my bag and left the room. As I scrambled down the stairs, past startled nurses carrying breakfast trays, I realized I'd left my toothbrush, towels, shampoo, soap, deodorant, makeup kit and face cream in the bathroom. So what, I thought, rushing through the prim, tidy entrance, so what! So what!

The street was empty with that fresh, gleaming look Parisian sidewalks boast early in the morning. I hailed a taxi and rode home.

July 16, 2002.

My baby. My baby was safe within me. I wanted to laugh and cry. I did. The taxi driver eyed me several times in the rearview mirror, but I didn't care. I was going to have this baby.

I MADE A ROUGH ESTIMATE, counting over two thousand people
grouped by the Seine, along the Bir-Hakeim bridge. The survivors.
The families. Children, grandchildren. Rabbis. The mayor of the city.
The prime minister. The minister of defense. Numerous politicians.
Journalists. Photographers. Franck Lévy. Thousands of flowers, a
soaring marquee, a white platform. An impressive gathering. Guillaume stood by my side, his face solemn, his eyes downcast.

Fleetingly, I recalled the old lady from the rue Nélaton. What was
it she had said? "Nobody remembers. Why should they? Those were
the darkest days of our country."

I suddenly wished she could be here now, gazing at the hundreds of
silent, emotional faces around me. From the stand, a beautiful
middle-aged woman with thick auburn hair sang. Her clear voice rose
above the roar of the nearby traffic. Then the prime minister began
his speech.

"Sixty years ago, right here, in Paris, but also throughout France,
the appalling tragedy began to take place. The march toward horror
was speeding up. Already, the Shoah's shadow darkened the innocent
people herded into the Vélodrome d'Hiver. This year, like every year,
we are gathered together in this place to remember. So as to forget
nothing of the persecutions, the hunting down, and shattered destiny
of so many French Jews."

An old man on my left took a handkerchief from his pocket and wept noiselessly. My heart went out to him. Who was he crying for? I wondered. Who had he lost? As the prime minister went on, my eyes moved over the crowd. Was there anyone here who knew and remembered Sarah Starzynski? Was she here herself? Right now, at this very moment? Was she here with a husband, a child, a grandchild? Behind me, in front of me? I carefully picked out women in their seventies, scanning wrinkled, solemn faces for the slanted green eyes. But I did not feel comfortable ogling these grieving strangers. I lowered my gaze. The prime minister's voice seemed to gain in strength and clarity, booming out over us.

"Yes, Vel' d'Hiv', Drancy, and all the transit camps, those antechambers of death, were organized, run, and guarded by Frenchmen. Yes, the first act of the Shoah took place right here, with the complicity of the French State."

The many faces around me appeared to be serene, listening to the prime minister. I watched them as he continued with the same powerful voice. But every one of those faces contained sorrow. Sorrow that could never be erased. The prime minister's speech was applauded for a long time. I noticed people crying, hugging each other.

Still with Guillaume, I went to speak to Franck Lévy, who was carrying a copy of *Seine Scenes* under his arm. He greeted me warmly, introduced us to a couple of journalists. A few moments later, we left. I told Guillaume I had found out who lived in the Tézac apartment, that somehow this had brought me closer to my father-in-law, who had kept a dark secret for over sixty years. And that I was trying to trace Sarah, the little girl who had escaped from Beaune-la-Rolande.

In half an hour, I was meeting Nathalie Dufaure in front of the Pasteur *métro* station. She was going to drive me to Orléans, to her grandfather. Guillaume kissed me warmly and hugged me. He said he wished me luck.

As I crossed the busy avenue, my palm caressed my stomach. If I had not left the clinic this morning, I would have been regaining consciousness by now in my cozy apricot room, watched over by the beaming nurse. A dainty breakfast—croissant, jam, and café au lait—

and I would have left the place alone in the afternoon, a little unsteadily, a sanitary pad between my legs, a dull pain in my lower abdomen. A void in my mind and in my heart.

I had not heard a word from Bertrand. Had the clinic telephoned him to inform him I'd left before the abortion? I did not know. He was still in Brussels, due back tonight.

I wondered how I'd tell him. How he would take it.

As I walked down the avenue Émile Zola, anxious not to be late for Nathalie Dufaure, I wondered if I still cared about what Bertrand thought, about what Bertrand felt? The unsettling thought frightened me.

WHEN I GOT BACK from Orléans in the early evening, the apartment felt hot and stuffy. I went to open a window, leaned out to the noisy boulevard du Montparnasse. It was strange to imagine that we'd soon be leaving for the quiet rue de Saintonge. We had spent twelve years here. Zoë had never lived anywhere else. It would be our last summer here, I thought fleetingly. I had grown fond of this apartment, the sunlight coming in every afternoon into the large white living room, the Luxembourg Garden just down the rue Vavin, the easiness of being situated in one of Paris's most active arrondissements, one of the places you could actually feel the city's heartbeat, its rapid, exciting pulse.

I kicked off my sandals and lay down on the soft, beige sofa. The fullness of the day weighed upon me like lead. I shut my eyes and was immediately startled back to reality by the phone. It was my sister, calling from her office overlooking Central Park. I imagined her behind her vast desk, her reading glasses perched on the end of her nose.

Briefly, I told her I had not gone through with the abortion.

"Oh, my God," breathed Charla. "You didn't do it."

"I couldn't," I said. "It was impossible."

I could hear her smiling down the phone, that wide, irresistible, smile.

"You brave, wonderful girl," she said. "I'm proud of you, honey."

"Bertrand still doesn't know," I said. "He won't be back till later on this evening. He probably thinks I've done it."

A transatlantic pause.

"You will tell him, won't you?"

"Of course. I'll have to, at some point."

After my conversation with my sister, I lay on the sofa for a long time, my hand folded over my stomach like a protective shield. Little by little, I felt vitality pumping back into me.

As ever, I thought of Sarah Starzynski, and of what I now knew. I had not needed to tape Gaspard Dufaure. Nor jot anything down. It was all written inside me.

A SMALL, NEAT HOUSE ON the outskirts of Orléans. Prim flower beds. An old, placid dog with failing eyesight A little old lady cutting up vegetables at the sink, and who nodded at me as I came in.

Gaspard Dufaure's gruff voice. His blue-veined hand patting the dog's wizened head. And what he had said.

"My brother and I knew there had been trouble during the war. But we were small then, and we didn't remember what the trouble was. It was only after my grandparents died that I found out from my father that Sarah Dufaure was in fact called Starzynski, and that she was Jewish. My grandparents had hidden her for all those years. There was something sad about Sarah, she was not a joyful, outgoing person. She was hard to get through to. We had been told she had been adopted by my grandparents because her parents had died during the war. That's all we knew. But we could tell she was different. When she came to church with us, her lips never moved during the 'Our Father.' She never prayed. She never received communion. She would stare in front of her with a frozen expression that frightened me. My grandparents would smile at us firmly and tell us to leave her alone. My parents did the same. Little by little, Sarah became part of our lives, the older sister we never had. And she grew into a lovely, melancholy young girl. She was very serious, mature for her years. Sometimes, after the war, we would go to Paris, with my parents, but Sarah never wanted to come. She said she hated Paris. She said she never wanted to go back there again."

"Did she ever talk about her brother? Her parents?" I asked.

Gaspard shook his head.

"Never. I only heard about her brother, and what happened, from my father, forty years ago. When I was living with her, I never knew."

Nathalie Dufaure's voice piped up.

"What happened to her brother?" she asked.

Gaspard Dufaure glanced at his fascinated granddaughter, hanging on to every word. Then he looked at his wife, who had not spoken during the entire conversation, but who looked on benignly.

"I will tell you about it another time, Natou. It's a very sad story."

There was a long pause.

"Monsieur Dufaure," I said, "I need to know where Sarah Starzynski is now. This is why I have come to see you. Can you help me?"

Gaspard Dufaure scratched his head and shot me a quizzical look.

"What *I* really need to know, Mademoiselle Jarmond," he grinned, "is why this is so important to you."

THE PHONE RANG AGAIN. It was Zoë from Long Island. She was having a great time, the weather was fine, she had a tan, a new bicycle, her cousin Cooper was "neat," but she missed me. I told her I missed her, too, that I'd be with her in less than ten days. Then she lowered her voice and asked if I had made any progress in locating Sarah Starzynski. I had to smile at the seriousness of her tone. I said that as a matter of fact, I had made progress, and I was going to tell her about it very quickly.

"Oh, Mom, what progress?" she panted. "I have to know! Now!"

"All right," I said, giving in to her enthusiasm. "Today I met a man who knew her well as a young girl. He told me that Sarah left France in 1952 for New York City, to become a nanny for an American family."

Zoë whooped.

"You mean she's in the States?"

"I guess so," I said.

A little silence.

"How are you going to find her in the States, Mom?" she asked, her voice clearly less cheerful. "The States are so much bigger than France."

"God knows, honey," I sighed. I kissed her fervently through the phone, sent all my love, and hung up.

"What *I* really need to know, Mademoiselle Jarmond, is why this is so important to you." I had decided, on the spur of the moment, to tell Gaspard Dufaure the truth. How Sarah Starzynski had come into my life. How I had discovered her terrible secret. And how she was linked to my in-laws. How, now that I knew about the events of the summer of 1942 (both the public events—the Vel' d'Hiv', Beaune-la-Rolande—and the private ones—little Michel Starzynski's death in the Tézac apartment), finding Sarah had become a major goal, something I strove for with all my might.

Gaspard Dufaure had been surprised at my doggedness. Why find her, what for? he had asked, shaking his grizzled head. I had replied, to tell her we care, to tell her we have not forgotten. "We," he had smiled, who was the "we"—my family-in-law, the French people? And then I had retorted, slightly irritated by his grin: no, me, just me, I wanted to say sorry, I wanted to tell her I could not forget the roundup, the camp, Michel's death, and the direct train to Auschwitz that had taken her parents away forever. Sorry for what? he had retaliated, why should I, an American, feel sorry, hadn't my fellow countrymen freed France in June 1944? I had nothing to be sorry for, he laughed.

I had looked at him straight in the eyes.

"Sorry for not knowing. Sorry for being forty-five years old and not knowing."

S ARAH HAD LEFT FRANCE in late 1952. She had gone to America. "Why the States?" I asked.

"She told us she had to get away, to a place that had not been touched directly by the Holocaust, in the way France was. We were all upset. Especially my grandparents. They loved her like the daughter they never had. But she would not be swayed. She left. And she never came back. At least, not that I know of."

"Then what happened to her?" I asked, sounding like Nathalie, using the same fervor, the same earnestness.

Gaspard Dufaure shrugged, sighed deeply. He had gotten up, followed by the blind, old dog. His wife had made me another cup of powerful, harsh coffee. Their granddaughter had remained silent, curled up in the armchair, her eyes going from him to me in a silent, endearing manner. She would remember this, I thought. She would remember it all.

Her grandfather came to sit down again with a grunt, handing me the coffee. He had looked around the small room, the faded photographs on the wall, the tired furniture. He had scratched his head and sighed. I waited, and Nathalie waited. Then he spoke at last.

They had never heard from Sarah after 1955.

"She wrote a couple of letters to my grandparents. And a year later, she sent a card to say she was getting married. I remember my father telling us Sarah was marrying a Yankee." Gaspard smiled. "We were delighted for her. But then, there were no more calls, no more letters.

Ever again. My grandparents tried to trace her. They did all they could to find her, called New York, wrote letters, sent telegrams. They tried to locate her husband. Nothing. Sarah had disappeared. It was dreadful for them. They waited, and waited, year after year, for a sign, a call, a card. Nothing came. Then my grandfather passed away in the early sixties, followed by my grandmother, a few years later. I think their hearts were broken."

"You know your grandparents could be declared 'Righteous among the Nations,'" I said.

"What does that mean?" he asked, puzzled.

"The Yad Vashem Institute in Jerusalem gives medals to those, non-Jewish, who saved Jews during the war. It can also be obtained posthumously."

He cleared his throat, looking away from me.

"Just find her. Please find her, Mademoiselle Jarmond. Tell her I miss her. My brother Nicolas, too. Tell her we send all our love."

Before I left, he handed me a letter.

"My grandmother wrote this to my father, after the war. Maybe you'd like to look at it. You can give it back to Nathalie, when you've read it."

Later on, at home, alone, I deciphered the old-fashioned handwriting. As I read, I cried. I managed to calm down, wiped away my tears, blew my nose.

Then I called Edouard and read it out loud to him on the phone. He sounded like he was crying, but he appeared to be doing everything he could to make me think he wasn't. He thanked me with a strangled voice and hung up.

September 8, 1946
Alain, my dear son,

When Sarah came back last week from spending the summer with you and Henriette, she had pink cheeks . . . and a smile. Jules and I were amazed, and thrilled. She will be writing to you herself to thank you, but I wanted to tell you how grateful I am for your help and hospitality. These have been four grim years, as you know. Four years of captivity, of fear, of deprivation. For all of us, for our country. Four years that have taken their toll, on Jules and me, but especially on Sarah. I do not think she has ever gotten over what happened in the summer of 1942, when we took her back to her family's apartment in the Marais. That day, something broke within her. Something collapsed.

None of this has been easy, and your support has been invaluable. Hiding Sarah from the enemy, keeping her safe from that long ago summer all the way to the Armistice, has been horrendous. But

Sarah now has a family. We are her family. Your sons, Gaspard and Nicolas, are her brothers. She is a Dufaure. She bears our name.

I know she will never forget. Behind the rosy cheeks and the smile, there is a hardness about her. She will never be a normal fourteen-year-old child. She is like a woman, a bitter woman. Sometimes it seems she is older than me. She never talks about her family, about her brother. But I know she carries them with her, always. I know she goes to the cemetery every week, sometimes more often, to visit her brother's grave. She wants to go alone. She refuses my company. Sometimes I follow her, just to make sure she's all right. She sits in front of the little tombstone, and she remains very still. She can sit there for hours, holding that brass key she carries around with her, always. The key to the cupboard where her poor little brother died. When she comes back home, her face is shut and cold. It is difficult for her to talk, to make contact with me. I try to give her all the love I have, for she is the daughter I never gave birth to.

She never talks about Beaune-la-Rolande. If ever we drive near the village, she goes white. She turns her head away and closes her eyes. I wonder if one day the world will know. If it will all come out into the open, what happened there. Or if it will stay a secret forever, buried in a dark, disturbed past.

In the past year, since the end of the war, Jules has been to the Lutétia often, sometimes with Sarah, to keep abreast of the people coming home from the camps. Hoping, always hoping. We all hoped, with all our might. But now we know. Her parents will never come back. They were killed at Auschwitz, during that terrible summer of 1942.

I sometimes wonder how many children, like her, went through hell and survived, and now have to go on, without their loved ones. So much suffering, so much pain. Sarah has had to give up everything she was: her family, her name, her religion. We don't ever talk about it, but I know how deep the void is, how cruel her loss is. Sarah talks of leaving the country, of starting anew, somewhere else, far away from everything she has known, everything she has gone through. She is too small now, too fragile to leave the farm, but the day will come. Jules and I will have to let her go.

Yes, the war is over, at last over, but for your father and me, nothing is the same. Nothing will ever be the same. Peace has a bitter taste. And the future is foreboding. The events that have taken place have changed the face of the world. And of France. France is still recovering from her darkest years. Will she ever recover, I wonder? This is no longer the France I knew when I was a little girl. This is another France that I don't recognize. I am old now, and I know my days are numbered. But Sarah, Gaspard, and Nicolas are still young. They will have to live in this new France. I pity them, and I fear what lies ahead.

My dear boy, this was not meant to be a sad letter; alas, it has turned out that way, and I am indeed sorry. The garden needs tending to, the chickens must be fed, and I shall sign off. Let me thank you again for everything you have done for Sarah. God bless you both, for your generosity, your faithfulness, and God bless your boys,

Your loving mother,
Geneviève

A NOTHER PHONE CALL. My cellular. I should have turned it off. It was Joshua. I was surprised to hear him. He didn't usually call this late.

"Just saw you on the news, sugar," he drawled. "Looking pretty as a picture. A trifle pale, but very glamoroso."

"The news?" I breathed. "What news?"

"Turned on my TV for the eight o'clock news on TF1 and there's my Julia, just below the prime minister."

"Oh," I said, "the Vel' d'Hiv' ceremony."

"Good speech, didn't you think?"

"Very good."

A pause. I heard the click of his lighter as he lit up a mild Marlboro, the silver-box ones, the kind you only get in the States. I wondered what he had to say to me. He was usually blunt. Too blunt.

"What is it, Joshua?" I asked warily.

"Nothing, really. Just called to say you did a good job. That Vel' d'Hiv' piece of yours is getting talked about. I just wanted to tell you. Bamber's photos are great, too. You guys pulled it off just fine."

"Oh," I said. "Thank you."

But I knew him better than that.

"Anything else?" I added carefully.

"There's one thing that bothers me."

"Go ahead," I said.

"One thing missing, in my opinion. You got the survivors, the witnesses, the old guy at Beaune-la-Rolande etc., all that is fine. Fine, fine. But you forgot a couple of things. The cops. The French cops."

"Well?" I asked, beginning to feel exasperation nibble at me. "What about the French cops?"

"It would have been perfect if you could have gotten those roundup cops to talk. If you could have found a couple of those guys, just to hear their side of the story. Even if they're old men now. What did these guys tell their kids? Did their families ever know?"

He was right, of course. It had never entered my head. The exasperation waned. I said nothing, crushed.

"Hey, Julia, no problem," Joshua chuckled. "You did a great job. Maybe those cops would never have talked, anyway. You probably didn't read much about them in your research, did you?"

"No," I said. "Come to think of it, there is nothing about how the French police felt in what I read. They were only doing their jobs."

"Yeah, their jobs," echoed Joshua. "But I sure would have liked to have known how they lived with that. And come to think of it, what about those fellas driving those endless trains from Drancy to Auschwitz. Did they know what they were carrying? Did they really think it was cattle? Did they know where they were taking these people, what was going to happen to them? And all the guys driving those buses? Did they know anything?"

He was right again, of course. I remained silent. A good journalist would have delved deep into those taboos. French police, French railway, French bus system.

But I had been obsessed with the Vel' d'Hiv' children. And one child, in particular.

"You OK, Julia?" came his voice.

"Peachy keen," I lied.

"You need some time off," he declared. "Time to climb into a plane and go home."

"That's exactly what I had in mind."

T HE LAST PHONE CALL of the evening had been from Nathalie Dufaure. She sounded ecstatic. I imagined her waiflike face lit up
with excitement, her brown eyes glowing.

"Julia! I looked through all Papy's papers, and I found it. I found
Sarah's card!"

"Sarah's card?" I repeated, lost.

"The card she sent to say she was getting married, the last card. She
gives the name of her husband."

I grabbed a pen, fumbled around in vain for a piece of paper. No
paper. I pointed the ball-point at the back of my hand.

"And the name is?"

"She wrote to say she was marrying Richard J. Rainsferd." She
spelled the name out. "The card is dated March 15, 1955. No address. Nothing else. Just that."

"Richard J. Rainsferd," I repeated, writing it in block letters on my
skin.

I thanked Nathalie, promised to keep her informed of my progress,
then dialed Charla's number in Manhattan. I got her assistant, Tina,
who put me on hold for a while. Then Charla's voice came through.

"You again, honey pie?"

I went straight to the point.

"How do you find someone in the States, get hold of someone?"

"Phone book," she said.

"Is it that easy?"

"There are other ways," she replied cryptically.

"What about a person who disappeared in 1955?"

"You got a Social Security number, license plate, or even an address?"

"Nope. Nothing."

She whistled through her teeth.

"It'll be tough. Might not work. I'll try, though, I have a couple of pals who could help. Give me the name."

At that moment, I heard the front door slam, the jangle of keys being tossed onto the table.

My husband, back from Brussels.

"I'll get back to you," I whispered to my sister, and hung up.

BERTRAND WALKED INTO THE ROOM. He looked tense, pale, his face was drawn. He came to me, took me in his arms. I felt his chin nestle on top of my head.

I felt I had to speak fast.

"I didn't do it," I said.

He hardly moved.

"I know," he answered. "The doctor phoned me."

I pulled away from him.

"I couldn't, Bertrand."

He smiled, a strange, desperate smile. He went over to the tray by the window where we kept liquor and poured cognac into a glass. I noticed how fast he drank it, his head snapping back. It was an ugly gesture and it stirred me.

"So what now?" he said, putting the glass down squarely. "What do we do now?"

I tried to smile, but I could fell it was a fake, cheerless one. Bertrand sat on the sofa, loosened his tie, opening the first two buttons of his shirt.

Then he said, "I can't face the idea of this child, Julia. I tried to tell you. You wouldn't listen."

Something in his voice made me look closer at him. He seemed vulnerable, rundown. For a split second I saw Edouard Tézac's weary face, the expression he had in the car, when he told me about Sarah coming back.

"I can't stop you having this baby. But I need you to know that I just can't come to terms with it. Having this child is going to destroy me."

I wanted to express pity—he seemed lost, defenseless—but instead an unexpected feeling of resentment took over me.

"Destroy you?" I repeated.

Bertrand got up, poured himself another drink. I glanced away as he swallowed it.

"Ever heard of midlife crisis, *amour*? You Americans are so fond of that expression. You've been wrapped up in your job, your friends, your daughter, you haven't even noticed what I've been going through. To tell the truth, you don't care. Do you?"

I stared at him, startled.

He lay back on the sofa, slowly, carefully, gazing up at the ceiling. Slow, precautious gestures I'd never seen him use. The skin of his face seemed crumpled. All of a sudden, I was looking at an aging husband. Gone was the young Bertrand. Bertrand had always been triumphantly young, vibrant, energetic. The kind of person who never sits still, always on the go, buoyant, fast, eager. The man I was staring at was like a ghost of his former self. When had this happened? How could I not have seen it? Bertrand and his tremendous laugh. His jokes. His audacity. Is that your husband? people would whisper, awed, galvanized. Bertrand at dinner parties, monopolizing conversations, but nobody cared, he was so riveting. Bertrand's way of looking at you, the powerful flicker of his blue eyes and that crooked, devilish smile.

Tonight there was nothing tight, nothing taut about him. He seemed to have let go. He sat there, flaccid, limp. His eyes were mournful, his lids drooped.

"You've never noticed, have you, what I've been going through. Have you?"

His voice was flat, toneless. I sat down next to him, stroked his hand. How could I ever admit I had not noticed? How could I ever explain how guilty I felt?

"Why didn't you tell me, Bertrand?"

The corners of his mouth turned down.

"I tried. It never worked."

"Why?"

Then his face went hard. He let out a small, dry laugh.

"You don't listen to me, Julia."

And I knew he was right. That awful night, when his voice had become hoarse. When he had expressed his greatest fear, growing old. When I realized he was fragile. Much more fragile than I had ever imagined. And I had looked away. It had disturbed me. It had repelled me. And he had sensed it. And he had not dared tell me how bad that had made him feel.

I said nothing, sitting next to him, holding his hand. The irony of the situation dawned upon me. A depressed husband. A failing marriage. A baby on the way.

"Why don't we go out for a bite to eat, down to the Select, or the Rotonde?" I said gently. "We can talk things over."

He heaved himself up.

"Another time, maybe. I'm tired."

It occurred to me that he had often been tired in the past months. Too tired to go to the movies, too tired to go jogging around the Luxembourg Garden, too tired to take Zoë to Versailles on a Sunday afternoon. Too tired to make love. Make love . . . When was the last time? Weeks ago. I watched him lumber across the room, his gait heavy. He had put on weight. I hadn't noticed that either. Bertrand was so careful about his appearance. *You've been wrapped up in your job, your friends, your daughter, you haven't even noticed. . . . You don't listen to me, Julia.* I felt shame race through me. Didn't I need to face up to the truth? Bertrand had not been part of my life in the past weeks, even if we shared the same bed, lived under the same roof. I hadn't told him about Sarah Starzynski. About my new relationship with Edouard. Hadn't I left Bertrand out of everything important to me? I had cut him out of my life, and the irony was that I was carrying his child.

From the kitchen, I heard him opening the fridge, caught the rustle of tinfoil. He came back to the living room, a chicken leg in one hand, foil in the other.

"Just one thing, Julia."

"Yes?" I said.

"When I told you I couldn't face this child, I meant it. You've made up your mind. Fine. Now this is my decision. I need time to myself. I need time off. You and Zoë will move into the rue de Saintonge after the summer. I'll find another place to live, nearby. Then we'll see how things go. Maybe by then, I can come to terms with this pregnancy. If not, we'll get a divorce."

This was no surprise. I had expected it all along. I got up, smoothed out my dress. I said, calmly, "The only thing that matters now is Zoë. Whatever happens, we will have to talk to her, you and I. We will have to prepare her. We have to do this right."

He put the chicken leg back into the foil.

"Why are you so tough, Julia?" he said. There was no sarcasm in his tone. Only bitterness. "You sound just like your sister."

I did not reply, heading out of the room. I went to the bathroom and turned on the water. Then it hit me: Hadn't I made my choice? I had chosen the baby over Bertrand. I had not been softened by his point of view, his inner fears, I had not been scared of his moving out for a couple of months, or indefinitely. Bertrand could not disappear. He was the father of my daughter, of the child within me. He could never completely walk out of our lives.

But as I looked at myself in the mirror, steam slowly filling the room, erasing my reflection with its misty breath, I felt everything had changed drastically. Did I still love Bertrand? Did I still need him? How could I want his child and not him?

I wanted to cry, but the tears did not come.

I WAS STILL IN the bath when he came in. He was holding the red Sarah file I had left in my bag.

"What is this?" he said, brandishing the file.

Startled, I moved abruptly, making the water slop over one side of the bath. His face was confused, flushed. He promptly sat down on the closed toilet. At any other time, I would have laughed outright at the ludicrousness of his position.

"Let me explain—," I began.

He raised his hand.

"You just can't help it, can you? You just can't leave the past alone."

He glanced through the file, leafed through the letters from Jules Dufaure to André Tézac, examined the photographs of Sarah.

"What is all this? Who gave this to you?"

"Your father," I answered quietly.

He stared at me.

"What does my father have to do with this?"

I stepped out of the bath, grabbed a towel, turned my back on him as I dried myself. Somehow I did not want his eyes on my naked skin.

"It's a long story, Bertrand."

"Why did you have to bring all this back? This stuff happened sixty years ago! It's all dead, it's all forgotten."

I swung around to face him.

"No, it isn't. Sixty years ago something happened to your family.

Something you don't know about. You and your sisters don't know anything. Neither does Mamé."

His mouth fell open. He seemed astounded.

"What happened? You tell me!" he demanded.

I snatched the file away from him, holding it against me.

"*You* tell me what you were doing going through my bag."

We sounded like kids fighting it out at recess. He rolled his eyes.

"I saw the file in your bag. I wondered what it was. That's all."

"I often have files in my bag. You've never looked at them before."

"That is not the issue. You tell me what all this is about. You tell me right now."

I shook my head.

"Bertrand, call your father. Tell him you found the file. Ask him."

"You don't trust me, is that it?"

His face sagged. I felt sudden pity for him. He seemed hurt, incredulous.

"Your father begged me not to tell you," I said gently.

Bertrand got up wearily from the toilet seat and reached over to put his hand on the doorknob. He looked beaten, spent.

He stepped back to stroke my cheek softly. His fingers were warm against my face.

"Julia, what happened to us? Where did it all go?"

Then he left the room.

The tears came, and I let them run down my face. He heard me sobbing, but he did not come back.

DURING SUMMER OF 2002, with the knowledge that Sarah Starzynski had left Paris for New York City fifty years ago, I felt propelled back across the Atlantic like a piece of steel pulled by a powerful magnet. I could not wait to leave town. I could not wait to see Zoë, and to search for Richard J. Rainsferd. I could not wait to board that plane.

I wondered if Bertrand called his father to find out what had happened in the rue de Saintonge apartment all those years ago. Bertrand said nothing. He remained cordial, but aloof. I felt he, too, was impatient for me to leave. So that he could think things over? See Amélie? I did not know. I did not care. I told myself I did not care.

A couple of hours before my departure to New York, I called my father-in-law to say good-bye. He did not mention having a conversation with Bertrand, and I did not ask him.

"Why did Sarah stop writing to the Dufaures?" Edouard asked. "What do you think happened, Julia?"

"I don't know, Edouard. But I am going to do my best to find out."

Those very questions haunted me night and day. When I boarded the plane a few hours later, I was still asking myself the same thing.

Was Sarah Starzynski still alive?

M Y SISTER, HER SHINY chestnut hair, her dimples, her beautiful
blue eyes. Her strong, athletic build, so like our mom's. *Les
soeurs* Jarmond. Towering above all the other women on the Tézac
side. The puzzled, bright smiles. A twinge of envy. Why are you
américaines so tall, is it something in your food, vitamins, hormones?
Charla was even taller than me. A couple of pregnancies had done
nothing to add padding to her powerful, sleek frame.

The minute she saw my face at the airport, Charla knew something
was on my mind, and that it had nothing to do with the baby I had decided to keep, or with marital difficulties. As we drove into the city,
her cell phone rang incessantly. Her assistant, her boss, her clients, her
kids, the babysitter; Ben, her ex-husband from Long Island; Barry, her
present husband on a business trip to Atlanta—the calls never
seemed to stop. I was so happy to see her I did not care. Just being
next to her, our shoulders brushing, made me happy.

Once we were alone in her narrow brownstone on East 81st Street,
in her spotless, chromed kitchen, and once she had poured out white
wine for her and apple juice for me (on account of my pregnancy), out
the entire story came. Charla knew little about France. She did not
speak much French, Spanish being the only other language she was
fluent in. Occupied France meant little to her. She sat in silence as I
explained the roundup, the camps, the trains to Poland. Paris in July
1942. The rue de Saintonge apartment. Sarah. Michel, her brother.

I watched her lovely face grow pale with horror. The glass of white wine remained untouched. She pressed her fingers hard upon her mouth, shook her head. I went right to the end of the story, to Sarah's last card, dated 1955, from New York City.

Then she said:

"Oh, my God." She took a quick sip of the wine. "You've come here for her, right?"

I nodded.

"How on earth are you going to start?"

"That name I called you about, remember? Richard J. Rainsferd. That's her husband's name."

"Rainsferd?" she said.

I spelled it.

Charla got up swiftly, took the cordless phone.

"What are you doing?" I said.

She held up her hand, motioning for me to keep quiet.

"Hi, operator, I'm looking for a Richard J. Rainsferd. New York State. That's right, R.A.I.N.S.F.E.R.D. Nothing? OK, can you check New Jersey please? . . . Nothing. . . . Connecticut? . . . Great. Yes, thank you. Just a minute."

She wrote something down on a scrap of paper. Then she handed it to me with a flourish.

"We got her," she said triumphantly.

Incredulous, I read the number and the address.

Mr. and Mrs. R. J. Rainsferd, 2299 Shepaug Drive, Roxbury, Connecticut.

"It can't be them," I muttered. "It's just not that easy."

"Roxbury," Charla mused. "Isn't that in Litchfield County? I used to have a beau there. You were gone by then. Greg Tanner. A real cutie. His dad was a doctor. Pretty place, Roxbury. About a hundred miles from Manhattan."

I sat on my high stool, flabbergasted. I simply could not believe that finding Sarah Starzynski had been so easy, so swift. I had barely landed. I hadn't even talked to my daughter. And I had already located Sarah. She was still alive. It seemed impossible, unreal.

"Listen," I said, "how do we know it's her, for sure?"

Charla was sitting at the table, busy powering up her laptop. She fished around in her bag for her glasses, and slid them over her nose.

"We're going to find out right away."

I came to stand behind her as her fingers ran deftly over the keyboard.

"What are you doing now?" I asked, mystified.

"Keep your hair on," she snapped, typing away. Over her shoulder, I saw she was already on the Internet.

The screen read: "Welcome to Roxbury, Connecticut. Events, social gatherings, people, real estate."

"Perfect. Just what we need," said Charla, studying the screen. Then she smoothly picked the scrap of paper from my fingers, took the phone again, and dialed the number on the paper.

This was going too fast. It was knocking the wind out of me.

"Charla! Wait! What the hell are you going to say, for God's sake!"

She cupped her palm over the receiver. The blue eyes went indignant over the rim of her glasses.

"You trust me, don't you?"

She used the lawyer's voice. Powerful, in control. I could only nod. I felt helpless, panicky. I got up, paced around the kitchen, fingering appliances, smooth surfaces.

When I looked back at her, she grinned.

"Maybe you should have some of that wine after all. And don't worry about caller ID, 212 won't show up." She suddenly held up a forefinger, pointed to the phone. "Yes, hi, good evening, is that, uh, Mrs. Rainsferd?"

I could not help smiling at the nasal whine. She had always been good at changing her voice.

"Oh, I'm sorry. . . . She's out?"

Mrs. Rainsferd was out. So there really was a Mrs. Rainsferd. I listened on, incredulous.

"Yes, uh, this is Sharon Burstall from the Minor Memorial Library on South Street. I'm wondering if you'd be interested in coming to our first summer get-together, scheduled on August 2. . . . Oh, I see. Gee, I'm sorry, ma'am. Hmm. Yes. I'm real sorry for the disturbance, ma'am. Thank you, good-bye."

She put the phone down and flashed a self-satisfied smile at me.

"Well?" I gasped.

"The woman I spoke to is Richard Rainsferd's nurse. He's a sick, old man. Bedridden. Needs heavy treatment. She comes in every afternoon."

"And Mrs. Rainsferd?" I asked impatiently.

"Due back any minute."

I looked at Charla blankly.

"So what do I do?" I said. "I just go there?"

My sister laughed.

"You got any other idea?"

THERE IT WAS. NUMBER 2299 Shepaug Drive. I turned the motor off and stayed in the car, clammy palms resting on my knees.

I could see the house from where I sat, beyond the twin pillars of gray stone at the gate. It was a squat, colonial-style place, probably built in the late thirties, I guessed. Less impressive than the sprawling million-dollar estates I had glimpsed on my way there, but tasteful and harmonious.

As I had driven up Route 67, I had been struck by the unspoiled, rural beauty of Litchfield County: rolling hills, sparkling rivers, lush vegetation, even during the full blast of summer. I had forgotten how hot New England could get. Despite the powerful air conditioner, I sweltered. I wished I had taken a bottle of mineral water with me. My throat felt parched.

Charla had mentioned Roxbury inhabitants were wealthy. Roxbury was one of those special, trendy, old time artistic places that no one tired of, she explained. Artists, writers, movie stars: there were a lot of them around there, apparently. I wondered what Richard Rainsferd did for a living. Had he always had a house here? Or had he and Sarah retired from Manhattan? And what about children? How many children had they had? I peered through the windshield at the wood exterior of the house and counted the number of windows. There were probably two or three bedrooms in there, I supposed, unless the back was bigger than I thought. Children who were perhaps my age. And grandchildren. I craned my neck to see if there were any cars parked in front of the house. I could only make out a closed detached garage.

I glanced at my watch. Just after two. It had only taken me a couple of hours to drive from the city. Charla had lent me her Volvo. It was as impeccable as her kitchen. I suddenly wished she could have been with me today. But she hadn't been able to cancel her appointments. "You'll do fine, Sis," she had said, tossing me the car keys. "Keep me posted, OK?"

I sat in the Volvo, anxiety rising with the stifling heat. What the hell was I going to say to Sarah Starzynski? I couldn't even call her that. Nor Dufaure. She was Mrs. Rainsferd now, she had been Mrs. Rainsferd for the past fifty years. Getting out of the car, ringing the brass bell I could see just on the right of the front door, seemed impossible. "Yes, hello, Mrs. Rainsferd, you don't know me, my name is Julia Jarmond, but I just wanted to talk to you about the rue de Saintonge, and what happened, and the Tézac family, and—"

It sounded lame, artificial. What was I doing here? Why had I come all this way? I should have written her a letter, waited for her to answer me. Coming here was ridiculous. A ridiculous idea. What had I hoped for anyway? For her to welcome me with open arms, pour me a cup of tea, and murmur: "Of course I forgive the Tézac family." Crazy. Surreal. I had come here for nothing. I should be leaving, right now.

I was about to back up and go, when a voice startled me.

"You looking for someone?"

I swiveled in my damp seat to discover a tanned woman in her midthirties. She had short, black hair and a stocky build.

"I'm looking for Mrs. Rainsferd, but I'm not sure I've got the right house."

The woman smiled.

"You got the right house. But my mom's out. Gone shopping. She'll be back in twenty minutes, though. I'm Ornella Harris. I live right next door."

I was looking at Sarah's daughter. Sarah Starzynski's daughter.

I tried to keep perfectly calm, managed a polite smile.

"I'm Julia Jarmond."

"Nice to meet you," she said. "Can I help in any way?"

I racked my brains for something to say.

"Well, I was just hoping to meet your mother. I should have phoned and all that, but I was passing through Roxbury, and I thought I'd drop by and say hi."

"You're a friend of Mom's?" she said.

"Not exactly. I met one of her cousins recently, and he told me she lived here."

Ornella's face lit up.

"Oh, you probably met Lorenzo! Was that in Europe?"

I tried not to look lost. Who on earth was Lorenzo?

"Actually, yes, it was in Paris."

Ornella chuckled.

"Yup, he's quite something, Uncle Lorenzo. Mom adores him. He doesn't come to see us much, but he calls a lot."

She cocked her chin toward me.

"Hey, you want to come in for some iced tea or something, it's damn hot out here. That way you can wait for Mom? We'll hear her car when she comes in."

"I don't want to be any trouble . . ."

"My kids are out boating on Lake Lillinonah with their dad, so please, feel free!"

I got out of the car, feeling more and more nervous, and followed Ornella to the patio of a neighboring house in the same style as the Rainsferd residence. The lawn was strewn with plastic toys, Frisbees, headless Barbie dolls, and Legos. As I sat down in the cool shade, I wondered how often Sarah Starzynski came here to watch her grandchildren play. As she lived next door, she probably came every day.

Ornella handed me a large glass of iced tea, which I accepted gratefully. We sipped in silence.

"You live around here?" she asked, finally.

"No, I live in France. In Paris. I married a Frenchman."

"Paris, wow," she cooed. "Beautiful place, eh?"

"Yeah, but I'm pretty glad to be back home. My sister lives in Manhattan, and my parents in Boston. I've come to spend the summer with them."

The phone rang. Ornella went to answer it. She murmured a few quiet words and came back to the patio.

"That was Mildred," she said.

"Mildred?" I asked blankly.

"My dad's nurse."

The woman Charla had spoken to yesterday. Who had mentioned an old, bedridden man.

"Is your dad . . . any better?" I asked tentatively.

She shook her head.

"No, he's not. The cancer is too advanced. He's not going to make it. He can't even talk anymore, he's unconscious."

"I'm very sorry," I mumbled.

"Thank God Mom is such a tower of strength. She's the one who's pulling me through this, not the other way around. She's wonderful. So is my husband, Eric. I don't know what I'd do without those two."

I nodded. Then we heard the crunch of car wheels on the gravel.

"That's Mom!" said Ornella.

I heard a car door slam and the scrunch of footsteps on the pebbles. Then a voice came over the hedge, high-pitched and sweet, "Nella! Nella!"

There was a foreign, lilting tone to it.

"Coming, Mom."

My heart walloped around in my rib cage. I had to put my hand on my sternum to quiet it. As I followed the swing of Ornella's square hips back across the lawn, I felt faint with excitement and agitation.

I was going to meet Sarah Starzynski. I was going to see her with my very eyes. Heaven knows what I was going to say to her.

Although she was standing right next to me, I heard Ornella's voice from a long way off.

"Mom, this is Julia Jarmond, a friend of Uncle Lorenzo's, she's from Paris, just passing through Roxbury."

The smiling woman coming toward me was wearing a red dress

that came down to her ankles. She was in her late fifties. She had the same stocky build as her daughter: round shoulders, plump thighs, and thick, generous arms. Black, graying hair caught up in a bun, tanned, leathery skin, and jet-black eyes.

Black eyes.

This was not Sarah Starzynski. That much I knew.

S<small>O YOU FRIEND OF</small> Lorenzo, *si*? Nice to meet you!"
The accent was pure Italian. No doubt about that. Everything about this woman was Italian.

I backed away, stuttering profusely.

"I am sorry, so very sorry."

Ornella and her mother stared at me. Their smiles hovered and vanished.

"I think I've got the wrong Mrs. Rainsferd."

"The wrong Mrs. Rainsferd?" repeated Ornella.

"I'm looking for a Sarah Rainsferd," I said. "I've made a mistake."

Ornella's mother sighed and patted my arm.

"Please don't worry. These things happen."

"I'll be leaving now," I muttered, my face hot. "I'm sorry to have wasted your time."

I turned and headed back to the car, trembling with embarrassment and disappointment.

"Wait!" came Mrs. Rainsferd's clear voice. "Miss, wait!"

I halted. She came up to me, put her plump hand on my shoulder.

"Look, you make no mistake, Miss."

I frowned.

"What do you mean?"

"The French girl, Sarah, she my husband's first wife."

I stared at her.

"Do you know where she is?" I breathed.

The plump hand patted me again. The black eyes seemed sad.

"Honey, she dead. She died 1972. So sorry to tell you this."

Her words took ages to sink in. My head was swimming. Maybe it was the heat, the sun pounding down on me.

"Nella! Get some water!"

Mrs. Rainsferd took my arm and guided me back to the porch, sat me on a cushioned, wooden bench. She gave me some water. I drank, teeth clattering against the rim, handing her the glass when I was through.

"So sorry to tell you this news, believe me."

"How did she die?" I croaked.

"A car accident. Richard and her were already living in Roxbury since the early sixties. Sarah's car skidded on black ice. Crashed into a tree. The roads very dangerous here in winter, you know. She killed instantly."

I could not speak. I felt utterly devastated.

"You upset, poor honey, now," she murmured, stroking my cheek with a strong motherly gesture.

I shook my head, mumbled something. I felt drained, washed out. An empty shell. The idea of the long drive back to New York made me want to scream. And after that . . . What was I going to tell Edouard, tell Gaspard? How? That she was dead? Just like that? That there was nothing to be done?

She was dead. She died at forty years old. She was gone. Dead. Gone.

Sarah was dead. I could never speak to her. I would never be able to tell her sorry, sorry from Edouard, tell her how much the Tézac family had cared. I could never tell her that Gaspard and Nicolas Dufaure missed her, that they sent their love. It was too late. Thirty years too late.

"I never met her, you know," Mrs. Rainsferd was saying. "I only met Richard couple of years later. He a sad man. And the boy—"

I raised my head, paying full attention.

"The boy?"

"Yes, William. You know William?"

"Sarah's son?"

"Yes, Sarah's boy."

"My half brother," said Ornella.

Hope dawned once more.

"No, I don't know him. Tell me about him."

"Poor bambino, he only twelve when his mother died, you see. A heartbroken boy. I raised him like he mine. I gave him love of Italy. He married Italian girl, from my home village."

She beamed with pride.

"Does he live in Roxbury?" I asked.

She smiled, patted my cheek again.

"*Mamma mia*, no, William lives in Italy. He left Roxbury in 1980, when he twenty. Married Francesca in 1985. Has two lovely girls. Comes back to see his father from time to time, and me and Nella, but not very often. He hates it here. Reminds him of his mother's death."

I felt much better all of a sudden. It was less hot, less stuffy. I found I could breathe easier.

"Mrs. Rainsferd—," I began.

"Please," she said, "call me Mara."

"Mara," I complied. "I need to talk to William. I need to meet him. It's very important. Could you give me his address in Italy?"

THE CONNECTION WAS BAD and I could barely hear Joshua's voice.
"You need an advance?" he said. "In the middle of summer?"
"Yes!" I shouted, cringing at the disbelief in his voice.
"How much?"
I told him.
"Hey, what's going on, Julia? Has that smooth operator of a husband turned stingy, or what?"
I sighed impatiently.
"Can I have it or not, Joshua? It's important."
"Of course you can have it," he snapped. "This is the first time in years you've ever asked me for money. Hope you're not having any problems?"
"No problems. I just need to travel. That's all. And I have to do it fast."
"Oh," he said, and I could feel his curiosity swelling. "And where are you going?"
"I'm taking my daughter to Tuscany. I'll explain another time."
My tone was flat and final. He probably felt it was useless trying to glean anything else from me. I could feel his annoyance pulse all the way from Paris. The advance would be in my account later this afternoon, he said curtly. I thanked him and hung up.
Then I put my hands under my chin and thought. If I told Bertrand what I was doing, he'd make a scene. He'd make everything complicated, difficult. I couldn't face that. I could tell Edouard . . . No, it

was too early. Too soon. I had to talk to William Rainsferd first. I had his address now, it would be easy locating him. Talking to him was another matter.

Then there was Zoë. How was she going to feel about her Long Island frolic being interrupted? And not going to Nahant, to her grandparents' place? That worried me, at first. Yet, I somehow did not think she would mind. She had never been to Italy. And I could let her into the secret. I could tell her the truth, tell her we were going to meet Sarah Starzynski's son.

And then there were my parents. What could I tell them? Where would I begin? They, too, were expecting me at Nahant after the Long Island stay. What on earth was I going to tell them?

"Yeah," drawled Charla later on when I explained all this, "yeah, sure, running off to Tuscany with Zoë, finding this guy, and just saying sorry sixty years later?"

I flinched at the irony in her voice.

"Well, why the hell not?" I asked.

She sighed. We were sitting in the large front room she used as an office on the second floor of her house. Her husband was turning up later on that evening. Dinner was waiting in the kitchen, we had made it together earlier. Charla craved bright colors, as did Zoë. This room was a melting pot of pistachio green, ruby red, and luminous orange. The first time I had seen it, my head had started to throb, but I had gotten used to it, and I secretly found it intensely exotic. I always tended to go for neutral, bland colors, like brown, beige, white, or gray, even in my dress code. Charla and Zoë preferred to overdose on anything bright, but they both carried it off, beautifully. I both envied and admired their audacity.

"Stop being the bossy older sister. You're pregnant, don't forget. I'm not sure all this traveling is the right thing to do at the moment."

I said nothing. She had a point. She got up and went to put an old Carly Simon record on. "You're So Vain," with Mick Jagger whining in the backup vocals.

Then she turned around and glared at me.

"Do you really have to find this man right now, this very minute? I mean, can't it wait?"

Again, she had a point.

I looked back at her.

"Charla, it's not that simple. And no, it can't wait. No, I can't explain. It's too important. It's the most important thing in my life right now. Apart from the baby."

She sighed again.

"That Carly Simon song always reminds me of your husband. 'You're so vain, I betcha think this song is about you . . .'"

I let out an ironic chuckle.

"What are you going to tell Mom and Dad?" she asked. "About not coming to Nahant? And about the baby?"

"God knows."

"Think it over, then. Think it over carefully."

"I am. I have."

She came up behind me and rubbed my shoulders.

"Does that mean you've got it all organized? Already?"

"Yup."

"You fast one."

Her hands felt good on my shoulders, making me drowsy and warm. I looked around at Charla's colorful work room, the desk covered with files and books, the light ruby curtains moving in the gentle breeze. The house was quiet without Charla's kids.

"And where does this guy live?" she asked.

"He has a name. William Rainsferd. He lives in Lucca."

"Where's that?"

"Small town between Florence and Pisa."

"What does he do for a living?"

"I looked him up on the Internet, but his stepmother told me anyway. He's a food critic. His wife is a sculptor. They have two kids."

"And how old is William Rainsferd?"

"You sound like a cop. Born in 1959."

"And you're just going to waltz into his life and set all hell loose."

I pushed her hands away, exasperated.

"Of course not! I just want him to know our side of the story. I want to make sure he knows nobody has forgotten what happened."

A wry grin.

"He probably hasn't either. His mom carried that with her all her life. Maybe he doesn't want to be reminded."

A door banged downstairs.

"Anyone home? The beautiful lady and her sister from Paree?"

The thud of steps coming up the stairs.

Barry, my brother-in-law. Charla's face lit up. So much in love, I thought. I felt happy for her. After a painful, trying divorce, she was truly happy again.

As I watched them kiss, I thought of Bertrand. What was going to happen to my marriage? Which way would it turn? Would it ever work out? I pushed it all away from my mind as I followed Charla and Barry downstairs.

Later on, in bed, Charla's words about William Rainsferd came back to me. *"Maybe he doesn't want to be reminded."* I tossed and turned most of the night. The following morning, I said to myself that I'd soon find out if William Rainsferd had a problem talking about his mother and her past. I was going to see him, after all. I was going to talk to him. In two days, Zoë and I were flying to Paris from JFK, then on to Florence.

William Rainsferd always spent his summer vacation in Lucca. Mara had told me that when she had given me his address. And Mara had phoned him to say I'd be looking him up.

William Rainsferd was aware that a Julia Jarmond was going to call him. That's all he knew.

TUSCAN HEAT HAD NOTHING to do with New England heat. It was overly dry, devoid of any humidity whatsoever. As I walked out of the Florence Peretola airport with Zoë in tow, the heat was so devastating, I thought I was going to shrivel up on the spot, dehydrated. I kept putting things down to my pregnancy, comforting myself, telling myself I didn't usually feel this drained, this parched. Jet lag didn't help, either. The sun seemed to bite into me, to eat into my skin and eyes despite a straw hat and dark glasses.

I had rented a car, a modest-looking Fiat, which was waiting for us in the middle of a sun-drenched parking lot. The air conditioner was more than meek. As I backed out, I wondered suddenly if I was going to make the forty-minute drive to Lucca. I craved a cool, shady room, drifting to sleep in soft, light sheets. Zoë's stamina kept me going. She never stopped talking, pointed out the color of the sky—a deep, cloudless blue—the cypress trees lining the highway, the olive trees planted in little rows, the crumbling old houses glimpsed in the distance, perched on hilltops. "Now that's Montecatini," she chirped knowingly, pointing and reading out from a guide book, "famous for its luxury spa and its wine."

As I drove, Zoë read aloud about Lucca. It was one of the rare Tuscan towns to have kept its famous medieval walls circling an unspoiled center where few cars were allowed. There was a lot to be seen, Zoë continued, the cathedral, the church of San Michele, the

Guinigui tower, the Puccini museum, the Palazzo Mansi. . . . I smiled at her, amused by her high spirits. She glanced back at me.

"I guess we don't have much time for sightseeing." She grinned. "We've got work to do, don't we, Mom?"

"We sure do," I agreed.

Zoë had already found William Rainsferd's address on her site map of Lucca. It wasn't far from the via Fillungo, the main artery of the town, a large pedestrian street where I had booked rooms in a small guesthouse, Casa Giovanna.

As we approached Lucca and its confusing maze of ring roads, I found I had to concentrate on the erratic driving methods of the cars surrounding me, which kept pulling out, stopping, or turning without any warning whatsoever. Definitely worse than Parisians, I decided, beginning to feel flustered and irritated. There was also a slow tug in the pit of my stomach that I did not like, that felt oddly like an oncoming period. Something I ate on the plane and that didn't agree with me? Or something worse? I felt apprehension flicker through me.

Charla was right. It was crazy coming here in my condition, not even three months pregnant. It could have waited. William Rainsferd could have waited another six months for my visit.

But then I looked at Zoë's face. It was beautiful, incandescent with joy and excitement. She knew nothing yet about Bertrand and me separating. She was preserved still, innocent of all our plans. This would be a summer she would never forget.

And as I drove the Fiat to one of the free parking lots near the city walls, I knew I wanted to make this part as wonderful as possible for her.

I TOLD ZOË I NEEDED to put my feet up for a while. While she chat-
ted away in the lobby with the amiable Giovanna, a buxom lady
with a sultry voice, I had a cool shower and lay down on the bed. The
ache in my lower abdomen slowly ebbed away.

Our adjoining rooms were small, high up in the towering, ancient
building, but perfectly comfortable. I kept thinking of my mother's
voice when I had called her from Charla's to say I wasn't coming to
Nahant, that I was taking Zoë back to Europe. I could tell, from her
brief pauses and the way she cleared her throat, that she was worried.
She finally asked me if everything was all right. I replied cheerfully
that everything was fine, I had an opportunity to visit Florence with
Zoë, I would come back to the States later to see her and Dad. "But
you've barely arrived! And why leave when you've only been with
Charla for a couple of days?" she protested. "And why interrupt Zoë's
vacation here? I simply don't understand. And you were saying how
much you missed the States. This is all so rushed."

I had felt guilty. But how could I explain the whole story to her and
Dad over the phone? One day, I thought. Not now. I still felt guilty, lying on the pale pink bedspread that smelled faintly of lavender. I
hadn't even told Mom about my pregnancy. I hadn't even told Zoë. I
longed to let them in on the secret, and Dad as well. But something
held me back. Some bizarre superstition, some deep-rooted apprehension I had never felt before. In the past few months, my life
seemed to have shifted subtly.

Was it to do with Sarah, with the rue de Saintonge? Or was it just a belated coming-of-age? I could not tell. I only knew that I felt as if I had emerged from a long-lasting, mellow, protective fog. Now my senses were sharpened, keen. There was no fog. There was nothing mellow. There were only facts. Finding this man. Telling him his mother had never been forgotten by the Tézacs, by the Dufaures.

I was impatient to see him. He was right here, in this very town, maybe walking down the bustling via Fillungo now, at this precise moment. Somehow, as I lay in my little room, the sounds of voices and laughter rising from the narrow street through the open window, accompanied by the occasional roar of a Vespa or the sharp clang of a bicycle bell, I felt close to Sarah, closer than I had ever been before, because I was about to meet her son, her flesh, her blood. This was the closest I would ever get to the little girl with the yellow star.

Just reach out your hand, pick up that phone, and call him. Simple. Easy. Yet I was incapable of doing it. I gazed at the obsolete black telephone, helpless, and sighed in despair and irritation. I lay back, feeling silly, almost ashamed. I realized I was so obsessed by Sarah's son that I hadn't even taken Lucca in, its charm, its beauty. I had trudged through it like a sleepwalker, trailing behind Zoë, who seemed to glide along the intricacy of the old winding streets as if she had always lived here. I had seen nothing of Lucca. Nothing mattered to me except William Rainsferd. And I wasn't even capable of calling him.

Zoë came in, sat on the edge of the bed.

"You all right?" she asked.

"I had a good rest," I answered.

She scrutinized me, her hazel eyes roving over my face.

"I think you should rest a little longer, Mom."

I frowned.

"Do I look that tired?"

She nodded.

"Just rest, Mom. Giovanna gave me something to eat. You don't have to worry about me. Everything is under control."

I couldn't help smiling at her seriousness. When she got to the door, she turned around.

"Mom . . ."

"Yes, sweetheart?"

"Does Papa know we're here?"

I hadn't told Bertrand yet about bringing Zoë to Lucca. No doubt he would explode when he found out.

"No, he doesn't, darling."

She fingered the door handle.

"Did you and Papa have a fight?"

No use lying to those clear, solemn eyes.

"Yes, we did, honey. Papa doesn't agree with me trying to find out more about Sarah. He wouldn't be happy if he knew."

"Grand-père knows."

I sat up, startled.

"You spoke to your grandfather about all this?"

She nodded.

"Yes. He really cares, you know, about Sarah. I called him from Long Island and told him you and I were coming here to meet her son. I knew you were going to call him at some point, but I was so excited, I had to tell him."

"And what did he say?" I asked, amazed at my daughter's forthrightness.

"He said we were right to come here. And he was going to tell Papa that if ever Papa made a fuss. He said you were a wonderful person."

"Edouard said that?"

"He did."

I shook my head, both baffled and touched.

"Grand-père said something else. He said you had to take it easy. He said I had to make sure you didn't get too tired."

So Edouard knew. He knew I was pregnant. He had spoken to Bertrand. There had probably been a long talk between father and son. And Bertrand was now aware of everything that had happened in the rue de Saintonge apartment in the summer of 1942.

Zoë's voice dragged me away from Edouard.

"Why don't you just call William, Mom? Make an appointment?"

I sat up on the bed.

"You're right, honey."

I took the slip of paper with William's number in Mara's handwriting and dialed it on the old-fashioned phone. My heart thumped away. This was surreal, I thought. Here I was, phoning Sarah's son.

I heard a couple of irregular rings, then the whir of an answering machine. A woman's voice in rapid Italian. I hung up quickly, feeling foolish.

"Now that was dumb," remarked Zoë. "Never hang up on a machine. You've told me that a thousand times."

I redialed, smiling at her grown-up annoyance with me. This time I waited for the beep. And when I spoke, it all came out beautifully, like something I'd rehearsed for days.

"Good afternoon, this is Julia Jarmond, I'm calling on behalf of Mrs. Mara Rainsferd. My daughter and I are in Lucca, staying at Casa Giovanna on the via Fillungo. We're here for a couple of days. Hope to hear from you. Thanks, bye."

I replaced the receiver in its black cradle, both relieved and disappointed.

"Good," said Zoë. "Now you go on with your rest. I'll see you later."

She planted a kiss on my forehead and left the room.

W E HAD DINNER IN a small, amusing restaurant behind the hotel, near the *anfiteatro*, a large circle of ancient houses that used to host medieval games centuries ago. I felt restored after my rest and enjoyed the colorful parade of tourists, Lucchesans, street vendors, children, pigeons. Italians loved children, I discovered. Zoë was called *principessa* by waiters, shopkeepers, fawned upon, beamed upon, her ears tweaked, her nose pinched, her hair stroked. It made me nervous at first, but she reveled in it, trying out her rudimentary Italian with ardor: *"Sono francese e americana, mi chiama Zoë."* The heat had abated, leaving cool drifts in its wake. However, I knew it would be hot and stuffy in our little rooms, high above the street. Italians, like the French, weren't keen on air-conditioning. I wouldn't have minded the icy blast of a machine tonight.

When we got back to Casa Giovanna, dazed with jet lag, there was a note pinned on our door. *"Per favore telefonare* William Rainsferd."

I stood, thunderstruck. Zoë whooped.

"Now?" I said.

"Well, it's only quarter to nine," Zoë said.

"OK," I answered, opening the door with trembling fingers. The black receiver stuck to my ear, I dialed his number for the third time that day. Answering machine, I mouthed to Zoë. Talk, she mouthed back. After the beep, I mumbled my name, hesitated, was about to hang up when a masculine voice said: "Hello?"

An American accent. It was him.

"Hi," I said, "this is Julia Jarmond."

"Hi," he said, "I'm in the middle of dinner."

"Oh, I'm sorry . . ."

"No problem. You want to meet up tomorrow before lunch?"

"Sure," I said.

"There's a nice café up on the walls, just beyond the Palazzo Mansi. We could meet there at noon?"

"Fine," I said. "Um . . . how do we find each other?"

He laughed.

"Don't worry. Lucca is a tiny place. I'll find you."

A pause.

"Good-bye," he said, and hung up.

THE NEXT MORNING, THE pain was back in my stomach. Nothing powerful, but it bothered me with a discreet persistence. I decided to ignore it. If it was still there after lunch, I'd ask Giovanna for a doctor. As we walked to the café, I wondered how I was going to broach the subject with William. I had put off thinking about it, and I realized now that I shouldn't have. I was going to stir sad, painful memories. Maybe he did not want to talk about his mother at all. Maybe it was something he had put behind him. He had his life here, far from Roxbury, far from the rue de Saintonge. A peaceful, bucolic life. And here I was bringing back the past. The dead.

Zoë and I discovered that one could actually walk on the thick medieval walls that circled the small city. They were high and wide, with a large path on their crest, hemmed in by a dense row of chestnut trees. We mingled with the incessant stream of joggers, walkers, cyclists, roller skaters, mothers with children, old men talking loudly, teenagers on scooters, tourists.

The café was a little farther on, shaded by leafy trees. I drew nearer with Zoë, feeling strangely light-headed, almost numb. The terrace was empty save for a middle-aged couple having an ice cream and some German tourists poring over a map. I lowered my hat over my eyes, smoothed out my crumpled skirt.

When he said my name, I was busy reading the menu to Zoë.

"Julia Jarmond."

I looked up to a tall, thickset man in his mid-forties. He sat down opposite Zoë and me.

"Hi," said Zoë.

I found I could not speak. I could only stare at him. His hair was dark blond, swept with gray. Receding hairline. Square jaw. A beautiful beak of a nose.

"Hi," he said to Zoë. "Have the tiramisu. You'll love it."

Then he lifted his dark glasses, gliding them back over his forehead to rest on top of his skull. His mother's eyes. Turquoise and slanted. He smiled.

"So you're a journalist, I gather? Based in Paris? Looked you up on the Internet."

I coughed, fingering my watch nervously.

"I looked you up as well, you know. That was a fabulous book, your last one, *Tuscan Feasts*."

William Rainsferd sighed and patted his stomach.

"Ah, that book contributed nicely to an extra ten pounds I've never been able to get rid of."

I smiled brightly. It was going to be difficult to switch from this pleasant, easy conversation to what I knew lay ahead. Zoë looked at me purposefully.

"It's very nice of you to come here and meet us . . . I appreciate it. . . ."

My voice sounded lame, lost.

"No problem." He grinned, clicking his fingers at the waiter.

We ordered tiramisu and a Coke for Zoë, and two cappuccinos.

"Your first time in Lucca?" he asked.

I nodded. The waiter hovered over us. William Rainsferd spoke to him in rapid, smooth Italian. They both laughed.

"I come to this café often," he explained. "I like hanging out here. Even on a hot day like this."

Zoë tried out her tiramisu, her spoon clicking against the small glass bowl. A sudden silence fell upon us.

"What can I do to help?" he asked brightly. "Mara mentioned something about my mother."

I praised Mara inwardly. She had made things easier, it seemed.

"I didn't know your mother had passed away," I said. "I'm sorry."

"That's all right." He shrugged, dropping a lump of sugar into his coffee. "Happened a long time ago. I was a kid. Did you know her? You look a little young for that."

I shook my head.

"No, I never met your mother. I happen to be moving into the apartment she lived in during the war. Rue de Saintonge, in Paris. And I know people who were close to her. That's why I'm here. That's why I came to see you."

He put his coffee cup down and looked at me quietly. The clear eyes were reflective, calm.

Under the table, Zoë placed a sticky hand on my bare knee. I watched a couple of cyclists wheel past. The heat was pounding down on us again. I took a deep breath.

"I'm not quite sure how to begin," I faltered. "And I know it must be difficult for you to have to think about this again, but I felt I had to. My in-laws, the Tézacs, met your mother in the rue de Saintonge, in 1942."

I thought the name Tézac might ring a bell, but he remained motionless. Rue de Saintonge did not seem to, either.

"After what happened, I mean, the tragic events of July '42, and the death of your uncle, I just wanted to assure you that the Tézac family has never been able to forget your mother. My father-in-law, especially, thinks of her every day."

There was a silence. William Rainsferd's eyes seem to shrink.

"I'm sorry," I said quickly, "I knew all this would be painful for you, I'm sorry."

When he finally spoke his voice sounded odd, almost smothered.

"What do you mean by tragic events?"

"Well, the Vél' d'Hiv' roundup," I stammered. "Jewish families, rounded up in Paris, in July '42 . . ."

"Go on," he said.

"And the camps. . . . The families sent to Auschwitz from Drancy . . ."

William Rainsferd spread his palms wide, shook his head.

"I'm sorry, but I don't see what this has to do with my mother."

Zoë and I exchanged uneasy glances.

A long minute dragged by. I felt acutely uncomfortable.

"You mentioned the death of an uncle?" he said at last.

"Yes . . . Michel. Your mother's little brother. In the rue de Saintonge."

Silence.

"Michel?" He seemed puzzled. "My mother never had a brother called Michel. And I've never heard of the rue de Saintonge. You know, I don't think we're talking about the same person."

"But your mother's name was Sarah, right?" I mumbled, confused.

He nodded.

"Yes, that's right. Sarah Dufaure."

"Yes, Sarah Dufaure, that's her," I said eagerly. "Or rather, Sarah Starzynski."

I expected his eyes to light up.

"Excuse me?" he said, eyebrows slanting downward. "Sarah what?"

"Starzynski. Your mother's maiden name."

William Rainsferd stared at me, lifting his chin.

"My mother's maiden name was Dufaure."

A warning bell went off in my head. Something was wrong. He did not know.

There was still time to leave, time to take off before I shattered the peace in this man's life to pieces.

I pasted a blithe smile on my face, murmured something about a mistake, and scraped my chair back a couple of inches, gently urging Zoë to leave her dessert. I wouldn't be wasting his time any longer, I was most sorry. I rose from my seat. He did as well.

"I think you've got the wrong Sarah," he said, smiling. "It doesn't matter, enjoy your stay in Lucca. It was nice meeting you, anyway."

Before I could utter a word, Zoë put her hand into my bag and handed him something.

William Rainsferd looked down at the photograph of the little girl with the yellow star.

"Is this your mother?" Zoë asked with a small voice.

It seemed that everything had gone quiet around us. No noise came from the busy path. Even the birds seemed to have stopped chirping. There was only the heat. And silence.

"Jesus," he said.

And then he sat down again, heavily.

T HE PHOTOGRAPH LAY FLAT between us on the table. William
Rainsferd looked from it to me, again and again. He read the
caption on the back several times, with an incredulous, startled expression.

"This looks exactly like my mother as a child," he said, finally. "That
I can't deny."

Zoë and I remained silent.

"I don't understand. This can't be. This is not possible."

He rubbed his hands together nervously. I noticed he wore a silver
wedding band. He had long, slim fingers.

"The star . . ." He kept shaking his head. "That star on her
chest . . ."

Was it possible this man did not know the truth about his mother's
past? Her religion? Was it possible that Sarah had not ever told the
Rainsferds?

As I watched his puzzled face, his anxiety, I felt I knew. No, she
had not told them. She had not revealed her childhood, her origins,
her religion. She had made a clean break with her terrible past.

I wanted to be far away. Far from this town, this country, this man's
incomprehension. How could I have been so blind? How could I have
not seen this coming? Not once had I ever thought that Sarah could
have kept all this secret. Her suffering had been too great. That was
why she had never written to the Dufaures. That was why she had

never told her son about who she really was. In America, she had wanted to start a new life.

And here I was, a stranger, revealing the stark truth to this man, a clumsy bearer of ill tidings.

William Rainsferd pushed the photograph back toward me, his mouth taut.

"What have you come here for?" he whispered.

My throat felt dry.

"To tell me my mother was called something else? That she was involved in a tragedy? Is this why you are here?"

I could sense my legs trembling under the table. This was not what I had imagined. I had imagined pain, sorrow, but not this. Not his anger.

"I thought you knew," I ventured. "I came because my family remembers what she went through, back in '42. That's why I'm here."

He shook his head again, raked agitated fingers through his hair. His dark glasses clattered to the table.

"No," he breathed. "No. No, no. This is crazy. My mother was French. She was called Dufaure. She was born in Orléans. She lost her parents during the war. She had no brothers. She had no family. She never lived in Paris, in that rue de Saintonge. This little Jewish girl cannot be her. You've got this all wrong."

"Please," I said, gently, "let me explain, let me tell you the whole story—"

He pushed his palms up to me, as if he meant to shove me away.

"I don't want to know. Keep the 'whole story' to yourself."

I felt the familiar ache tug at my insides, plucking at my womb with a deft gnaw.

"Please," I said, feebly. "Please listen to me."

William Rainsferd was on his feet, a quick, supple gesture for such a big man. He looked down at me, his face dark.

"I'm going to be very clear. I don't want to see you again. I don't want to talk about this again. Please don't call me."

And he was gone.

Zoë and I stared after him. All this, for nothing. This whole trip, all these efforts, for this. For this dead end. I could not believe Sarah's story could end here, so quickly. It could not just dry out.

We sat in silence for a long moment. Then, shivering despite the heat, I paid the bill. Zoë did not say a word. She seemed stunned.

I got up, weariness hindering every move. What now? Where to go? Back to Paris? Back to Charla's?

I trudged on, my feet as heavy as lead. I could hear Zoë's voice calling out to me, but I did not want to turn around. I wanted to get back to the hotel, fast. To think. To get going. To call my sister. And Edouard. And Gaspard.

Zoë's voice was loud now, anxious. What did she want? Why was she whining? I noticed passersby staring at me. I swiveled around to my daughter, exasperated, telling her to hurry up.

She rushed to my side, grabbed my hand. Her face was pale.

"Mom . . . ," she whispered, her voice strained thin.

"What? What is it?" I snapped.

She pointed at my legs. She started to whimper, like a puppy.

I glanced down. My white skirt was soaked with blood. I looked back to my seat, imprinted with a crimson half moon. Thick red rivulets trickled down my thighs.

"Are you hurt, Mom?" choked Zoë.

I clutched my stomach.

"The baby," I said, aghast.

Zoë stared at me.

"The baby?" she screamed, her fingers biting into my arm. "Mom, what baby? What are you talking about?"

Her pointed face loomed away from me. My legs buckled. I landed chin first on the hot, dry path.

Then silence. And darkness.

I OPENED MY EYES to Zoë's face, a few inches from mine. I could smell the unmistakable scent of a hospital around me. A small, green room. An IV in my forearm. A woman wearing a white blouse scribbling something on a chart.

"Mom . . . ," whispered Zoë, squeezing my hand. "Mom, everything is OK. Don't worry."

The young woman came to my side, smiled and patted Zoë's head.

"You will be all right, Signora," she said, in surprisingly good English. "You lost blood, a lot, but you are fine now."

My voice came out like a groan.

"And the baby?"

"The baby is fine. We did a scan. There was problem with placenta. You need to rest now. No getting up for a while."

She left the room, closing the door quietly behind her.

"You scared the shit out of me," said Zoë. "And I can say 'shit' today. I don't think you'll scold me."

I pulled her close, hugging her as hard as I could despite the IV.

"Mom, why didn't you tell me about the baby?"

"I was going to, sweetie."

She looked up at me.

"Is the baby why you and Papa are having problems?"

"Yes."

"You want the baby and Papa doesn't, right?"

"Something like that."

She stroked my hand gently.

"Papa is on his way."

"Oh, God," I said.

Bertrand here. Bertrand in the aftermath of all this.

"I phoned him," said Zoë. "He'll be here in a couple of hours."

Tears welled up in my eyes, slowly trickled down my cheeks.

"Mom, don't cry," pleaded Zoë, frantically wiping my face with her hands. "It's OK, everything is OK now."

I smiled wearily, nodding my head to reassure her. But my world felt hollow, empty. I kept thinking of William Rainsferd walking away. *"I don't want to see you again. I don't want to talk about this again. Please don't call me."* His shoulders, rounded, stooped. The tightness of his mouth.

The days, weeks, months to come stretched ahead, bleak and gray. Never had I felt so despondent, so lost. The core of me had been nibbled away. What was left for me? A baby my soon to be ex-husband did not want and that I'd have to raise on my own. A daughter who would shortly become a teenager, and who might no longer remain the marvelous little girl she was now. What was there to look forward to, all of a sudden?

Bertrand arrived, calm, efficient, tender. I put myself in his hands, listened to him talking to the doctor, watching him reassure Zoë with an occasional, warm glance. He took care of all the details. I was to stay here till the bleeding stopped completely. Then I was to fly back to Paris and take it easy until fall, till my fifth month. Bertrand did not mention Sarah once. He did not ask a single question. I retreated into a comfortable silence. I did not want to talk about Sarah.

I began to feel like a little old lady, shipped here and there, like Mamé was shipped here and there, within the familiar boundaries of her "home," receiving the same placid smiles, the same stale benevolence. It was easy, letting someone else control your life. I had nothing much to fight for, anyway. Except this child.

The child that Bertrand did not once mention either.

WHEN WE LANDED IN Paris a few weeks later, it felt like an entire
year had gone by. I still felt tired and sad. I thought of
William Rainsferd every day. Several times, I reached out for the
phone, or pen and paper, meaning to talk to him, to write, to explain,
to say something, to say sorry, but I never dared.

I let the days slip by, the summer move into fall. I lay on my bed
and read, wrote my articles on my laptop, spoke to Joshua, Bamber,
Alessandra, to my family and friends on the telephone. I worked from
my bedroom. It had all seemed complicated at first, but it had worked
out. My friends Isabelle, Holly, and Susannah took turns coming and
making me lunch. Once a week, one of my sisters-in-law would go to
the nearby Inno or Franprix for groceries with Zoë. Plump, sensual
Cécile would make fluffy crêpes oozing with butter, and aesthetic,
angular Laure would create exotic low-calorie salads that were surprisingly savory. My mother-in-law came less often but sent her
cleaning lady, the dynamic and odorous Madame Leclère, who vacu-
umed with such terrifying energy it gave me contractions. My parents
came to stay for a week in their favorite little hotel on the rue Delambre, ecstatic at the idea of becoming grandparents again.

Edouard came to visit every Friday, with a bouquet of pink roses.
He would sit in the armchair next to the bed, and again and again, he
would ask me to describe the conversation that took place between
William and me in Lucca. He would shake his head and sigh. He

said, over and over, that he should have anticipated William's reaction, how was it that neither himself, nor I, could possibly have imagined that William never knew, that Sarah had never breathed a word?

"Can we not call him?" he would say, his eyes hopeful. "Can I not telephone him and explain?" Then he would look at me and mumble, "No, of course, I can't do that, how stupid of me. How ridiculous of me."

I asked my doctor if I could host a small gathering, lying down on my living-room sofa. She accepted and made me promise not to carry anything heavy and to remain horizontal, à la Récamier. One evening in late summer, Gaspard and Nicolas Dufaure came to meet Edouard. Nathalie Dufaure was there as well. And I had invited Guillaume. It was a moving, magical moment. Three elderly men who had an unforgettable little girl in common. I watched them pore over the old photos of Sarah, the letters. Gaspard and Nicolas asked us about William, Nathalie listened, helping Zoë pass around drinks and food.

Nicolas, a slightly younger version of Gaspard, with the same round face and wispy white hair, spoke of his particular relationship with Sarah, how he used to tease her because her silence pained him so, and how any reaction, albeit a shrug, an insult, or a kick, was a triumph because she had for one instant emerged from her secrecy, her isolation. He told us about the first time she had bathed in the sea, at Trouville, in the beginning of the fifties. She had stared out at the ocean in absolute wonder, and then she had stretched out her arms, whooped with delight, and rushed to the water on her nimble, skinny legs, and dashed into the cool, blue waves with screeches of joy. And they had followed her, hollering just as loud, entranced by a new Sarah they had never seen.

"She was beautiful," Nicolas recalled, "a beautiful eighteen-year-old glowing with life and energy, and I felt that day for the first time that there was happiness within her, that there was hope for her ahead."

Two years later, I thought, Sarah was out of the Dufaures' lives, forever, carrying her secret past to America. And twenty years later she was dead. What had those twenty years in America been like, I mused. Her marriage, the birth of her son. Had she been happy in Roxbury? Only William had those answers, I thought. Only William could tell us. My eyes met Edouard's, and I could tell he was thinking the same thing.

I heard Bertrand's key in the lock and my husband appeared, tanned, handsome, exuding Habit Rouge, smiling breezily, shaking hands smoothly, and I couldn't help remembering the lyrics of that Carly Simon song that reminded Charla of Bertrand: "You walked into the party like you were walking onto a yacht."

BERTRAND HAD DECIDED TO postpone the move to the rue de Saintonge because of the problems with my pregnancy. In this odd, new life I still couldn't get used to, he was physically present in a friendly, useful way, but not there spiritually. He traveled more than usual, came home late, left early. We still shared a bed, but it was no longer a marital bed. The Berlin wall had sprouted in its middle.

Zoë seemed to take all this in her stride. She often talked about the baby, how much it meant to her, how excited she was. She had been shopping with my mother during my parents' stay, and they had gone crazy at Bonpoint, the outrageously expensive and exquisite baby-wear boutique on the rue de l'Université.

Most people reacted like my daughter, my parents and sister, and my in-laws and Mamé: they were thrilled by the upcoming birth. Even Joshua, infamous for his scorn toward babies and sick leaves, seemed interested. "I didn't know one could have kids at middle age," he had said snidely. No one ever mentioned the crisis my marriage was going through. No one seemed to notice it. Did they all secretly believe that Bertrand, once the child was born, would come to his senses? That he would welcome this child with open arms?

I realized that both Bertrand and I had locked each other into a state of numbness, of not talking, of not telling. We were both waiting for the baby to be born. Then we'd see. Then we'd have to move on. Then decisions would have to be made.

One morning, I felt the baby start to move deep within me, to give those first tiny kicks one mistakes for gas. I wanted the baby out of me, into my arms. I hated this state of silent lethargy, this waiting. I felt trapped. I wanted to zoom to winter, to early next year, to the birth.

I hated the end of summer that lingered on, the fading heat, the dust, the stealthy minutes that oozed by with the laziness of molasses. I hated the French word for the beginning of September, back to school, and the new start after summer: *la rentrée,* repeated over and over again on the radio, on television, in the newspapers. I hated people asking me what the baby was going to be called. The amniocentesis had revealed its sex, but I had not wanted to be told. The baby did not have a name, yet. Which did not mean I wasn't ready for it.

I crossed out every day on my calendar. September merged into October. My stomach rounded out nicely. I could get up now, go back to the office, pick Zoë up at school, go to the movies with Isabelle, meet Guillaume at the Select for lunch.

But although my days felt fuller, busier, the emptiness and the ache remained.

William Rainsferd. His face. His eyes. His expression when he had looked down at the little girl with the star. *"Jesus."* His voice when he had said that.

What was his life like now? Had he erased everything from his mind the moment he turned his back on Zoë and me? Had he already forgotten once he had reached home?

Or was it different? Was it hell for him because he could not stop thinking about what I had said, because my revelations had changed his entire life? His mother had become a stranger. Somebody with a past he knew nothing about.

I wondered whether he had said anything to his wife, his daughters. Anything about an American woman turning up in Lucca with a kid, showing him a photo, telling him his mother was a Jew, that she had been rounded up during the war, that she had suffered, lost a brother, parents he'd never heard of.

I wondered if he had researched information concerning the Vel' d'Hiv', if he had read articles, books about what took place in July 1942 in the heart of Paris.

I wondered if he lay awake in bed at night and thought of his mother, of her past, of the truth of it, of what remained secret, unspoken, shrouded in darkness.

THE RUE DE SAINTONGE apartment was nearly ready. Bertrand had arranged for Zoë and me to move in just after the baby's birth, in February. It looked beautiful, different. His team had done a wonderful job. It no longer bore Mamé's imprint, and I imagined it was a far cry from what Sarah had known.

But as I wandered through the freshly painted, empty rooms, the new kitchen, my private office, I asked myself if I could bear living here. Living where Sarah's little brother had died. The secret cupboard did not exist anymore, it had been destroyed when two rooms had been made into one, but somehow that changed nothing for me.

This is where it had happened. And I could not erase that from my mind. I had not told my daughter about the tragedy that had taken place here. But she sensed it, in her particular, emotional way.

On a damp November morning, I went to the apartment to start working on curtains, wallpaper, carpeting. Isabelle had been particularly helpful and had escorted me around shops and department stores. To Zoë's delight, I had decided to ignore the quiet, placid tones I had resorted to in the past, and make a wild go at new, bold colors. Bertrand had waved a careless hand: "You and Zoë make the decisions, it's your home, after all." Zoë had decided on lime green and pale purple for her bedroom. It was so reminiscent of Charla's taste that I had to smile.

A cluster of catalogues awaited me on the bare, polished floorboards. I was leafing through them studiously when my cell phone rang. I recognized the number: Mamé's nursing home. Mamé had been tired lately, irritable, sometimes unbearable. It was difficult to make her smile, even Zoë had a hard time doing so. She was impatient with everybody. Going to see her recently had almost become a chore.

"Miss Jarmond? This is Véronique, at the nursing home. I'm afraid I don't have good news. Madame Tézac is not well, she has had a stroke."

I sat up straight, shock reeling through me.

"A stroke?"

"She is a bit better, with Docteur Roche now, but you must come. We have reached your father-in-law. But we cannot get hold of your husband."

I hung up feeling flustered, panicky. Outside, I heard rain pattering against the windowpanes. Where was Bertrand? I dialed his number and got his voice mail. At his office near the Madeleine, nobody seemed to know where he was, not even Antoine. I told Antoine I was at the rue de Saintonge, and could he have Bertrand call me ASAP. I said it was very urgent.

"*Mon dieu,* the baby?" he stammered.

"No, Antoine, not the *bébé,* the *grand-mère,*" I replied and hung up.

I glanced outside. The rain was falling thickly now, a gray, glistening curtain. I'd get wet. Too bad, I thought. Who cared. Mamé. Wonderful, darling Mamé. My Mamé. No, Mamé could not possibly go now, I needed her. This was too soon, I was unprepared. But how could I ever be prepared for her death, I thought. I looked around me, at the living room, remembering that this had been the very place where I had met her for the first time. And once again I felt overwhelmed by the weight of all the events that had taken place here, and that seemed to be coming back to haunt me.

I decided to call Cécile and Laure to make sure they knew and were on their way. Laure sounded businesslike and curt, she was already in her car. She'd see me there, she said. Cécile appeared more emotional, fragile, a hint of tears in her voice.

"Oh, Julia, I can't bear the idea of Mamé . . . You know . . . It's too awful. . . ."

I told her I couldn't get hold of Bertrand. She sounded surprised.

"But I just spoke to him," she said.

"Did you reach him on his cell phone?"

"No," she replied, her voice hesitant.

"At the office, then?"

"He's coming to pick me up any minute. He's taking me to the nursing home."

"I wasn't able to contact him."

"Oh?" she said carefully. "I see."

Then I got it. I felt anger surge through me.

"He was at Amélie's, right?"

"Amélie's?" she repeated blandly.

I stamped impatiently.

"Oh, come on, Cécile. You know exactly who I'm talking about."

"The buzzer's going, that's Bertrand," she breathed, rushed.

And she hung up. I stood in the middle of the empty room, cell phone clenched in my hand like a weapon. I pressed my forehead against the coolness of the windowpane. I wanted to hit Bertrand. It was no longer his never-ending affair with Amélie that got to me. It was the fact his sisters had that woman's number and knew where to reach him in case of an emergency like this one. And I did not. It was the fact that even if our marriage was dying, he still did not have the courage to tell me he was still seeing this woman. As usual, I was the last to know. The eternal, *vaudevillesque* wronged spouse.

I stood there for a long time, motionless, feeling the baby kick within me. I did not know whether to laugh or to cry.

Did I still care for Bertrand, was this why it still hurt? Or was it just a question of wounded pride? Amélie and her Parisian glamour and perfection, her daringly modern apartment overlooking the Trocadéro, her well-mannered children—*"Bonjour, Madame"*—and her powerful perfume that lingered in Bertrand's hair and his clothes. If he loved her, and no longer me, why was he afraid of telling me? Was he afraid of hurting me? Hurting Zoë? What made him so frightened? When would he realize that it wasn't his infidelity I couldn't bear, but his cowardice?

I went to the kitchen. My mouth felt parched. I turned on the tap and drank directly from the faucet, my cumbersome belly brushing against the sink. I peered out again. The rain seemed to have abated. I slipped my raincoat on, grabbed my purse, and headed to the door.

Somebody knocked, three short blows.

Bertrand, I thought, grimly. Antoine or Cécile had probably told him to call or come.

I imagined Cécile waiting in the car below. Her embarrassment. The nervous, tight silence that would ensue as soon as I would get into the Audi.

Well, I'd show them. I'd tell them. I wasn't going to play timid, nice French wife. I was going to ask Bertrand to tell me the truth from now on.

I flung the door open.

But the man waiting for me on the threshold was not Bertrand.

I recognized the height, the broad shoulders immediately. Ash blond hair darkened by the rain plastered back over his skull.

William Rainsferd.

I stepped back, startled.

"Is this a bad moment?" he said.

"No," I managed.

What on earth was he doing here? What did he want?

We stared at each other. Something in his face had changed since the last time I'd seen him. He seemed gaunt, haunted. No longer the easygoing gourmet with a tan.

"I need to talk to you," he said. "It's urgent. I'm sorry, I couldn't find your number. So I came here. You weren't in last night, so I thought I'd come back this morning."

"How did you get this address?" I asked, confused. "It's not listed yet, we haven't moved in yet."

He took an envelope out of the pocket of his jacket.

"The address was in here. The same street you mentioned in Lucca. Rue de Saintonge."

I shook my head.

"I don't get it."

He handed the envelope to me. It was old, torn at the corners. There was nothing written on it.

"Open it," he said.

I pulled out a slim, tattered notebook, a faded drawing and a long, brass key that fell to the floor with a clank. He bent to pick it up, nestling it in the palm of his hand for me to see.

"What is all this?" I asked warily.

"When you left Lucca, I was in a state of shock. I could not get that photograph out of my mind. I could not stop thinking about it."

"Yes," I said, my heart beating fast.

"I flew to Roxbury, to see my dad. He's very ill, as I think you know. Dying of cancer. He can't speak anymore. I looked around, I found this envelope in his desk. He had kept it, after all these years. He had never shown it to me."

"Why are you here?" I whispered.

There was pain in his eyes, pain and fear.

"Because I need you to tell me what happened. What happened to my mother as a child. I need to know everything. You're the only person who can help me."

I looked down at the key in his hand. Then I glanced at the drawing. An awkward sketch of a little boy with fair, curly hair. He seemed to be sitting in a small cupboard, with a book on his knee and a toy bear next to him. On the back, a faded scrawl, "Michel, 26, rue de Saintonge." I leafed through the notebook. No dates. Short sentences scribbled like a poem, in French, difficult to make out. A few words jumped out at me: *"le camp," "la clef," "ne jamais oublier," "mourir."*

"Did you read this?" I asked.

"I tried. My French is bad. I can only understand parts of it."

The phone in my pocket rang, startling us. I fumbled for it. It was Edouard.

"Where are you, Julia?" he asked, gently. "She's not well. She wants you."

"I'm coming," I replied.

William Rainsferd looked down at me.

"You have to go?"

"Yes. A family emergency. My husband's grandmother. She's had a stroke."

"I'm sorry."

He hesitated, then put a hand on my shoulder.

"When can I see you? Talk to you?"

I opened the front door, turned back to him, looked down at his hand on my shoulder. It was strange, moving, to see him on the threshold of that apartment, the very place that had caused his mother so much pain, so much sorrow, and to think he did not yet know, he did not yet know what had happened here, to his family, his grandparents, his uncle.

"You're coming with me," I said. "There's someone I want you to meet."

MAMÉ'S TIRED, WITHERED FACE. She seemed asleep. I spoke to her, but I wasn't sure she heard me. Then I felt her fingers encircle my wrist. She held on tight. She knew I was there.

Behind me, the Tézac family stood around the bed. Bertrand. His mother, Colette. Edouard. Laure and Cécile. And behind them, hesitating in the hall, stood William Rainsferd. Bertrand had glanced at him once or twice, puzzled. He probably thought he was my new boyfriend. At any other time than this, I would have laughed. Edouard had looked at him several times, curious, eyes screwed up, then back at me with insistence.

It was later, when we were filing out of the nursing home, that I took my father-in-law's arm. We had just been told by Docteur Roche that Mamé's condition had stabilized. But she was weak. There was no telling what would happen next. We had to prepare ourselves, he had said. We had to convince each other this was probably the end.

"I'm so sad and sorry, Edouard," I murmured.

He stroked my cheek.

"My mother loves you, Julia. She loves you dearly."

Bertrand appeared, his face glum. I glanced at him, briefly thinking of Amélie, toying with the idea of saying something that would hurt, that would sting, and finally letting go. After all, there would be time ahead to discuss it. It did not matter right now. Only Mamé mattered now, and the tall silhouette waiting for me in the hall.

"Julia," said Edouard, looking back over his shoulder, "who is that man?"

"Sarah's son."

Awed, Edouard gazed at the tall figure for a couple of minutes.

"Did you phone him?"

"No. He recently discovered some papers that his father had hidden all this time. Something Sarah wrote. He's here because he wants to know the whole story. He came today."

"I would like to speak to him," said Edouard.

I went to fetch William, I told him my father-in-law wanted to meet him. He followed me, dwarfing Bertrand and Edouard, Colette, her daughters.

Edouard Tézac looked up at him. His face was calm, composed, but there was a wetness in his eyes.

He held out his hand. William took it. It was a powerful, silent moment. No one spoke.

"Sarah Starzynski's son," murmured Edouard.

I shot a glance at Colette, Cécile, and Laure looking on in polite, curious incomprehension. They could not understand what was going on. Only Bertrand understood, only he knew the whole story, although he had never discussed it with me since the evening he had discovered the red "Sarah" file. He had not even brought it up after having met the Dufaures in our apartment, a couple of months before.

Edouard cleared his throat. Their hands were still clasped. He spoke in English. Decent English, with a strong French accent.

"I am Edouard Tézac. This is a difficult time to meet you. My mother is dying."

"Yes, I'm sorry," said William.

"Julia will tell you the whole story. But your mother, Sarah—"

Edouard paused. His voice broke. His wife and daughters glanced at him, surprised.

"What is all this about?" murmured Colette, concerned. "Who is Sarah?"

"This is about something that happened sixty years ago," said Edouard, fighting to control his voice.

I fought an urge to reach out and slip an arm around his shoulder. Edouard took a deep breath and some color came back into his face. He smiled up at William, a small, timid smile I had not seen him use before.

"I will never forget your mother. Never."

His face twitched, the smile vanished, and I saw the pain, the sadness make him breathe once again with difficulty, like he had on the day he'd told me.

The silence grew heavy, unbearable, the women looked on, puzzled.

"I am most relieved to be able to tell you this today, all these years later."

William Rainsferd nodded.

"Thank you, sir," he said, his voice low. His face was pale, too, I noticed. "I don't know much, I came here to understand. I believe my mother suffered. And I need to know why."

"We did what we could for her," said Edouard. "That I can promise you. Julia will tell you. She will explain. She will tell you your mother's story. She will tell you what my father did for your mother. Good-bye."

He drew back, an old man all of a sudden, shrunken and wan. Bertrand's eyes watching him, curious, detached. He had probably never seen his father so moved. I wonder what it did to him, what it meant to him.

Edouard walked away, followed by his wife, his daughters, bombarding him with questions. His son trailed after them, hands in pockets, silent. I wondered if Edouard was going to tell Colette and his daughters the truth. Most likely, I thought. And I imagined their shock.

WILLIAM RAINSFERD AND I stood alone in the hall of the nursing
home. Outside, on the rue de Courcelles, it was still raining.

"How about some coffee?" he said.

He had a beautiful smile.

We walked under the drizzle to the nearest café. We sat down, ordered two espressos. For a moment, we sat there in silence.

Then he asked: "Are you close to the old lady?"

"Yes," I said. "Very close."

"I see you're expecting a baby?"

I patted my plump stomach. "Due in February."

At last he said, slowly, "Tell me my mother's story."

"This isn't going to be easy," I said.

"Yes. But I need to hear it. Please, Julia."

Slowly, I began to talk, in a low hushed voice, only glancing up at
him from time to time. As I spoke, my thoughts went to Edouard,
probably sitting in his elegant, salmon-colored living room on the rue
de l'Université, telling the exact same story to his wife, his daughters,
his son. The roundup. The Vel' d'Hiv'. The camp. The escape. The little
girl who came back. The dead child in the cupboard. Two families,
linked by death, and a secret. Two families linked by sorrow. Part of
me wanted this man to know the entire truth. Another yearned to protect him, to shield him from blunt reality. From the awful image of the
little girl and her suffering. Her pain, her loss. His pain, his loss. The

more I talked, the more details I gave, the more questions I answered, the more I felt my words enter him like blades and wound him.

When I finished, I looked up at him. His face and lips were pale. He took out the notebook from the envelope and gave it to me in silence. The brass key lay on the table between us.

I held the notebook between my hands, looking back at him. His eyes egged me on.

I opened the book. I read the first sentence to myself. Then I read out loud, translating the French directly into our mother tongue. It was a slow process; the writing, a thin, slanted scribble, was hard to read.

> *Where are you, my little Michel? My beautiful Michel.*
> *Where are you now?*
> *Would you remember me?*
> *Michel.*
> *Me, Sarah, your sister.*
> *The one who never came back. The one who left you in the cup-*
>   *board. The one who thought you'd be safe.*
>
> *Michel.*
> *The years have gone by and I still have the key.*
> *The key to our secret hiding place.*
> *You see, I've kept it, day after day, touching it, remembering you.*
> *It has never left me since July 16, 1942.*
> *No one here knows. No one here knows about the key, about you.*
> *About you in the cupboard.*
> *About Mother, about Father.*
> *About the camp.*
> *About summer 1942.*
> *About who I really am.*
>
> *Michel.*
> *Not one day has gone by without me thinking of you.*

Remembering 26, rue de Saintonge.
I carry the burden of your death like I would a child.
I will carry it till the day I die.
Sometimes, I want to die.
I cannot bear the weight of your death.
Of Mother's death, of Father's death.
Visions of cattle trains carrying them to their deaths.
I hear the train in my mind, I have heard it over and over again for
  the past thirty years.
I cannot bear the weight of my past.
Yet I cannot throw away the key to your cupboard.
It is the only concrete thing that links me to you, apart from your
  grave.

Michel.
How can I pretend I am someone else.
How can I make them believe I am another woman.
No, I cannot forget.
The stadium.
The camp.
The train.
Jules and Geneviève.
Alain and Henriette.
Nicolas and Gaspard.

My child cannot make me forget. I love him. He is my son.
My husband does not know who I am.
What my story is.
But I cannot forget.
Coming here was a terrible mistake.
I thought I could change. I thought I could put it all behind me.
But I cannot.

They went to Auschwitz. They were killed.
My brother. He died in the cupboard.

There is nothing left for me.
I thought there was but I was wrong.
A child and a husband are not enough.
They know nothing.
They don't know who I am.
They will never know.

Michel.
In my dreams, you come and get me.
You take me by the hand and you lead me away.
This life is too much for me to bear.
I look at the key and I long for you and for the past.
For the innocent, easy days before the war.
I know now my scars will never heal.
I hope my son will forgive me.
He will never know.
No one will ever know.

Zakhor. Al Tichkah.
Remember. Never forget.

T HE CAFÉ WAS A noisy, lively place, yet around William and me
grew a bubble of total silence.

I put the notebook down, devastated at what we now knew.

"She killed herself," William said flatly. "There was no accident.
She drove that car straight into the tree."

I said nothing. I could not speak. I did not know what to say.

I wanted to reach out and take his hand, but something held me
back. I took a deep breath. But still the words did not come.

The brass key lay between us on the table, a silent witness of the
past, of Michel's death. I sensed him closing up, like he had done once
before in Lucca, when he had held up his palms as if to push me away.
He did not move, but I clearly felt him drawing away. Once again, I re-
sisted the powerful, compulsive urge to touch him, to hold him. Why
did I feel there was so much I could share with this man? Somehow he
was no stranger to me, and more bizarre still, I felt even less a stranger
to him. What had brought us together? My quest, my thirst for truth,
my compassion for his mother? He knew nothing of me, knew nothing
of my failing marriage, my near miscarriage in Lucca, my job, my life.
What did I know of him, of his wife, his children, his career? His present was a mystery. But his past, his mother's past, had been etched out
to me like fiery torches along a dark path. And I longed to show this
man that I cared, that what happened to his mother had altered my
life.

Thank you," he said, at last. "Thank you for telling me all this."

His voice seemed odd, contrived. I realized I had wanted him to break down, to cry, to show me some form of emotion. Why? No doubt because I myself needed release, needed tears to wash away pain, sorrow, emptiness, needed to share my feelings with him, in a particular, intimate communion.

He was leaving, getting up from the table, gathering up the key and the notebook. I could not bear the idea of him going so soon. If he walked out now, I was convinced I would never hear from him again. He would not want to see me, or talk to me. I would lose the last link to Sarah. I would lose him. And for some godforsaken, obscure reason, William Rainsferd was the only person I wanted to be with at that very moment.

He must have read something in my face because he hesitated, hovered over the table.

"I will go to these places," he said. "Beaune-la-Rolande, and rue Nélaton."

"I could come with you, if you want me to."

His eyes rested upon me. Again, I perceived the contrast of what I knew I inspired in him, a complex bundle of resentment and thankfulness.

"No, I prefer to go alone. But I'd appreciate it if you gave me the Dufaure brothers' addresses. I'd like to see them, too."

"Sure," I replied, looking at my agenda and scribbling the addresses down on a piece of paper for him.

Suddenly he sat down again, heavily.

"You know, I could do with a drink," he said.

"Fine. Of course," I said, signaling to the waiter. We ordered some wine for William and a fruit juice for me.

As we drank in silence, I noticed inwardly how comfortable I felt with him. Two fellow Americans enjoying a quiet drink. Somehow we did not need to talk. And it did not feel awkward. But I knew that as soon as he had finished the last dregs of his wine, he'd be gone.

The moment came.

"Thank you, Julia, thank you for everything."

He did not say, *Let's keep in touch, send each other e-mails, talk on the phone from time to time.* No, he said nothing. But I knew what his silence spelled out, loud and clear. *Don't call me. Don't contact me, please. I need to figure my entire life out. I need time and silence, and peace. I need to find out who I now am.*

I watched him walk away under the rain, his tall figure fading into the busy street.

I folded my palms over the roundness of my stomach, letting loneliness ebb into me.

W HEN I CAME HOME that evening, I found the entire Tézac family waiting for me. They were sitting with Bertrand and Zoë in our living room. I immediately picked up the stiffness of the atmosphere.

It appeared they had divided into two groups: Edouard, Zoë, and Cécile, who were on "my side," approving of what I had done, and Colette and Laure, who disapproved.

Bertrand said nothing, remaining strangely silent. His face was mournful, his mouth drooping at the sides. He did not look at me.

How could I have done such a thing, Colette exploded. Tracing that family, contacting that man, who in the end knew nothing of his mother's past.

"That poor man," echoed my sister-in-law Laure, quivering. "Imagine, now he finds out who he really is, his mother was a Jew, his entire family wiped out in Poland, his uncle starved to death. Julia should have left him alone."

Edouard stood up abruptly, threw his hands into the air.

"My God!" he roared. "What has come over this family!" Zoë took shelter under my arm. "Julia did something brave, something generous," he went on, quaking with anger. "She wanted to make sure that the little girl's family knew. Knew we cared. Knew that my father cared enough to ensure Sarah Starzynski was looked after by a foster family, that she was loved."

"Oh Father, please," interrupted Laure. "What Julia did was pathetic. Bringing back the past is never a good idea, especially whatever happened during the war. No one wants to be reminded of that, nobody wants to think about that."

She did not look at me, but I perceived the full weight of her animosity. I read her mind easily. Just the sort of the thing an American would do. No respect for the past. No idea of what a family secret is. No manners. No sensitivity. Uncouth, uneducated American: *l'Américaine avec ses gros sabots*.

"I disagree!" said Cécile, her voice shrill. "I'm glad you told me what happened, *Père*. It's a horrid story, that poor little boy dying in the apartment, the little girl coming back. I think Julia was right to contact that family. After all, we did nothing we should be ashamed of."

"Perhaps!" said Colette, her lips pinched. "But if Julia had not been so nosy, Edouard would never have mentioned it. Right?"

Edouard faced his wife. His face was cold, so was his voice.

"Colette, my father made me promise I'd never reveal what happened. I respected his wish, with difficulty, for the past sixty years. But now I am glad you know. Now I can share this with you, even if it apparently disturbs some of you."

"Thank God Mamé knows nothing," sighed Colette, patting her ash blond hair into place.

"Oh, Mamé knows," piped up Zoë's voice.

Her cheeks turned beet red but she faced us bravely.

"She told me what happened. I didn't know about the little boy, I guess Mom didn't want me to hear that part. But Mamé told me all about it."

Zoë went on.

"She's known about it since it happened, the concierge told her Sarah came back. And she said Grand-père had all these nightmares about a dead child in his room. She said it was horrible, knowing, and never being able to talk about it with her husband, her son, and later, with the family. She said it had changed my great-grandfather, that it had done something to him, something he could not talk about, even to her."

I looked at my father-in-law. He stared at my daughter, incredulous.

"Zoë, she knew? She's known about it all these years?"

Zoë nodded.

"Mamé said it was a dreadful secret to carry, that she never stopped thinking about the little girl, she said she was glad I now knew. She said we should have talked about it much earlier, we should have done what Mom did, we should not have waited. We should have found the little girl's family. We were wrong to have kept it hidden. That's what she told me. Just before her stroke."

There was a long, painful silence.

Zoë drew herself up. She gazed at Colette, Edouard, at her aunts, at her father. At me.

"There's something else I want to tell you," she added, smoothly switching from French to English and accentuating her American accent. "I don't care what some of you think. I don't care if you think Mom was wrong, if you think Mom did something stupid. I'm really proud of what she did. How she found William, how she told him. You have no idea what it took, what it meant to her. What it means to me. And probably what it means to him. And you know what? When I grow up, I want to be like her. I want to be a mom my kids are proud of. *Bonne nuit.*"

She made a funny little bow, walked out of the room, and quietly closed the door.

We remained in silence for a long time. I watched Colette's face grow stony, almost rigid. Laure checked her makeup in a pocket mirror. Cécile seemed petrified.

Bertrand had not said one word. He was facing the window, hands joined behind his back. He had not looked at me once. Or at any of us.

Edouard got up, patted my head in a tender, paternal gesture. His pale blue eyes twinkled down at me. He murmured something in French, in the crook of my ear.

"You did the right thing. You did well."

But later on that evening, as I lay in my solitary bed, unable to read, to think, to do anything but lie back and examine the ceiling, I wondered.

I thought of William, wherever he was, trying to fit the new pieces of his life together.

I thought of the Tézac family, for once having to come out of their shell, for once having to communicate, the sad, dark secret out in the open. I thought of Bertrand turning his back to me.

"*Tu as fait ce qu'il fallait. Tu as bien fait,*" Edouard had said.

Was Edouard right? I did not know. I wondered, still.

Zoë opened the door, crept into my bed like a long silent puppy, nestling up to me. She took my hand, slowly kissed it, rested her head on my shoulder.

I listened to the muffled roar of the traffic on the boulevard du Montparnasse. It was getting late. Bertrand was with Amélie, no doubt. He felt so far from me, like a stranger. Like somebody I hardly knew.

Two families that I had brought together, just for today. Two families that would never be the same again.

Had I done the right thing?

I did not know what to think. I did not know what to believe.

Zoë fell asleep next to me, her slow breath tickling my cheek. I thought of the child to come, and I felt a sort of peace come over me. A peaceful feeling that soothed me for a while.

But the ache, the sadness remained.

New York City, 2005

"Z OË!" I YELLED. "For God's sake hold your sister's hand. She is going to fall off that thing and break her neck!"

My long-legged daughter scowled at me.

"You are one hell of a paranoid mother."

She grabbed the baby's plump arm and shoved her back onto her
tricycle. Her little legs pumped furiously along the track, Zoë hurdling
behind her. The toddler gurgled with delight, craning her neck back to
make sure I was watching, with the overt vanity of a two-year-old.

Central Park and the first tantalizing promise of spring. I stretched
my legs out, tilted my face back to the sun.

The man at my side caressed my cheek.

Neil. My boyfriend. A trifle older than me. A lawyer. Divorced.
Lived in the Flatiron district with his teenage sons. Introduced to me
by my sister. I liked him. I wasn't in love with him, but I enjoyed his
company. He was an intelligent, cultivated man. He had no intention
of marrying me, thank God, and he put up with my daughters from
time to time.

There had been a couple of boyfriends since we had come to live
here. Nothing serious. Nothing important. Zoë called them my suit-
ors, Charla, my beaux, in Scarlett-like fashion. Before Neil, the latest
suitor was called Peter, he had an art gallery, a bald spot on the back
of his head that pained him, and a drafty loft in Tribeca. They were
decent, slightly boring, all-American middle-aged men. Polite,
earnest, and meticulous. They had good jobs, they were well-

educated, cultivated, and generally divorced. They came to pick me up, they dropped me off, they offered their arm and their umbrella. They took me out to lunch, to the Met, MoMA, the City Opera, the NYCB, to shows on Broadway, out to dinner, and sometimes to bed. I endured it. Sex was something I now did because I felt I had to. It was mechanical and dull. There, too, something had vanished. The passion. The excitement. The heat. All gone.

I felt like someone—me?—had fast-forwarded the film of my life, and there I appeared like a wooden Charlie Chaplin character, doing everything in a hasty and awkward way, as if I had no other choice, a stiff grin pasted on my face, acting like I was happy with my new life.

Sometimes Charla would steal a look at me and say, "Hey, you OK?"

She would nudge me and I'd mumble, "Oh, sure, fine." She did not seem convinced, but for the moment she let me be.

My mother, too, would let her eyes roam over my face and purse her lips with worry. "Everything all right, sugar?"

I'd shrug away her anxiety with a careless smile.

A GLORIOUS, CRISP NEW YORK morning. The kind you never get in Paris. Sharp fresh air. Stark blue sky. The city's skyline hemming us in above the trees. The Dakota's pale mass, facing us. The smell of hotdogs and pretzels wafting through the breeze.

I reached out my hand and stroked Neil's knee, eyes still closed against the sun's increasing heat. New York and its fierce, contrasted weather. Sizzling summers. Freezing white winters. And the light that fell over the city, a hard, bright silvery light that I had grown to love. Paris and its damp gray drizzle seemed to come from another world.

I opened my eyes and watched my daughters cavort. Overnight, or so it seemed, Zoë had sprouted into a spectacular teenager, towering over me with lissome strong limbs. She looked like Charla and Bertrand, she'd inherited their class, their allure, their charm, that feisty, powerful combination of Jarmond and Tézac that enchanted me.

The little one was something else. Softer, rounder, more fragile. She needed cuddling, kissing, more fuss and attention than Zoë had demanded at her age. Was it because her father was not around? Because Zoë, the baby, and I had left France for New York, not long after the birth? I did not know. I did not question myself too much.

It had been strange, coming back to live in America, after many years in Paris. It still felt strange, sometimes. It did not yet feel like home. I wondered how long that would take. But it had happened. There had been difficulty. It had not been an easy decision to make.

The baby's birth had been premature, a cause for panic and pain. She was born just after Christmas, two months before her due date. I underwent a gruesomely long C-section in the emergency room at Saint-Vincent de Paul Hospital. Bertrand had been there, oddly tense, moved, despite himself. A tiny, perfect little girl. Had he been disappointed? I wondered. I wasn't. This child meant so much to me. I had fought for her. I had not given in. She was my victory.

Shortly after the birth, and just before the move to the rue de Sain-tonge, Bertrand summoned up the courage to tell me he loved Amélie, that he wanted to live with her from now on, that he wanted to move into the Trocadéro apartment with her, that he could no longer lie to me, to Zoë, that there would have to be a divorce, but it could be quick, and easy. It was then, watching him go through with his longwinded, complicated confession, watching him pace the room up and down, his hands behind his back, his eyes downcast, that the first idea of moving to America dawned upon me. I listened to Bertrand till the end. He looked drained, wrecked, but he had done it. He had been honest with me, at last. And honest with himself. And I had looked back at my handsome, sensual husband and thanked him. He had seemed surprised. He admitted he had expected a stronger, more bitter reaction. Shouts, insults, a fuss. The baby in my arms had moaned, waving her tiny fists.

"No fuss," I said. "No shouts, no insults. All right?"

"All right," he said. And he kissed me, and the baby.

He already felt like he was out of my life. Like he had already left.

That night, every time I rose to feed the hungry child, I thought of the States. Boston? No, I hated the idea of going back to the past, to my childhood city.

And then I knew.

New York. Zoë, the baby, and I could go to New York. Charla was there, my parents not far. New York. Why not? I didn't know the city all that well, I had never lived there for a long spell, apart from my annual visits to my sister's.

New York. Perhaps the only city that could rival Paris because of its complete and utter difference. The more I thought about it, the more the idea secretly appealed to me. I didn't talk it over with my friends. I knew Hervé, Christophe, Guillaume, Susannah, Holly, Jan, and Isabelle would be upset at the idea of my departure. But I knew they would understand and accept it, too.

And then Mamé had died. She had lingered on since her stroke in November, she had never been able to speak again, although she had regained consciousness. She had been moved to the intensive care unit, at the Cochin hospital. I was expecting her death, gearing myself up to face it, but it still came as a shock.

It was after the funeral, which took place in Burgundy, in the sad little graveyard, that Zoë had said to me, "Mom, do we have to go live in the rue de Saintonge?"

"I think your father expects us to."

"But do *you* want to go live there?" she asked.

"No," I said truthfully. "Ever since I've known what happened there, I don't want to."

"I don't want to either."

Then she said, "But where could we move to then, Mom?"

And I replied, lightly, jokingly, expecting her to snort with disapproval, "Well, how about New York City?"

IT HAD BEEN AS easy as that, with Zoë. Bertrand had not been
happy about our decision. About his daughter moving so far
away. But Zoë was firm about leaving. She said she'd come back
every couple of months, and Bertrand could come over, too, to see
her, and the baby. I explained to Bertrand that there was nothing
set, nothing definitive about the move. It wasn't forever. It was just
for a couple of years. To let Zoë grasp the American side of her. To
help me move on. To start something new. He had now established
himself with Amélie. They formed a couple, an official one.
Amélie's children were nearly adults. They lived away from home
and also spent time with their father. Was Bertrand tempted by the
prospect of a new life without the everyday responsibility of
children—his, or hers—to raise on a daily basis? Perhaps. He finally said yes. And then I got things going.

After an initial stay at her house, Charla had helped me find a
place to live, a simple, white, two-bedroom apartment with an "open
city view" and a doorman, on West 86th Street, between Amsterdam
and Columbus. I sublet it from one of her friends who had moved to
Los Angeles. The building was full of families and divorced parents, a
noisy beehive of babies, kids, bikes, strollers, scooters. It was a comfortable, cozy home, but there, too, something was missing. What? I
could not tell.

Thanks to Joshua, I'd been hired as the New York City correspondent for a hip French Web site. I worked from home and still used Bamber as a photographer when I needed shots from Paris.

There had been a new school for Zoë, Trinity College, a couple of blocks away. "Mom, I'll never fit in, now they call me the Frenchy," she complained, and I couldn't help smiling.

NEW YORKERS WERE FASCINATING to watch, their purposeful step, their banter, their friendliness. My neighbors said hi in the elevator, had offered us flowers and candy when we moved in, and joked with the doorman. I had forgotten about all that. I was so used to Parisian surliness and people living on the same doorstep barely giving each other curt nods in the staircase.

Perhaps the most ironic thing about it all was that despite the exciting whirlwind of a life I now had, I missed Paris. I missed the Eiffel Tower lighting up on the hour, every evening, like a shimmering, bejeweled seductress. I missed the air sirens howling over the city, every first Wednesday, at noon, for their monthly drill. I missed the Saturday outdoor market along the boulevard Edgar-Quinet, where the vegetable man called me *"ma p'tite dame"* although I was probably his tallest feminine customer. Like Zoë, I felt I was a Frenchy, too, despite being American.

Leaving Paris had not been as easy as I had anticipated. New York and its energy, its clouds of steam billowing from its manholes, its vastness, its bridges, its buildings, its gridlock, was still not home. I missed my Parisian friends, even if I'd made some great new ones here. I missed Edouard, who I had become close to and who wrote to me monthly. I especially missed the way French men check women out, what Holly used to call their "naked" look. I had gotten used to it over there, but now, in Manhattan, there were only cheerful bus drivers to yell "Yo, slim!" at Zoë and "Yo, blondie!" at me. I felt like I had become invisible. Why did my life feel so empty? I wondered. As if a hurricane had hit it. As if the bottom had dropped out of it.

And the nights.

Nights were forlorn, even those I spent with Neil. Lying in bed listening to the sounds of the great, pulsating city and letting the images come back to me, like the tide creeping up the beach.

S ARAH.
    She never left me. She had changed me, forever. Her story, her suffering, I carried them within me. I felt as if I knew her. I knew her as a child. As a young girl. As the forty-year-old housewife who crashed her car into a tree on an icy New England road. I could see her face, perfectly. The slanted green eyes. The shape of her head. Her posture. Her hands. Her rare smile. I knew her. I could have stopped her on the street, had she still been alive.

Zoë was a sharp one. She had caught me red-handed.

Googling William Rainsferd.

I had not realized she was back from school. One winter afternoon, she had sneaked in without me hearing her.

"How long have you been doing this?" she asked, sounding like a mother coming across her teenager smoking pot.

Flushed, I admitted that I'd looked him up regularly in the past year.

"And?" she went on, arms crossed, frowning down at me.

"Well, it appears he has left Lucca," I confessed.

"Oh. Where is he, then?"

"He's back in the States, has been for a couple of months."

I could no longer bear her stare, so I stood up and went to the window, glancing down to busy Amsterdam Avenue.

"Is he in New York, Mom?"

Her voice was softer now, less harsh. She came up behind me, put her lovely head on my shoulder.

I nodded. I could not face telling her how excited I'd been when I found out he was here, too. How thrilled, how amazed I'd felt about ending up in the same city as him, two years after our last meeting. His father was a New Yorker, I recalled. He had probably lived here as a little boy.

He was listed in the phone book. In the West Village. A mere fifteen-minute subway ride from here. And for days, for weeks, I had agonizingly asked myself whether I should call him, or not. He had never tried to contact me since Paris. I had never heard from him since then.

The excitement had petered out after a while. I did not have the courage to call him. But I went on thinking about him, night after night. Day after day. In secret, in silence. I wondered if I'd ever run into him one day, in the park, in some department store, bar, restaurant. Was he here with his wife and girls? Why had he come back to the States, like I had? What had happened?

"Have you contacted him?" Zoë asked.

"No."

"Will you?"

"I don't know, Zoë."

I started to cry, silently.

"Oh, Mom, please," she sighed.

I wiped the tears away, angrily, feeling foolish.

"Mom, he knows you live here now. I'm sure he knows. He's looked you up as well. He knows what you do here, he knows where you live."

That thought had never occurred to me. William Googling *me*. William checking out *my* address. Was Zoë right? Did he know I lived in New York City, too, on the Upper West Side? Did he ever think of me? What did he feel, exactly, when he did?

"You have to let go, Mom. You have to put it behind you. Call Neil, see him more often, just get on with your life."

I turned to her, my voice ringing out loud and harsh.

"I can't, Zoë. I need to know if what I did helped him. I need to know that. Is that too much to ask? Is that such an impossible thing?"

The baby wailed from the next room. I'd disturbed her nap. Zoë went to get her and came back with her plump, hiccupping sister.

Zoë stroked my hair gently over the toddler's curls.

"I don't think you'll ever know, Mom. I don't think he'll ever be ready to tell you. You changed his life. You turned it upside down, remember. He probably never wants to see you again."

I plucked the child from her arms and pressed her fiercely against me, relishing her warmth, her plumpness. Zoë was right. I needed to turn the page, to get on with my life.

How, was another matter.

I KEPT MYSELF BUSY. I did not have a minute to myself, what with Zoë, her sister, Neil, my parents, my nephews, my job, and the never-ending string of parties Charla and her husband Barry invited me to, and to which I relentlessly went. I met more new people in two years than I had in my entire Parisian stay, a cosmopolitan melting pot that I reveled in.

Yes, I had left Paris for good, but whenever I returned for my work or to see my friends or Edouard, I always found myself in the Marais, drawn back again and again, as if my footsteps could not help bringing me there. Rue des Rosiers, rue du Roi-de-Sicile, rue des Ecouffes, rue de Saintonge, rue de Bretagne, I saw them file past with new eyes, eyes that remembered what had happened here, in 1942, even if it had been long before my time.

I wondered who lived in the rue de Saintonge apartment now, who stood by the window overlooking the leafy courtyard, who ran their palm along the smooth marble mantelpiece. I wondered if the new tenants had any inkling that a little boy had died within their home, and that a young girl's life had been changed that day, forever.

In my dreams, I went back to the Marais, too. In my dreams, sometimes the horrors of the past that I had not witnessed appeared to me with such starkness that I had to turn on the light, in order to drive the nightmare away.

It was during those sleepless, empty nights, when I lay in bed, jaded by the social talk, dry-mouthed after the extra glass of wine I should not have given in to, that the old ache came back and haunted me.

His eyes. His face when I had read Sarah's letter out loud. It all came back and drove sleep away, delving into me.

Zoë's voice dragged me back to Central Park, the beautiful spring day, and Neil's hand on my thigh.

"Mom, this monster wants a Popsicle."

"No way," I said. "No Popsicle."

The baby threw herself face forward on the grass and bawled.

"Quite something, isn't she?" mused Neil.

JANUARY 2005 ALSO BROUGHT me back, again and again, to Sarah, to William. The importance of the sixtieth commemoration of Auschwitz's liberation made every headline around the world. It seemed that never before had the word "Shoah" been pronounced so often.

And every time I heard it, my thoughts leaped painfully to him, to her. And I wondered, as I watched the Auschwitz memorial ceremony on TV, if William ever thought of me when he, too, heard the word, when he, too, saw the monstrous black-and-white images of the past flicker across the screen, the lifeless skeletal bodies piled high, the crematoriums, the ashes, the horror of it all.

His family had died in that hideous place. His mother's parents. How could he not think of it, I mused. On the screen, with Zoë and Charla at my side, I watched the snowflakes fall on the camp, the barbed wire, the squat watchtower. The crowd, the speeches, the prayers, the candles. The Russian soldiers and their particular dancing gait.

And the final, unforgettable vision of nightfall, and the railway tracks aflame, glowing through the darkness with a poignant, sharp mixture of grief and remembrance.

THE CALL CAME ONE May afternoon, when I was least expecting it. I was at my desk, struggling with a new computer's whims. I picked up the phone, my "yes" sounding curt even to me.

"Hi. This is William Rainsferd."

I sat up straight, heart aflutter, trying to remain calm.

William Rainsferd.

I said nothing, dumbstruck, clutching the receiver to my ear.

"You there, Julia?"

I swallowed.

"Yes, just having some computer problems. How are you, William?"

"Fine," he said.

A little silence. But it did not feel tense, or strived.

"It's been a while," I said lamely.

"Yes, it has," he said.

Another silence.

"I see you're a New Yorker now," he said, at last. "Looked you up."

So Zoë had been right, after all.

"Well, how about getting together?" he asked.

"Today?" I said.

"If you can make it."

I thought of the sleeping child in the next room. She had been to day care this morning, but I could take her along. She wasn't going to like having her nap interrupted, though.

"I can make it," I said.

"Great. I'll ride up to your part of town. Got any ideas where we could meet?"

"Do you know Café Mozart? On West 70th Street and Broadway?"

"I know it, fine. See you there in half an hour?"

I hung up. My heart was beating so fast I could hardly breathe. I went to wake the baby, ignored her protests, bundled her up, unfolded the stroller, and took off.

H<small>E WAS ALREADY THERE</small> when we arrived. I saw his back first, the powerful shoulders, and his hair, silver and thick, no longer bearing any trace of blond. He was reading a newspaper, but he swivelled around as I approached, as if he could feel my eyes upon him. Then he was up on his feet, and there was an awkward, amusing moment when we didn't know whether to shake hands or kiss. He laughed, I did, too, and he finally hugged me, a great big bear hug, slamming my chin against his collarbone and patting the small of my back, and then he bent down to admire my daughter.

"What a beautiful little girl," he crooned.

She solemnly handed him her favorite rubber giraffe.

"And what's your name, then?" he asked.

"Lucy," she lisped.

"That's the giraffe's name—," I began, but William had already started to press the toy and loud squeaks drowned out my voice, making the baby shriek with glee.

We found a table and sat down, keeping the child in her stroller. He glanced at the menu.

"Ever had the Amadeus cheesecake?" he asked, raising one eyebrow.

"Yes," I said, "it's positively diabolical."

He grinned.

"Hey, you look fabulous, Julia. New York certainly suits you."

I blushed like a teenager, imagining Zoë looking on and rolling her eyes.

Then his mobile rang. He answered it. I could tell by his expression it was a woman. I wondered who. His wife? One of his daughters? The conversation went on. He seemed flustered. I bent over the child, playing with the giraffe.

"Sorry," he said, tucking the phone away. "That was my girlfriend."

"Oh."

I must have sounded confused because he snorted with laughter.

"I'm divorced now, Julia."

He looked straight at me. His face sobered.

"You know, after you told me, everything changed."

At last. At last he was telling me what I needed to know. The aftermath. The consequences.

I did not quite know what to say. I was afraid that if I uttered one word, he'd stop. I kept busy with my daughter, handing her her bottle of water, making sure she didn't spill it all over herself, fumbling with a paper napkin.

The waitress came to take our orders. Two Amadeus cheesecakes, two coffees, and a pancake for the child.

William said, "Everything went to pieces. It was hell. A terrible year."

We said nothing for a couple of minutes, looking around us at the busy tables. The café was a noisy, bright place, with classical music emanating from hidden speakers. The child cooed to herself, smiling up at me and at William, brandishing her toy. The waitress brought us our food.

"Are you OK now?" I asked tentatively.

"Yes," he said, swiftly. "Yes I am. It took me a while to get used to this new part of me. To understand and accept my mother's history. To deal with the pain of it. Sometimes I still can't. But I work at it, hard. I did a couple of very necessary things."

"Like what?" I asked, feeding sticky bits of crumbled pancake to my daughter.

"I realized I could no longer bear all this alone. I felt isolated, broken. My wife could not understand what I was going through. And I just could not explain, the communication between us was nonexistent. I took my daughters to Auschwitz with me, last year, before the sixtieth anniversary celebration. I needed to tell them what had happened to their great-grandparents, it wasn't easy and that was the only way I could do it. Showing them. It was a moving, tearful trip, but I felt at peace, at last, and I felt my daughters understood."

His face was sad, thoughtful. I did not speak, I let him do the talking. I wiped the baby's face and gave her more water.

"I did one last thing, in January. I went back to Paris. There's a new Holocaust memorial in the Marais, maybe you know that." I nodded. I had heard of it and planned to go there on my next trip. "Chirac inaugurated it at the end of January. There's a wall of names, just by the entrance. A huge, gray stone wall, engraved with 76,000 names. The names of every single Jew deported from France."

I watched his fingers play with the rim of his coffee cup. I felt it hard to look him fully in the face.

"I went there to find their names. And there they were. Wladyslaw and Rywka Starzynksi. My grandparents. I felt the same peace I had found at Auschwitz. The same pain. I felt grateful that they were remembered, that the French remembered them and honored them this way. There were people crying in front of that wall, Julia. Old people, young people, people of my age, touching the wall with their hands, and crying."

He paused, breathed carefully through his mouth. I kept my eyes on the cup, on his fingers. The baby's giraffe squeaked but we hardly heard it.

"Chirac gave a speech. I did not understand it, of course. I looked it up later on the Internet and read the translation. A good speech. Urging people to remember France's responsibility during the Vel' d'Hiv' roundup and what followed. Chirac pronounced the same words my mother had written at the end of her letter. *Zakhor, Al Tichkah*. Remember. Never forget. In Hebrew."

He bent down and retrieved a large manila envelope from the back-pack at his feet. He handed it to me.

"These are my photos of her, I wanted to show them to you. I suddenly realized I didn't know who my mother was, Julia. I mean, I knew what she looked like, I knew her face, her smile, but nothing about her inner life."

I wiped the maple syrup off my fingers in order to be able to handle them. Sarah, on her wedding day. Tall, slender, her small smile, her secret eyes. Sarah, cradling William as a baby. Sarah with William as a toddler, holding him by the hand. Sarah, in her thirties, wearing an emerald ball dress. And Sarah, just before her death, a large color close-up. Her hair was gray, I noticed. Prematurely gray and oddly becoming. Like his, now.

"I remember her as being tall, and slim, and silent," said William as I looked at each photo with growing emotion. "She didn't laugh much, but she was an intense person, and a loving mother. But no one ever mentioned suicide after her death. Ever. Not even Dad. I guess Dad never read the notebook. No one did. Maybe he found it a long time after her death. We all thought it was an accident. No one knew who my mother was, Julia. Not even me. And that's what I still find so hard to live with. What brought her to her death, on that cold snowy day. How she made that decision. Why we never knew anything about her past. Why she chose not to tell my father. Why she kept all her suffering, all her pain, to herself."

"These are beautiful pictures," I said at last. "Thank you for bringing them."

I paused.

"There's something I must ask you," I said, putting the photos away, gathering courage and looking at him at last.

"Go ahead."

"No harsh feelings against me?" I asked with a weak smile. "I've been feeling like I destroyed your life."

He grinned.

"No harsh feelings, Julia. I just needed to think. To understand. To put all the pieces back together. It took a while. That's why you never heard from me during all that time."

I felt relief sweep over me.

"But I knew where you were all along." He smiled. "Spent quite some time keeping track of you." *Mom, he knows you live here now. He's looked you up as well. He knows what you do here, he knows where you live.* "When did you move to New York exactly?" he asked.

"A little while after the baby was born. Spring 2003."

"Why did you leave Paris? If you don't mind telling me . . ."

I gave a rueful half smile.

"My marriage had fallen apart. I'd just had this baby. I couldn't bring myself to live in the rue de Saintonge apartment after everything that had happened there. And I felt like moving back to the States."

"So how did you actually do it?"

"We stayed with my sister for a while, on the Upper East Side, then she found me a place to sublet from one of her friends. And my ex-boss found me a great job. What about you?"

"Same story. Life in Lucca just didn't seem possible. And my wife and I. . . ." His voice trailed off. He made a little gesture with his fingers as if to say farewell, bye-bye. "I lived here as a boy, before Roxbury. And the idea had been passing through my head, for a while. So I finally got 'round to it. I stayed at first with one of my oldest friends, in Brooklyn, then I found a place in the Village. I do the same job here. Food critic."

William's phone rang. The girlfriend, again. I turned away, trying to give him the privacy he needed. He finally put the phone down.

"She's a little possessive," he said, sheepishly. "I think I'll turn it off for a while."

He fumbled with the phone.

"How long have you been together?"

"A couple of months." He looked at me. "What about you? Are you seeing someone?"

"Yes, I am." I thought of Neil's courteous, bland smile. His careful gestures. The routine sex. I nearly added it was not important, that it was just for the company, because I could not stand being alone, because every night I thought of him, William, and of his mother, every single night, for the past two-and-a-half years, but I kept my mouth shut. I just said, "He's a nice person. Divorced. A lawyer."

William ordered fresh coffee. As he poured out mine, I noticed, once again, the beauty of his hands, his long, tapered fingers.

"About six months after our last meeting," he said, "I went back to the rue de Saintonge. I had to see you. To talk to you. I didn't know where to reach you, I had no number for you and couldn't remember your husband's name, so I couldn't even look you up in the phone book. I thought you'd still be living there. I had no idea you'd moved."

He paused, ran a hand through his thick, silver hair.

"I read all about the Vel' d'Hiv' roundup, I'd been to Beaune-la-Rolande, and to the street the stadium was on. I'd been to see Gaspard and Nicolas Dufaure. They took me to my uncle's grave, in the Orléans cemetery. Such kind men. But it was difficult, hard to go through. And I wished you'd been there with me. I should never have done all that alone, I should have said yes when you asked to come along."

"Maybe I should have insisted," I said.

"I should have listened to you. It was too much to bear alone. And then, when I finally went back to the rue de Saintonge, and when those unknown people opened your door, I felt you'd let me down."

He lowered his eyes. I set my coffee cup back in its saucer, resentment sweeping through me. How could he, I thought, after all I'd done for him, after all the time, the effort, the pain, the emptiness?

He must have deciphered something in my face because he quickly put his hand on my sleeve.

"I'm sorry I said that," he murmured.

"I never let you down, William."

My voice sounded stiff.

"I know that, Julia. I'm sorry."

His was deep, vibrant.

I relaxed. Managed a smile. We sipped in silence. Sometimes our knees brushed against each other under the table. It felt natural, being with him. As if we had been doing this for years. As if this was not just the third time in our lives we were seeing each other.

"Is your ex-husband OK about you living here with the kids?" he asked.

I shrugged. I looked down at the child who'd fallen asleep in her stroller.

"It wasn't easy. But he's in love with someone else. Has been for some time. That helped. He doesn't see the girls much, though. He comes here from time to time, and Zoë spends her vacations in France."

"Same thing with my ex-wife. She's had a new child. A boy. I go to Lucca as often as I can to see my daughters. Or they come here, but more rarely. They're quite grown up now."

"How old are they?"

"Stefania is twenty-one and Giustina, nineteen."

I whistled.

"You sure had them young."

"Too young, maybe."

"I don't know," I said. "I sometimes feel awkward with the baby. I wish I'd had her earlier. There's such a gap between her and Zoë."

"She's a sweet baby," he said, taking a healthy bite out of his cheesecake.

"Yes, she is. The apple of her doting mother's eye."

We both chuckled.

"Do you miss not having a boy?" he asked.

"No, I don't. Do you?"

"No. I love my girls. Maybe they'll have grandsons, though. She's called Lucy, then?"

I glanced across at him. Then down at her.

"No, that's the toy giraffe," I said.

There was a little pause.

"Her name is Sarah," I said quietly.

He stopped chewing, put his fork down. His eyes changed. He looked at me, at the sleeping child, said nothing.

Then he buried his face in his hands. He remained like that for minutes. I did not know what to do. I touched his shoulder.

Silence.

I felt guilty again, felt as if I had done something unforgivable. But I had known all along this baby was to be called Sarah. As soon as I had been told it was a girl, at the moment of her birth, I had known her name.

There was no other name my daughter could have had. She was Sarah. My Sarah. An echo to the other one, to the other Sarah, to the little girl with the yellow star who had changed my life.

At last he drew his hands away and I saw his face, wrecked, beautiful. The acute sadness, the emotion in his eyes. He was not afraid of letting me see them. He did not fight the tears. It seemed that he wanted me to see it all, the beauty and ache of his life, he wanted me to see his thanks, his gratitude, his pain.

I took his hand and pressed it hard. I could not bear to look at him any longer, so I closed my eyes and put his hand against my cheek. I cried with him. I felt his fingers grow wet with my tears, but I kept his hand there.

We sat there for a long time, till the crowd around us thinned, till the sun shifted and the light changed. Till we felt our eyes could meet again, without the tears.

❧ *Acknowledgments* ❧

Above all, I need to thank Héloïse d'Ormesson and Gilles Cohen-Solal. This book would never have been published without their talent, energy, and enthusiasm.

I thank you to my wonderful husband Nicolas Jolly for his support and his patience. Thank you: Andrea Stuart, Hugh Thomas, Peter Viertel, Catherine Rambaud, and Laure du Pavillon who believed in this book from the very start.

At St. Martin's Press, thank you to a fabulous team: Jennifer Weis, Lisa Senz, Sarah Goldstein, Stefanie Lindskog, Elizabeth Wildman, Hilary Rubin Teeman, and Colleen Schwartz

Thank you: Charla Carter-Halabi, Jan Pfeiffer, and Carol Dufaure, my real-life inspiration for Julia Jarmond.

Thank you: Holly Dando, Julia Harris-Voss, Sarah Hirsch, Tara Kaufman, Hélène Le Beau, Emma Parry, and Susanna Salk, for their help and their fervor.

Thank you: Marilyn Amerson, Laura Durnell, Marie Edwards, Sandy Flitterman-Lewis, Marion Higgins, Dr. Marcia Horn, Leon Jedeikin, Isaac Levendel, and Barbara Mix for believing in *Sarah's Key*.

Reading
Group
Gold

SARAH'S KEY
by Tatiana de Rosnay

In Her Own Words
- A Conversation with Tatiana de Rosnay

Keep on Reading
- Reading Group Questions

A
*Reading
Group Gold
Selection*

For more reading group suggestions
visit www.readinggroupgold.com

 ST. MARTIN'S GRIFFIN

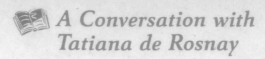

A Conversation with Tatiana de Rosnay

What was the inspiration for Sarah's Key?

I have always been interested in places and houses. And how places and houses keep memories, how walls can talk. I was browsing on the Internet about places in Paris where dark deeds had happened, and fell upon a Web site describing the rue Nélaton, in the 15th arrondissement, not far from where I live. That was where the great Vel' d'Hiv' roundup took place on July 16, 1942.

How much did you know about what happened before you started writing?

I realized I didn't know much about what exactly happened that day. I was not taught about this event at school, during the '70s. And it still seemed to be shrouded by some kind of taboo. So I started reading and researching.

And what did you learn? How did it make you feel?

As I progressed through my research, I was moved, appalled by what I discovered concerning the Vel' d'Hiv' roundup, especially about what happened to those 4,000 Jewish children, and I knew I had to write about it. I needed to write about it. But I also knew it could not be a historical novel, it had to have a more contemporary feel to it. And that's how I imagined Julia's story taking place today, linked to Sarah's, back in the '40s.

Are there any parallels between you and Julia? Can you tell us a bit about your French husband and his family? What do they think of your novel, and the issues it raises?

Julia is American and I am French, born in France, of a French father and a British mother. I based her on my

"I was not taught about [Vel' d'Hiv'] at school ... it still seemed to be shrouded by some kind of taboo."

American friends living in Paris. However, most of my readers are convinced I *am* Julia. At first this annoyed me somewhat, but in the end, I take it to be a magnificent compliment that I have created a character who could really exist and that women can identify with! The only thing Julia and I have in common is our age, our job (I'm also a journalist), and I "gave" Julia the horror I felt when I first discovered what happened to the Vel' d'Hiv' children.

My husband's family has nothing to do with Betrand Tézac's family, they are far more relaxed! Nor does my wonderful husband, Nicolas, have anything to do with arrogant Bertrand. I think—and hope—that my in-laws approve of my book and the issues it raises, and are proud of me. As for Nicolas, he is my first reader, and he believed in *Sarah's Key* from the moment he read the first pages.

In Her Own Words

Speaking of your writing career, who are your top three favorite authors and/or books—and why?

I am in awe of Daphne du Maurier, the author of *Rebecca,* for the way she is able to mix sheer psychological suspense with aspects of ordinary life. Émile Zola, whom I have been reading since my teens, is my favorite French author: I love his powerful descriptions of old, forgotten Paris. His first novel, *Thérèse Raquin,* with its terrifying ending, is in my eyes a masterpiece. On a more contemporary note, I admire Tracy Chevalier's work (*Girl with a Pearl Earring*), and the way she is able to plunge her reader into the past using a perfect balance of emotion and history.

When did you start writing?

I first started writing novels when I was eleven years old, in 1972. I was an avid bookworm

Photo Credit: Arnaud Février

and several books inspired me: Anne Frank's diary, *Rebecca* by Daphne du Maurier, and *The Young Visitors* by nine-year-old Daisy Ashford. For my mother's upcoming birthday, I decided to write her a novel and she was most encouraging when she read "A Girl Named Carey," an eighty-page, hand-written story of a poor little rich girl in nineteenth-century London. So from then on, I wrote a book a year for my family. I was already firmly convinced I was going to be a writer.

Describe your writing process.

"Most of my readers are convinced I am Julia."

I start writing each of my novels on small black Moleskine notebooks and then continue with the computer, but go back to the notebook if I get stuck. I write my book everyday, even on weekends and holidays (but this upsets my family, so I try not to). I hate it when someone talks to me while I'm writing or if the phone rings and I can get quite irritable, so I often write late at night or early in the morning. I read out loud from my book and sometimes cringe when I do so. I get back to work till I don't cringe at the next reading. I have three first readers, Nicolas (my husband), Julia, and Laure. I wouldn't dream of letting anyone else read my work before they do.

I'm often asked if, as a writer, I have any quirks and idiosyncrasies. Well, yes I do. I can't stand it if a door is opened behind me and someone walks in as I'm writing. I like to have a window in front of me, not a blank wall. I eat Cachou Lajaunies as I write, and if you're not French, you won't know what that is (subtle hint: your tongue goes black after a couple . . .). I drink Earl Grey while I write and when the tea gets cold, I make another pot. I can't listen to music while I work. I admire writers who are able to do this. When I feel I'm getting nowhere in my book, I come back to it later and write something else, an article, a blog post, an e-mail, a short story. A poem? Nope, haven't written a poem since the '80s. Thank God!

Please share a few words about the process of writing *Sarah's Key*.

Writing *Sarah's Key* was a powerful experience. First of all, reverting to my mother tongue, English, after years of writing novels in French felt exhilarating, like coming home after a long trip.

English is a language that is more emotional to me, because it's linked to my mother. My mother is British and my father is French—actually he's not very French, he's Mauritian and Russian, so I'm not that French after all. I was born in France, but English is the first language I learned. Also, with my heroine Julia Jarmond being American, I couldn't envision her speaking in French, it would be like seeing a dubbed movie. And finally, writing from my English side gave me the distance I needed in order to explore this black episode of French history.

Researching those dark times of France's past, the Occupation, the Vichy years, was tremendously enriching. But sobering, too. Writing *Sarah's Key* took me to Drancy and Beaune-la-Rolande, places around Paris which have a dreaded precedent that cannot be forgotten despite time going by. My visits there were poignant and memorable.

Sarah's Key has two interwoven stories: Sarah's in 1942 and Julia's in the present. Which part did you most enjoy writing?

I am not a historian and did not wish to write a historical novel. I also wanted to have a modern-day heroine in order to reveal the shame and taboo that the Vel' d'Hiv' round-up still sparks today. And I did feel that alternating Julia's and Sarah's stories gave a certain pace to the book, and made Sarah's part less "heavy."

*In Her Own
Words*

The Sarah part set in 1942 was difficult to write, but I learned so much from it, from my research, for one thing, but also from Sarah's bravery, her relentlessness. She was a wonderful and moving character to create. Julia's modern story was easier in a way, and I did enjoy imagining her life as an American in Paris.

Is Sarah based on a real-life person?

Sarah is a fictional character, but she bears an uncanny resemblance to my daughter Charlotte, who was ten years old when I was researching this novel between 2001 and 2003. I remember thinking, watching my daughter laugh and play, Sarah was exactly this age when horror came into her life.

Are there any other "forgotten" moments of history that interest you?

Yes, I'm interested in aspects of the French Revolution and in particular the ransacking and looting of all the royal remains at the Saint-Denis Cathedral which is not a very well known fact even here in France. The Haussmann era also draws me. And I recently read *Tokyo* by Mo Hayder and realized I did not know much about the Nanking massacre. The Great Fire of London is also one my interests, and Jack the Ripper—all very macabre, I must say!

1. What did you know about France's role in World War II—and the Vel' d'Hiv' roundup in particular—before reading *Sarah's Key*? How did this book teach you about, or change your impression of, this important chapter in French history?

2. *Sarah's Key* is composed of two interweaving story lines: Sarah's, in the past, and Julia's quest in the present day. Discuss the structure and prose style of each narrative. Did you enjoy the alternating stories and time frames? What are the strengths or drawbacks of this format?

3. Which "voice" did you prefer: Sarah's or Julia's? Why? Is one more or less authentic than the other? If you could meet either of the two characters, which one would you choose?

4. How does the apartment on la rue de Saintonge unite the past and present action—and all the characters—in *Sarah's Key*? In what ways is the apartment a character all its own?

5. What are the major themes of *Sarah's Key*?

6. Tatiana de Rosnay's novel is built around several "key" secrets that Julia unearths. Discuss the element of mystery in these pages. What types of narrative devices does the author use to keep the reader guessing?

*Keep on
Reading*

7. How do you imagine what happens after the end of the novel? What do you think Julia's life will be like now that she knows the truth about Sarah? What truths do you think she'll learn about herself?

8. Among modern Jews, there is a familiar mantra about the Holocaust; they are taught, from a very young age, that they must "remember and never forget" (as the inscription on the Rafle du Vel' d'Hiv' memorial also informs). Discuss the events of *Sarah's Key* in this context. Who are the characters doing the remembering? Who are the ones who choose to forget?

9. What does it take for a novelist to bring a historical event to life? To what extent do you think de Rosnay took artistic liberties with this work?

10. Why *do* modern readers enjoy novels about the past? How and when can a powerful piece of fiction be a history lesson in itself?

11. We are taught, as young readers, that every story has a "moral." Is there a moral to *Sarah's Key*? What can we learn about our world—and ourselves—from Sarah's story?